The Never-Ending Storm

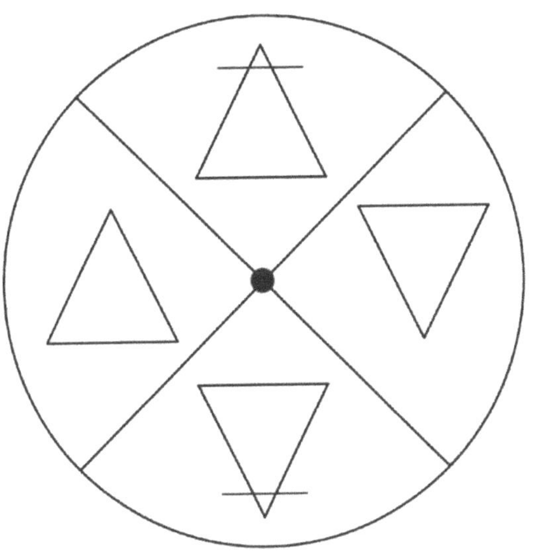

TRENT GERBERS

DEDICATION

Thank you to my children for the inspiration
that got me started

Thank you to my wife for the encouragement and support
that kept me going

Thank you to my grandfather for the drive
that I needed to finish

ACKNOWLEDGMENTS

Special thanks to Kristina McNeish for the wonderful artwork
Special thanks to Cameron Gerbers, my brother, for his questions,
comments, edits, and final review

Prologue

The families three, they shall combine
Across the planes of space and time

To bestow or to retrieve
The gift of immortality

For Gods made shall roam the Earth
Aiding in mankind's birth

But when man's need is at its end,
The Gods shall be unmade again

For Gods unmade shall then be free,
Regaining their mortality

All but one who must remain,
To keep the dead in his domain

~ Notes on the Godmaker Prophecy found in the margin of page 1,097 of Dr. Amity Auster's text, *Collecting Souls: A Guide Through the Underworld*, from the Weston Family Library. The date and source of the notation is unknown.

PART 1
JILLIAN RACHAEL WESTON

1

Jillian watched her father manically pace around the room as he muttered nonsense to himself. The night air was cold, colder than it should have been, and the fire that had been burning in the fireplace had long gone out. The only source of light in the room came from the torches on the wall producing flickers of dancing flame. Jillian's father cast a monstrous shadow that seemed to move independently of the man himself.

"There's only one thing to do, and I must be the one to do it!" Jillian's father exclaimed to no one in particular. "He simply must be stopped."

"Dad, what are you…"

"Quiet, Jillian!" her father snapped. "We are all in grave danger, and I need to think!"

As the evening continued, and after several trips to the beverage cart, Morris Weston's behavior became more erratic. He scribbled random thoughts on every loose piece of paper he could find, only to throw the note into the trash as soon as he finished writing. He would catch a glimpse of his shadow in the corner of his eye and turn to yell at it for attempting to sneak up on him. He would even raise a finger to his lips to call for silence when no one was making any noise. When Jillian would attempt to protest, he would fly into a rage, but not at his daughter, never at her. He lashed out at the air as though voices were traveling on the wind and invisibly invading his mind.

Then, there was the book. At least once every fifteen minutes or so, Morris would stumble towards his desk and open a very unusual text. During one agonizingly silent period, while Morris stared into the heart of the nearest torch flame, Jillian stealthily crept over to her father's desk to inspect the book he had been periodically referencing. To her horror, a repulsive eyeball protruded from the cover and stared right back at her. She barely managed to stifle a scream as she turned the cover with one hand while holding her mouth closed with the other. Jillian was shocked to find that every page was blank. She was positive that she had chosen the correct book. It was the only one on her father's desk, and every time he examined it, he studied something on the pages, but there wasn't a single word written anywhere. In fact, there were no markings of any kind — just blank pages on smooth paper. Disappointed, Jillian closed the book without looking at the eye on the cover and returned to her seat.

With nothing else to do to keep her mind occupied, Jillian began to think back to when her father first introduced her to the world that had been hiding in plain sight. Only a month or so had passed, but in that short time, Jillian had been given transformative knowledge about who she really was and who she might someday become. Still, there were so many questions left unanswered and so many secrets to reveal.

***

It was the early morning of Jillian's thirteenth birthday when her father had woken her up and whisked her away to the horse stables. Jillian was still rubbing the sleep out of her eyes when she noticed a glow coming from the last stall that had been unoccupied the day before. As they moved closer to the closed stall door, the mysterious light began to intensify. Jillian instinctively put her hand on the door to open it but was stopped abruptly.

"I've longed for this day," Morris said lovingly. "I wish your mother could be here with us for this important celebration."

Jillian took a moment to read her father's face. He was excited for whatever was inside the horse stall, but there was something else that he was trying not to show. Sadness? Fear? She couldn't tell.

"What are we doing out here, Dad? Where is that light coming from?"

"Take a peek inside and see for yourself."

With that, Morris stepped aside and allowed his daughter to proceed. Jillian nervously put both hands on the stall door and slid it open in one quick motion. Inside the enclosure was something so extraordinary that Jillian could not believe her own eyes.

The hair on the animal was whiter than any cloud she had ever seen and gave off a glow of bright, pure light. The mane and tail were perfectly strung silver. And right in the middle of the creature's forehead was a horn that looked sharp enough to pierce anything that stood in the beast's way. There was no doubt about it. Jillian was in the presence of a real, live unicorn.

"How is this possible?" Jillian asked quietly as tears began streaming down her cheeks.

With her hand extended, Jillian started to inch closer to the beautiful creature lying before her. She wanted nothing more than to run her fingers through the silver mane, but the unicorn had other ideas and aggressively snapped its teeth at the young girl. Jillian jumped back in shock as the sweating unicorn thrashed its head back and forth anxiously.

"Dad, there's something wrong. I think she's in distress."

Morris excitedly moved towards his daughter until he was directly behind her. "Very good," he said softly. "Tell me why."

"It's obvious, Dad. She's scared. She doesn't want us here. That's why she keeps shifting her weight and moving her head back and forth. It's almost like she's…" Jillian's voice trailed off.

"Yes, my love. Finish your thought! She's…"

"She's pregnant," Jillian finished. "She's going to have a baby right now."

"Well done, my love! Well done! Your first Cryptozoology lesson, and you didn't even need it. This particular unicorn is carrying your birthday present, and we are going to help deliver it together."

"Wait. What did you just say? I can't deliver a baby unicorn, and what in the world is Crypto-something-ology? Is that even a word?"

Morris laughed at his daughter's confusion as he put on a long pair of gloves.

"I understand that you have questions, and I am happy to answer them, but right now, this baby needs to come out, and I need your help to deliver it."

Jillian nodded in agreement and put on a pair of gloves.

The delivery of the foal went as smoothly as possible. Jillian took instructions from her father about where to put her hands and when to pull, and she carried out each task as carefully as she could. She was surprised to find that she wasn't nervous or scared, as though she had been delivering unicorns her entire life. When the final push came, and the baby emerged, Jillian felt a wave of happiness wash over her.

"Do you feel that?" Morris asked knowingly. "Do you feel the moment filling you up inside? A new creature of pure goodness and magic has entered the world, and that light is part of you now. You helped deliver this little miracle, so I think it's only right that you name her."

Jillian's face lit up, and she smiled wide as she held the baby in her arms. The foal already had its own glow, and its features strongly resembled her mother's in every way except one. The tip of the baby unicorn's horn was shaded a pale green color. Jillian looked back at the mother and saw that her horn was entirely ivory.

"I want to call her, Jade," Jillian said thoughtfully.

"Ah yes. Good eye, my love. Some unicorns have slightly colored horns at birth. Your great aunt studied unicorns extensively, and her research concluded that colored horns represent powerful traits in the creature."

"What does a green horn mean?

"Well, let me ask you this. How did you feel while you were delivering this girl?"

"I felt strong and confident. I felt happy."

Morris smiled and nodded in agreement.

"That makes sense. A unicorn with a green-tipped horn will help support and protect loving heart energy. I believe that as the bond between you and Jade grows, she will help to keep your spirit nourished and make you brave in the face of adversity."

Jillian held the unicorn close and buried her face in its silver mane as she said a silent prayer that everything she had just experienced wasn't some sort of crazy dream.

"We really should get going, my love. This mother and baby need some time together, and I'm sure you have more than a few questions for me."

To Jillian's surprise, she didn't have that many questions for her father. Despite being presented with something impossible, her brain was ready to accept the existence of unicorns because its beauty and elegance didn't seem worth debating. It was just easier to embrace the magic of the moment than deny it.

Jillian gave her new friend one final squeeze and whispered, "I love you, Jade."

Then, both Jillian and Morris returned to the house and discussed the extraordinary traits of unicorns long into the night.

2

The next day, Jillian woke with unusual vigor and excitement. Her father had opened her eyes to an ocean of endless possibilities, and she wanted to dive right in. Of course, a million questions raced through her mind, not the least of which was to figure out the meaning of the word her father had casually used the night before - Crypto something or other. She was also dying to know what her place in this new world would be.

As Jillian peaked into her father's study, she found him sitting in his favorite chair and reading the morning paper while enjoying a cup of black English tea.

"Dad, last night was the best!" Jillian said sweetly as she danced into the room. "Thank you so much for Jade and for letting me help with her! She is the best birthday present ever!"

Morris put down his tea and his paper and extended his arms toward his daughter. She fell into his lap and embraced him with a long hug and several cheek kisses.

"You are very welcome, my love. Nothing makes me happier than when you are happy."

"So, what happens next?"

"What do you mean, Dear?"

Jillian chuckled and snuggled up even closer to her father.

"You know. What are we doing today? I'm ready to take the next step. I'm ready to do whatever it is you do."

Morris shifted uncomfortably in his seat as he picked up his ornate cup and sipped lightly at his near scalding beverage.

After he put the cup back down, he said firmly, "Jillian, last night was a magical evening. It was everything I hoped it would be and more. You have real talent, and I think you will become a brilliant Cryptozoologist, but you have much to learn before you are ready to do the types of things that I do. As vast as your potential might be, what you don't know in my line of work is likely to get you killed."

Jillian had been so caught up in the euphoria from the night before that she had not considered that her father's work could be harmful in any way, let alone lethal.

"How is what you do dangerous?" Jillian asked, annoyed and slightly confused. "We weren't in any danger last night, were we?"

"Oh yes, love. Considerable danger. Like most mythical creatures, unicorns are incredibly powerful. I had taken every possible precaution, but when I saw how distressed the mother was, I admit that I found myself a bit nervous."

"Yeah, I mean, she was thrashing around a lot, but she was in the middle of having a baby. I don't think she could have gotten up to hurt me even if she wanted to."

"Ah yes, but that's the very thing, Jillian. She didn't have to get up. I'm sure you noticed the sharpness of the horn on her head. Well, in addition to running you through, one stab from a unicorn's horn will turn you into stone."

Jillian gasped with terror.

"Are you serious?! Why would you let me help you if I could have been turned into a statue?"

"I almost didn't let you help me, but the moment was too perfect to pass up. Besides, I had taken several precautions, including the procurement of a very expensive and very rare elixir that could cure any wound you may have suffered. Luckily, that particular potion was not necessary, and we had a wonderful evening."

Jillian wasn't sure what to say. She was furious that her father could be so careless with her life, but she also wasn't willing to trade the memory of the previous night for anything in the world. Ultimately, she decided to forgive her father's lapse in judgment but resolved to be more aware of possible dangers and threats going forward.

The morning was not going as Jillian had hoped, and the excitement that carried her into the room had been dampened significantly.

"Okay, well, back to my original question. What happens next?"

"Well, I thought we might venture out for some birthday breakfast and then look in on Jade at the stables. How would that be?"

Jillian let out a heavy sigh as she rose from her father's lap.

"That's not what I mean, Dad. What happens next with me? I get what you're saying that what you do is dangerous, but I was serious when I said that I was ready to take the next step. I want to be like you. I want to be a…"

Jillian paused as she searched her mind for the correct term, but when nothing came to her, she became flustered and half-heartedly blurted out, "A Cryptopsycologist."

Morris folded his paper and set it aside.

"Jillian, my love, you have taken your first step into a world of unbelievable magic and creatures of magnificent power and beauty beyond your comprehension. It is only natural after seeing what you saw last night that you would want more. I am touched that you want to be like me, flawed as I am, but this role we play in the world, this position of ours, is a tremendous responsibility. A Cryptozoologist is part scientist, part activist, and part historian whose job is to protect the creatures and beings of mythology from the world and protect the world from the creatures and beings of mythology. When I told you that what you don't know could get you killed, that was no exaggeration."

Jillian stared at her father blankly, letting one or two questions form partially in her mind but never enough to travel to her lips.

After a few moments of trying to make sense of her father's explanation of things, she gave up and replied in frustration, "Dad, I have no idea what you just said."

Morris burst out laughing as he rose from his chair.

"Forgive me, my dear. I sometimes forget my audience. All I'm saying is that we have work to do. I will teach you everything I know, not just about mythical creatures, but also about acquiring and using spells, mixing a variety of potions, and some of the moral and ethical dilemmas we face in the line of duty. I have no doubt that you will pick it up quickly. Don't worry. It won't be as boring as you think."

Morris took his daughter to their favorite local diner, Flappy Jack's, for an extravagant birthday breakfast. For as long as Jillian could remember, she and her father had gone to Flappy Jack's every weekend and ordered enough food to feed a small army. As per their tradition, they chose one empty plate for themselves and filled it with the food they wanted for their meal. The rest of the feast was then immediately packed up and delivered to the nearest homeless shelter for distribution among the occupants. Once Jillian and her father made their selections, several waiters worked to clear the excessive food while Morris excused himself from the table to converse with the establishment's owner for a few moments. When he returned, the extra plates and people were gone, and the birthday business resumed.

"What do you have in mind for a birthday wish this year?" Morris asked while cutting up his french toast.

Jillian replied with a mouthful of eggs, "Kind of tough to top a unicorn, Dad."

"Manners, Dear. Chew, swallow, speak."

Jillian rolled her eyes and made a show of swallowing her food.

"I feel like there is this whole side of you I don't even know. Until last night, you'd always just been my dad. Now, I don't know what to think. I guess my wish this year is just to get to know you better."

Being the gentleman that he was, Morris did not outwardly show his emotions, but he was sad to learn that his daughter felt like she didn't know him. It had never been his intention to keep her any further from him than a safe distance, but he realized that even that much space had created a void that would require a bridge to cross.

"You have my word, Dear, from this day on, no more secrets or lies. Whatever you want to know, ask it."

Without hesitating, Jillian asked the question that was always in her heart.

"Where is Mom?"

Morris dropped his fork, and it clanged loudly off the table and onto the floor. There was a slight pause, and Jillian stared expectedly at her father. After a moment, Morris removed the napkin from his lap and gently dabbed at his lips while carefully avoiding his daughter's gaze.

"Excuse an old man, my love. It seems I need another fork."

Without waiting for Jillian's reply, Morris stood from the table and walked towards a collection of diner employees.

Jillian felt a sharp pain in her heart as she watched her father walk away from the one thing she was dying to know. Hadn't he just promised her truth? Hadn't he just made a vow that there would be no more secrets? Jillian wanted to leave, but she was too far from home to walk and was uncomfortable taking a bus or Uber alone. Instead, she decided to do the only thing she felt like she could do, which was sulk and move her eggs back and forth across her plate without eating them.

Morris returned with a new fork and immediately resumed eating his meal.

A few minutes of wordless, uncomfortable silence passed before Morris pointed at his daughter's plate with his knife and said, "Your eggs are going to get cold, Dear."

Jillian shrugged.

Morris let out a long sigh and set the silverware down on his plate.

"I don't think you're ready for the answer to the question you asked."

"I need to know."

"It's not the right time."

"Dad, please," Jillian said pleadingly. "I need to know."

Morris could see tears forming in his daughter's eyes even though she was doing everything she could to keep herself composed. He had taught her how to keep her emotions in check so they could never be used against her, but now, seeing Jillian struggle so mightily not to feel everything she was feeling, he wished that he had left well enough alone.

"I made you a promise today, and I intend to keep it, but before I answer your question, know this; this new world you are so desperate to learn about is dangerous. When we are training together, there are some things I will tell you and some things I will not for specific reasons that mostly have to do with your safety. With that in mind, you cannot question me about these things, and you must do exactly as I say when I say it. Do you understand?"

Jillian nodded vigorously.

"I understand, Dad. I'll do everything you say. Please, tell me where Mom is."

The moment of truth had finally come. There was no more time to wait, no more excuses to make. Morris knew his daughter well enough to know that she would not be denied, so with exaggerated effort, he cleared his throat, straightened a little in his seat, and said, "Your mother is the spiritual leader and keeper of stories and oral traditions for a tribe of humans who live on another planet called, Aryn. Many of the mythical creatures that inhabit our world were originally from Aryn, and it was on this planet that I met and fell in love with your mother. You were conceived and born there."

"Are… are you serious?"

Morris's impossible words floated around Jillian's brain. She tried to think back. She tried to grab on to any memory of being in another world, but there was nothing.

"Yes, Sweetheart. I'm serious. To the best of my knowledge, your mother is still living there now. As you can imagine, communication with her is difficult. I only get to see her once a year when the gate opens between our worlds. Even then, we take a huge risk because if you are caught on one side of the gate after it closes, you are trapped there until the following year when it opens again."

"Wait. Wait. If you and Mom get to each other once a year, why isn't she here with us now? Or why aren't we with her?"

"Nothing would make me happier than the three of us being together, and I promise you that your mother suffers greatly from missing out on your life. The problem is, her role as a spiritual leader is incredibly important for her tribe. The knowledge she possesses and passes on is vital to the survival of humanity on Aryn."

"Then let's go live on Aryn! I mean, if I was born there, then why shouldn't I grow up there? I would rather be with you and Mom in a completely different world than live my life here and never see her again!"

Morris reached out and wiped the tears from his daughter's face. He marveled at how much she was beginning to look like her mother.

His heart ached with regret, and he suddenly felt overwhelmed with the horrible possibility that every decision he had made to protect Jillian had been wrong.

"Jillian, now that you know about all of this, you will be able to see your mother every year as I do. Usually, the gate stays open for at least a few hours, but living on Aryn is out of the question."

"Why?! Why is it out of the question?!" Jillian demanded as her sorrowful expression turned to one of simmering fury.

"We're part of the Weston family. More importantly, you are the youngest Weston, and while that doesn't mean much to you yet, I can tell you that your position is one of great importance."

"What is so important about being a Weston that I have to live my whole life only seeing Mom once a year?"

"This is one of those moments where I cannot tell you the whole truth for your well-being, but I will say what I can. Our family is one of three that can trace their lineage directly back to the dawn of one of the great civilizations. If you search throughout history, you will always find three families at the heart of leadership, beginning in Mesopotamia and then to Egypt, China, Greece, Rome, and countless other empires, extending all the way to us in the United States of America. Over time, members of the three families became known in the magical community as 'the Godmakers'."

"But you're not an important leader or anything. You don't even work for the government."

"Appearances can be deceiving, my dear. The Godmaker families are not always seated in the most obvious places of power. In fact, in the last century, it has been quite the opposite. When my great, great grandfather first immigrated to this country from Greece, he decided to use his power and influence behind the scenes and not out in the open to protect his family. We have kept a low profile since that time, but I assure you, the members of our family still play an important role in the world of magic and myth."

"That still doesn't explain why we can't go live with Mom."

"All I can say is that being the youngest member of one of the three families of power is a distinct honor. You may or may not be called upon to fulfill certain responsibilities, but that is all I can tell you for the time being. Unfortunately, you must be here on this earth to perform those tasks if the time comes, and the world can't risk you being away if you're needed."

Jillian deflated in her seat and put her face in her hands to conceal the tears she was no longer able to hold back. Morris got up and joined his daughter on her side of the booth.

"My poor love. I know it hurts. I do, but you have a destiny that is bigger than you know. Plus, your mother and I have been preparing for this day ever since you and I left Aryn when you were two years old. She has written you so many letters and recorded countless video messages. In fact, through pre-recorded lessons she gave me last year, she will be your instructor regarding many mythical animals on which she is the foremost expert in her world and ours."

Jillian couldn't help but smile at the idea of her mom acting as one of her teachers. Even though they would only be able to see each other in person once a year, there was still a way for them to communicate through letters and recorded messages, and that was better than nothing.

"How long until the gate to Aryn opens?" Jillian asked hopefully.

"Three months from today," Morris answered with a smile.

"I want to go there. I want to go and be with Mom."

Morris kissed his daughter on the forehead and replied, "I wouldn't have it any other way."

3

My Dearest Jillian,

If you are reading this letter, then it means you have finally learned the truth about who and where I am, and soon, we will be together again. Your father has been good enough to provide me with countless photos and videos, and I have watched you grow from a precocious toddler into an intelligent, confident, and beautiful young woman. Alas, I am only a spectator of your life, an obsessed voyeur who would give anything to see you achieve each important milestone firsthand.

As I'm sure your father has explained, the world is more complicated than you realized. There are reasons, good reasons, for us to spend so much of our lives apart, but I would be lying if I said there weren't days when I would trade everything I am and everything I have to be with you. Together, you and I will explore the mysteries of our worlds. I will teach you what I have learned. I will guide you with my knowledge and experience. I will help prepare you to take up the mantle of your father's name, your name. Just know that who you are is not a matter of what you know, but rather, the people you love and love you in return. You will forever be in my heart, and I cannot wait to see you again.

Your Loving Mother,

Brityn

***

Much to Jillian's displeasure, Morris insisted that she begin her education slowly with pre-recorded lessons from her mother regarding several animal species native to Aryn that had made their way to Earth.

"The platypus, or platypulse as it is called on Aryn, does not possess the same level of power or ability on Earth that it does on its native world, but it is the only mammal on your planet capable of using electroreception for hunting prey in the water. On Aryn, the platypulse is also able to channel that electric energy into a

lightning strike that is capable of killing small animals or temporarily immobilizing a larger threat."

For several weeks, Jillian was an excellent student. She took copious notes and memorized everything presented to her. Still, as much as she enjoyed learning her family's trade from her mom, she was growing restless to begin practical, hands-on training. Morris did what he could to put off his daughter's growing ambitions and tried to refocus her on Cryptozoology, but it was no use.

After nearly a month of lectures from her mother, Jillian finally found herself in her father's library with nervous anticipation. Having been homeschooled since she was five years old, the Weston Family Library also doubled as Jillian's classroom. Each day, she received instruction from a variety of excellent tutors on all the usual subjects, but in addition to her formal education, she was also given lessons in Latin, archery, horseback riding, hunting, etiquette, social norms across a variety of cultures, and dance.

Jillian's socialization was deemed very important and was a high priority, but not for the purpose of making friends. Instead, Morris wanted his daughter to understand people so she could learn how to read and, ultimately, manipulate them. He arranged several play dates for Jillian each week where she would be given an emotional objective such as obtaining a secret from the other child or genuinely crying in front of a stranger. After the playdate, Jillian would wave goodbye to her new friend whom she would never see again and review observational notes with her father.

This highly productive and regimented upbringing resulted in two significant outcomes. The first was that Jillian became an exceptional human being, fluent in several languages, proficient in hand-to-hand combat, as well as armed combat, incredibly strategic, resourceful, and physically fit. The second outcome was that she tended to be headstrong, arrogant, and she often had difficulty making a genuine connection with people.

As Jillian waited anxiously for her father's arrival, she ambled around the library, taking in all of the titles and wondering what magic she might be able to find hidden within the pages. Up until that moment, she had known that her father often paid extravagant amounts of money for books on unusual topics such as alchemy, folklore from obscure cultures, and anything he could get his hands on related to dragons. The books and manuscripts he purchased were often in poor condition, which used to make Jillian wonder why her father would pay so much for made-up stories and theories from occult sciences. Now, she understood. All of the information her father had obtained throughout his life were not mere bedtime stories but rather, powerful spells, unbreakable curses, and the exact recipe for a potion that could make you live forever.

"I know what you are thinking, my love."

Jillian spun around, looking guilty even though she hadn't done anything wrong.

"You're thinking about which spell you are going to learn first. You're thinking about the power you could accumulate. You're thinking about doing incredible things like flying, becoming invisible, or maybe even cheating death. Am I right?"

Jillian was too embarrassed to make eye contact with her father, so she nodded while staring down at his shoes.

"No, my dear. Do not feel ashamed. Your feelings are completely normal and natural, especially given your lack of understanding about how everything works. While the Weston family has mostly contained itself to the preservation and well-being of mythical animals, there are many other facets to our hidden world that we will explore. Just as your mother has been taking the lead on the Cryptozoology portion of your education, I will give you a broader view of the various components of magic."

Returning to his previous examples, Morris continued, "Believe it or not, it is possible to fly and become invisible. Cheating death is, well, death is always paid what he is owed one way or another, but it is possible to delay him for a time. Even more incredible, this power is available to everyone in the entire world."

"Oh, come on, Dad. If everyone could learn how to fly, then why aren't we having this conversation on the Weston Family Cloud?"

"Excellent point, love, and coincidently, you've found your way to the subject of your very first lesson, which is the exploration of the origin of magic and how it works."

Jillian rolled her eyes and let out a heavy sigh.

"Are you serious?! I can already feel my eyes getting heavy. Can't you just give me a summary of the intro chapters so we can move on to the good stuff?"

"Jillian, skipping to the end of your training on the very first day is not only irresponsible, but it's also dangerous. Magic may be accessible to everyone, but acquiring that knowledge and power requires years of study and physical preparation. Even the strongest in our ranks usually only acquire a handful of truly powerful spells because of how dangerous it can be to achieve that power. Many well-trained and well-armed mages, or as they are often called, Elementals, die in the pursuit of that power."

Jillian softened her stance and began regaining the work ethic and composure that had been drilled into her over the years.

"I don't understand, though. If these books have all the answers, then why is learning magic dangerous?"

"There are hundreds of books in this library. All of them are pieces to an intricate puzzle, brushstrokes of an artist's masterpiece. That said, there is quite a leap from theory to practical application. Do you remember when you first began your archery lessons? How many times did you hit the target on your first day?"

"I never hit the target. Not even once."

"Precisely! And you had one of the finest instructors in New England teaching you exactly what to do, but being told how to do something is much different than actually doing it. Now imagine that I just handed you a book about archery and then told you to fire an arrow. How would that have gone?"

"I would probably still be out there trying to hit the target for the first time."

"Correct again. Nothing worth learning happens overnight, Jillian. Do not commit the sin of laziness. You are a talented young woman, but you did not get to where you are through dumb luck or coincidence. The only difference between everything you've done before and everything you are about to do is that the step you are willing to skip is likely the one that will lead to your death."

Jillian's eyes widened at her father's ominous words.

"Well, that's horrifying. Where do we start that's slightly less intense than everything you just said?"

It was Morris's turn to relax a little, and he gave a slight smile as he gestured Jillian toward her school desk while assuming his usual position in front of a chalkboard.

"Let's come at this from a different direction. What do you know about magic and myth? Tell me anything."

Jillian moved slowly towards her seat and sat down cautiously as though any sudden movements may lead to her demise.

"Well, on more than one occasion, I've heard you mention something about me being a Godmaker, and that made me think about some of the lessons we've had about polytheistic cultures. What exactly is a Godmaker, anyways?"

"Ah yes, the Gods. Fascinating beings. This is an excellent place to begin. Tell me what you remember."

"Umm. Not much. Just a few random stories from the Greeks. I remember some facts about Zeus, Poseidon, and Hades because they ran the whole world for a while. I remember the story about the Trojan Horse because I always thought it made more sense to fight a war for love than anything else. For some reason, I also remember stories about Pan, the God of the Forest. I don't know why, but he always stuck with me."

Morris flashed a knowing grin at his only daughter.

"You know, my dear, Pan's flute is quite the rare and magical item. One of a kind and lost to the ages after Pan's mysterious death. It's said that with the proper spell, Pan's flute can put nearly any mythical creature to sleep or, perhaps, a crying baby in the middle of the night."

"Yeah, right," Jillian said sarcastically. "Come on. Be serious."

Unfazed by his daughter's taunt, Morris went on, "It took me half my adult life to track the flute down. I fought acolytes of nearly a dozen Greek Gods, spent a fortune, traveled around the world three times, and finally, I found, not only the magical flute but Pan himself!"

"Wait...What?!" Jillian cried out in shocked disbelief. "Pan's real?!"

"As real as you and me. Pan is an immortal God, Jillian! He cannot be killed in the conventional sense."

Morris began pacing around the room excitedly as he spoke.

"To answer your original question, my love, the Godmakers are the youngest members of the three families of power. Quite simply, when the Godmakers come together, they have the ability to either create or destroy immortal Gods."

The words and their implications felt impossibly heavy, and Jillian felt as though all the oxygen were being sucked from her body as a violent sense of vertigo threatened to throw her from her seat.

Without realizing that his daughter was in distress, Morris continued, "When I found Pan, he was frail for a God, not much more than an ordinary, middle-aged man with a goat's legs. We spoke at length about his deeds, and he humored me as I told him some stories of my own. In the end, we struck a bargain wherein I would temporarily take possession of his flute with two conditions. Condition one was that the flute only be used for the protection or safety of a creature in peril. The second condition was that I return his property to him should the day ever come when the Gods return to power."

Jillian stood so quickly that she knocked her chair over. She began breathing frantically while her mind drowned in a sea of a million different thoughts at once.

"Wow. Okay. So, let me see if I understand what you're saying. On top of everything else you have piled on me, and that pile is pretty big at this point, you're telling me that there are Gods out there in the world, and I have the power to destroy them?"

Morris put his hands on his daughter's shoulders, but she shrugged them off.

"I know this news probably feels overwhelming, but you need to try and remain calm."

"Remain calm?! How am I supposed to remain calm when I have to worry that Zeus is going to zap me with a lightning bolt every time it rains?"

Morris could see that his daughter was unraveling quickly. It was only in that moment, watching her hyperventilate while muttering nonsense to herself about the Gods, that he stopped and thought about how much he had laid in Jillian's lap. Only weeks ago, she had been free from the burden of truth. Yes, she had questions about her mother, but she was happy. Now, the weight of magic spells, mythical creatures, different worlds, and living Gods was taking up all the space in her mind, and it was too much for her to bear. Morris realized that all of his planning and preparation had revolved around making Jillian the optimal student. He never considered that he might not be the optimal teacher.

Jillian continued to spin out as she walked and talked herself in circles, trying to make sense of everything. There was a big picture somewhere. She just couldn't get enough distance to see it. Now, she was lost in a vast ocean of information, drifting with no anchor to ground her and no compass to guide her, but through her panic, Jillian also noticed that there was something else. A noise was trying to break through, but she couldn't quite hear it, so she stopped pacing and closed her eyes while she concentrated on the sound in her mind. It only took a moment for Jillian to recognize the melody of a song she had heard many times before, but she couldn't remember when or where. She opened her eyes and saw her father sitting at his desk, casually playing a pan flute.

Jillian felt her heart rate begin to slow, and her breathing was returning to normal. She picked her chair up from off the ground and returned it to her desk.

"Is that what I think it is?"

Morris ignored his daughter's question and continued to play the soft, sweet tune. Jillian felt the calming music wash over her as she stood and listened to the familiar song.

When Morris could see that his daughter had fully recovered herself, he ended the song and put the pan flute down on his desk.

"Pan's flute is a very powerful, one-of-a-kind item. I keep it locked in our family's vault. This is a replica of that flute," Morris said as he gestured towards the instrument on his desk. "Your mother and I used it to soothe you as a baby until you fell asleep. It has no inherent magical ability, but I think you will find that the music can be peacefully hypnotic."

Jillian nodded in relaxed agreement.

"Jillian, you have repeatedly asked me to explain to you what comes next. Your thirst for knowledge and your dedication to mastering every endeavor you undertake are admirable. These traits will not only help you succeed but will also help keep you alive. As your teacher, I have prepared you well, but I fear that I have failed you as a father."

Jillian's face twisted with confusion. "But, Dad, that's not…"

"No dear, let me finish. Being a Godmaker is a large responsibility, but it is a duty that has been unfulfilled for many generations, partly because making or unmaking an immortal God is a very complex undertaking, but also because you must have all three Godmakers willingly participating in the ritual, and one of the three families has been lost to the ages for quite some time. Someday, we will talk in-depth about the Godmakers and what you might be called upon to do, but today is not that day."

Jillian opened her mouth to start a new series of questions, but Morris quickly raised his hand and continued, "What I do, what you will eventually do, is our job. It's an important job, and the world depends on us to do it well, not to mention the creatures we protect, but there is more to life than that. In the end, what's in your heart will always be more important than what's in your head."

When Morris finished his speech, Jillian did not try to ask any of her questions. Instead, she let her father's words sink in, and she reflected on what she was feeling, not what she was thinking.

"Mom wrote something like that to me in one of her letters. I have it framed in my room."

Morris shrugged his shoulders and grinned.

"Well, your mother is a wise woman. I probably stole that line from her."

Rather than continue the lesson about Gods, Morris told his daughter stories about her mother and their time together in Aryn. For the first time in her life, Jillian forgot about taking notes or memorizing facts. Instead, she allowed herself to be swept away by her father's words. She imagined herself as a baby, playing with magical animals like the

Permafox, a snow-covered creature with shards of ice protruding from its body like a porcupine's quills.

Hours slipped by in what felt like mere moments. Morris seemed to have no end to his collection of stories and adventures, each more thrilling than the last. Jillian was the perfect audience, drinking in his words, clutching a pillow with fear at the scary parts, and falling out of her seat with laughter at the funny ones. Her favorite stories, though, were the ones about when her parents had first met on Aryn. According to Morris, Jillian's mother initially thought of him as little more than an arrogant jerk.

"It took more than a little convincing and a rather unfortunate run-in with a gorilla who set my trousers on fire for your mother to see me as a friend, but eventually, we found love in one another."

Morris was in the middle of an interesting anecdote about a Tortwist, a particular breed of turtle that uses vines to swing from tree to tree through the forests of Aryn, when he was interrupted by a phone call on his private line.

"This is Morris Weston. How can I be of assistance?"

Jillian watched her father's facial expression rapidly change from cheerful to furious.

"You can't be serious. Right now?!"

The man's face continued to darken, and Jillian knew that whoever was on the other end of the phone was not delivering good news.

"Fine. I will call you back shortly."

Morris slammed the phone down onto the receiver and closed his eyes as he clenched his fists so tight that his knuckles turned white.

"Dad, what's wrong? What's going on?!"

"A fool is doing foolish things, Jillian. I need to make a few phone calls from my office."

"Can I come with you?"

"No!"

The refusal came out harsher than Morris had intended, making Jillian recoil from the sudden rebuke. Feeling guilty for his outburst, Morris quickly composed himself and approached his daughter more gently.

"I'm sorry, my love, but this is no lesson or game. A man, a powerful man, is playing with forces beyond his abilities, and I must put an end to it. Wait for me here. I will return after I make my calls, and I will tell you what I can."

With that, Morris exited the library, leaving Jillian alone with a room full of books about magic. It was the opportunity that she had longed for at the start of the day, but now, found that she no longer had any interest in seeking out the power on the pages of the varied texts. Instead, Jillian found a book of fables and made herself comfortable on one of the couches near the fireplace. She barely noticed when her eyelids grew too heavy to stay open, and the pan flute's melody began playing in the back of her mind as she fell asleep.

4

"Damn that man to the deepest caverns of hell!" Morris growled as he threw open the large library door. Jillian wasn't sure how long she had been asleep, but her father's thunderous entrance had frightened her so badly that she nearly fell out of her chair.

"Dad, what's wrong?" Jillian asked timidly.

Morris ignored his daughter's question and marched over to his desk, aggressively opening each drawer and slamming it shut when he failed to find what he was looking for.

"Where is the damn book?!" Morris demanded. "I can never find the thing when I…" Then, with a sudden fury, he used both arms to clear every single item from the desk's surface, scattering papers, folders, and books around the room.

For a few moments, Jillian stood motionless, unsure of what to say or do. Morris continued his destructive search, leaving a mess of broken artifacts and furniture in his wake. Not wanting to put herself in her father's path, Jillian dropped to her hands and knees and began picking up the fallen papers when she saw the mysterious book with the eye on the cover hiding beneath the desk's filing cabinet.

"Dad, look! I found your book!"

Morris dropped a stack of old parchment he had been examining and stalked over to his daughter. Without acknowledging her at all, he snatched the book from her hands and opened it on his desk.

"Aren't you even going to…"

"Not now!" Morris interrupted. "I have work to do, and time is of the essence."

For the next several hours, Jillian tried everything she could think of to calm her father down. She even toyed with the idea of playing the pan flute in the hopes that it would get through to him in the same way that it had worked for her, but she didn't know how to play any tunes, so she gave up on the notion. Jillian had never seen her father so broken down in this way. Even at his angriest, he always managed to maintain his composure, but his current mood could only be described as chaotic. He continually paced around the room while cursing himself and the man with whom he was quarreling. He drank more than a gentleman should. The worst thing, though, was that he wouldn't even let Jillian get a word in of any kind.

Finally, after a long period of horrible silence, with the occasional expletive directed at no one in particular, Morris turned his attention to his deflated daughter who had refused to leave despite the abuse he had hurled at her throughout the evening. He marveled at the young woman sitting before him. Only a year ago, she had seemed like such a little girl, but now there was no denying that a young woman had taken that little girl's place. With each passing day, Jillian's resemblance to her mother grew. Both women had the same strawberry blond hair, the same bright blue eyes, and the same full lips that could quickly turn into a playful pout.

Morris lamented the fact that he had only been training Jillian for a month, and the world was already ending. Worse than that, he had made a promise to be completely honest with her, and he was already facing a situation that would almost certainly require a lie, or at best, the omission of several details. He knew well enough not to underestimate Jillian. She was already searching for answers, and he had seen her inspecting the Weston Family Book when she thought he wasn't paying attention. Luckily, she wasn't ready for the information contained within the book, so there was nothing there for her to find, but that wouldn't stop Jillian for long. She was intelligent, resourceful, and clever; all traits engrained in her by Morris himself and by her many tutors throughout the years. On top of that, he couldn't be sure that he hadn't let some detail slip in his rage.

Morris took a deep breath and prepared to begin his made-up explanation of events but was interrupted before he could start.

"Don't do it, Dad," Jillian said softly.

"Don't do what, Dear?"

"Don't lie to me."

Jillian sat up straight in the large armchair where she had been resting and assertively stared into her father's tired eyes.

"We both know that whatever you were about to say was either going to be partial or complete nonsense, so let me save you from yourself. I would rather you say nothing than tell me something pretty that wasn't true."

Morris fell to his knees in front of his daughter and took her hands in his own. "You are too smart for me, my love," he said as tears welled up in his eyes.

Jillian wanted to be mad at her father for his attempted betrayal, but she knew how seriously he took his promises. For as long as she could remember, he had told her that a person's word is a powerful and sacred oath and should not be given lightly. For him to break that oath meant that things were worse than she could imagine, and he only wanted to spare her from the fear of a situation where she probably wouldn't even be able to help him.

"I have to go, Sweetheart."

"Where? Take me with you," Jillian pleaded.

Morris squeezed his daughter's hands tighter.

"Not this time, my love."

"Dad, please! I promise I'll stay out of the way! I promise!"

"Jillian, you are exactly what this man will use to hurt me. If you went, you wouldn't just be in danger; you would be his primary target. I need you to stay here, out of harm's way, while I handle this problem. I don't think the man I'm going to see is beyond reason, so hopefully, this will go no further than words."

"But what if it does? What if he tries to hurt you?"

It was Jillian's turn to lose her composure. She felt the tears streaming down her face, and her straight posture had all but melted into the flailing movements of a child's tantrum. When she could no longer hold herself upright, she fell into her father's waiting arms.

"Daddy, don't go."

It had been several years since Jillian had referred to her father as "daddy". The tactic did not go unnoticed as Morris could feel the pain in his heart resonate throughout his entire body. It was a cheap move, but then again, so was lying. He squeezed Jillian with the perfect mixture of strength and tenderness that only a father can achieve. Then, he kissed his daughter on the forehead and walked out of the room, leaving the poor girl to sob alone on the floor of the dim library in the middle of the night.

With each step he took, Morris began to regain himself and his determination to end a threat before it could begin. In his mind, the difficult part of leaving Jillian had been handled as honestly and delicately as possible. When he first began indoctrinating her into the world of magic, he had been completely candid about the real dangers they would encounter. Still, he had not yet explained that, occasionally, the whole world could face that same level of peril, and tonight was one of those nights.

As Morris passed by one of the manor's many attendants, and without breaking his stride or even turning to face the man, he said, "See her off to bed, please. And call security. I want at least two men posted at her door until I return."

The attendant nodded in the affirmative and quickly entered the library to carry out the orders he had been given. By the time Morris reached the carport, he had all but shaken the soft, sympathetic father and had once again found the unbreakable composure and focus that gave him a mental and emotional advantage over every person he faced.

The snow was already falling by the time Morris made it to the main road. With a two-hour drive ahead of him, he realized that he should have left sooner, but he didn't believe that his former friend would be crazy enough to use his power just to blackmail him into an unwanted face-to-face confrontation. Now, it was all too clear that the threat he had received earlier over the telephone was not a bluff after all.

An unforeseen snowstorm in June was not only completely unexplainable, but it was also incredibly dangerous. No one would be prepared to deal with the sudden change in weather, and it wouldn't take long for panic to set in. With each passing hour, the snow would fall harder, and the accumulation would quickly become unmanageable. Fear would spread quickly. People would make bad choices in the interest of self-preservation, which could lead to accidents, looting, and maybe even death.

When he arrived at the Easton estate, Morris found an empty security kiosk, and the large iron gate was wide open. He knew that he was willingly entering a trap, but there was no alternative. He had to try and talk sense into a deluded man who had once been like a brother to him.

In their youth, Morris Weston and Cecil Easton had been constant companions. Despite their many differences, Morris being tall, athletic, and outgoing, and Cecil being overweight, shy, and awkward, the boys were close friends. They accompanied their parents on important business trips worldwide, attended the same private school, and were the youngest members of two of the three Godmaker families. Morris and Cecil were also welcomed into the magical world at the early age of ten, rather than the usual age of thirteen, with the thought that the shared secret would bring the young men closer together and make them better, more well-rounded mages.

The Weston family boasted a long line of Cryptozoologists and adventurers, so George Easton, Cecil's father, hoped that his son would learn a little courage and daring from the Weston boy. The Easton family focused more on academic scholarship and produced many notable historians and occult scientists. It was even rumored that some of the only successful alchemists in history stemmed from the Easton family line.

Morris often heard his father joke to George Easton, "I'm sure there are many things your son could teach mine, but I don't know if Morris would even know what to do with a book if you handed it to him."

Then both men would laugh, and Morris would sulk away, wishing he cared more about the family texts and the lessons, but he just didn't. He wanted to soar with dragons and communicate with forest spirits. He wanted to live an exciting life, not read about the exciting things other people had done. Whenever Morris got down about his father's perception of him, he'd find Cecil, usually in a library somewhere, and ask his friend for advice.

"You know, Morris, you could take the time to learn some of this stuff."

"Gee. Thanks, Dad. That helps," Morris said sarcastically as he punched his friend in the arm.

Cecil dropped his book and rubbed his hurt shoulder.

"I'm serious. You're looking at this all wrong."

"What do you mean?" Morris asked in a bored monotone.

"You want to be a Cryptozoologist, right?"

Morris nodded.

"Well, the people in your field are discovering new mythical animal species every day. Every culture on our planet has had its fair share of beasts, monsters, Gods, mages, and everything else you can think of."

"So, what's your point?" Morris retorted unenthusiastically.

"My point is, every animal you encounter has strengths and weaknesses. When you go out into the world, how will you know how to defend yourself from a charging unicorn or what magical antivenom to use if you are stung by a buzzlebee if you don't study it? What you don't know is likely to be the thing that will get you killed."

Cecil's words washed over Morris like the burning waters from a hot spring, painful but also renewing.

"Wow. You're absolutely right. I'll die on my first day if I don't know what I'm doing."

Without thinking, Morris reached over and grabbed his friend's book right out of his hands. Cecil threw his arms up in protest.

"No, that's fine. It's not like I was reading that or anything."

Morris ignored the objection and began trying to read the text out loud but quickly found it impossible.

"What is this?" Morris asked as he turned the book over to inspect the cover. "I can't read any of it."

Cecil smiled, and replied, "That, dear boy, is a botanist's guide to possible species of plant life on Earth-like planets, in Latin."

Morris dropped the book and looked at his smirking friend with disgust.

"I hate you so much right now."

"Take your muscles over to the kid's section and grab a coloring book. Only the mind has power here."

Both boys laughed, and Cecil helped Morris find a beginner's guide to understanding the differences and commonalities between North American dragon species.

Those memories felt like a lifetime ago. Now, the only bond between the two men was a shared responsibility to use their magic and wisdom to protect the people and creatures of the world. Cecil had gradually cast that responsibility aside in favor of power. It was no secret in the magical community that Cecil had spent several years attempting to strengthen and consolidate his influence and authority. As a member of one of the Godmaker families, he felt that leadership was his right. In his search for new artifacts and spells, he systematically drove all of his friends and family away. Morris was one of the last people to try and stand by the man and help bring him back to his senses, but every conversation they had quickly became an argument. Their last encounter came on the night Morris told his best friend about his wife's pregnancy.

Cecil had always been slightly overweight as a teenager, but he had completely let himself go as an adult. Morris remembered how crazed his friend looked that evening, dressed in a shabby suit that barely fit him with an unkempt beard and bloodshot eyes. They were the same age, but somehow, Cecil looked twenty years older than he should. It seemed that in his search for power, he had lost all sense of himself. When Morris delivered the happy news of his impending fatherhood, Cecil exploded with fury that his "so-called friend" would dare to bring another Godmaker into the world without his consent. That was the final straw. Morris could feel the rage building within him, but he did not want to be drawn into a confrontation, so he tried to soothe his friend's ego, but he received nothing but venom in return. After a few more attempts at restoring order, Morris tried to leave, but Cecil blocked the exit.

"You will terminate that child, Morris!"

Morris attempted to move around Cecil without putting his hands on him, but the man was just too huge, and there wasn't enough space.

"Who are you to make such a demand?"

"I am a Godmaker," Cecil replied with zealous conviction.

"So am I you arrogant, power-crazed fool. You are a disgrace to…"

Before Morris could finish his insult, Cecil used all of his considerable weight to barrel into his friend, and both men fell back into the room.

As the two wrestled and rolled across the floor, Morris shouted, "You will never have my child!"

Cecil yelled and kicked and clawed at his opponent, but he tired quickly, and Morris was eventually able to get enough distance to stand, leaving his friend gasping for breath. Without waiting to see if Cecil would attempt another assault, Morris turned to move towards the door but felt a hand grab him by the shoulder. A wave of energy pulsed from his back and shot out like a cannon, throwing the would-be assailant across the room. Morris turned to see Cecil lying on pieces of a broken coffee table and groaning in pain.

With shock and anger in his voice, Cecil cried out, "You used magic against me?!"

Morris took a few steps towards Cecil but stopped just short in case a retaliatory attack was coming.

"I'm sorry. It's a defensive spell that I learned last year to keep people from sneaking up behind me. It only works if the person grabbing you is intending to hurt you."

There was silence. Cecil attempted to get up from the broken table but found that he was unable to do so. Morris extended his hand, but his friend brushed it aside with a wave and a grunt.

"You're making a huge mistake, Morris. You can't just give up your Godmaker title! My plan won't work if we don't do it together!"

For a moment, Morris saw his old friend as the funny, excited young man that he once was, fueled by knowledge just for the sake of knowing something, not power. He felt pity for the man before him now.

"I'm having this baby, Cecil. I don't care about your plan. I don't care about being a Godmaker. Now, I'm just going to be a father, and I'm going to teach my child everything he or she needs to know. You're living your life like you've got a dozen more coming to you, but you don't, Cecil. You're wasting your days with your foolish ambition and your lust for power. If you know what's good for you, you'll go back to being the smartest guy in the room and leave my family alone."

With that, Morris turned and walked out the door. As he left, he could hear Cecil screaming obscenities mixed with vows of revenge, but Morris blocked them all out and never looked back.

5

The unmistakable melody of Toccata and Fugue in D minor blared through the external speakers of a public address system. Morris feigned amusement, but the dark tones found their way inside him, taking sharp jabs at his courage. Like the iron gate on the property outskirts, the front door to the manor was wide open. Several inches of snow had already piled up inside the entryway.

"What game are you playing, Cecil?" Morris muttered to himself.

He continued to linger outside, trying to decide if he should follow the path that his adversary had laid out for him.

"You're no use to me dead, old friend," Cecil's voice boomed through the speakers. "Come join me in my study. I want to talk through a new proposition with you."

Morris looked around and spotted a camera pointed directly at him. He turned his head slightly and found a second camera aimed in his direction and then a third. There was no point in trying to gain the element of surprise. Every move he made was being carefully watched.

"Please close the door on your way in, Morris. We aren't animals, you know."

Cecil chuckled with amusement as Bach's masterpiece continued to play through the speakers.

As Morris made his way through the enormous house, he tried to take mental notes that could be useful to him, like which rooms contained weapons or the locations of the most accessible places to escape. The trouble was, he couldn't seem to shake the feeling that something terrible was about to happen, and somehow, Jillian would get caught in the crossfire. Morris tried to remember what it was like to do dangerous things before becoming a father. In those days, he didn't think. He just set his mind to what needed to be done, and his body responded flawlessly and without fail. Since Jillian, though, Morris's tactics had changed. He read more, studied more, and planned more. He had a compulsion to know every detail of each situation by heart, and even the slightest miscalculation or unknown element would likely result in him aborting his objective. He hated Cecil for forcing this moment on him. He hated feeling defenseless and unprepared. What he hated most, though, was the fear of not knowing what would happen next.

When Morris reached the door of the study, he paused for the briefest of moments, wondering if it was too late to turn back. After all, there was no way Cecil was crazy enough to follow through with his summer snowstorm. But then Morris thought of Jillian again, home alone and probably terrified. It was his job to protect her, and on the off chance that Cecil wasn't bluffing, her life, and the lives of many others, would be in danger. That was all the resolve Morris needed. He ran his hands through his hair, took a deep breath, and straightened himself to his full height. Then, he calmly and casually entered the room.

"Morris Weston, my oldest friend! I'm so glad you could make it!"

Cecil practically skipped over and threw his arms around his guest as though there had never been any bad blood between them.

Morris did not return the embrace and responded coolly, "Yes, well, to be honest, I had some trouble getting here. The roads are already getting dangerous for travel."

Cecil released his friend and threw his head back with laughter. "A joke! Just a joke! I thought you would find it amusing. After all, you were always the one with the real power, right? I thought it would be fun to show you that I finally made my way to your level."

Morris eyed Cecil with heavy suspicion and dread. Despite his cheerful tone, there was no hiding the anger and intensity in Cecil's eyes. Even the lines on his face seemed to strain with each fake smile. A conflict was coming. It was only a matter of time.

"Yes, it would seem you've picked up a spell or two, but the Cecil I knew believed that knowledge was the real power, not magic tricks."

The smile on Cecil's face faded a little, and Morris could see that his words, for better or worse, had hit the mark.

"This storm is no mere trick, old friend. I have the power to white out the whole world if I wished."

Morris continued to act unimpressed as he walked towards the beverage cart. He picked up the most expensive bottle he could find and poured himself a generous dram.

"I'm glad to see your taste in scotch is still quite excellent," Morris said nonchalantly. "Regarding your threat, well, walk me through it. Why end the world? Being the last man standing in a tundra is its own kind of victory, I suppose, but there will be no one around to see it, so I'm not sure I understand the point of all this."

With that, Morris threw back his drink in one swallow and helped himself to another pour.

"Oh, my short-sighted fool of a friend, I have no intention of destroying the world with this storm. I merely meant to show you what I was capable of so that you would come to speak with me." Cecil flashed an evil grin. "Besides, why kill every person when I need only to kill the right person?"

Before Morris had a chance to react, Cecil snapped his fingers, and chains made from solid ice materialized from the floor, binding Morris's wrists and ankles.

"You'll have to forgive the restraints, but I can't risk you doing something clever like the last time when you sucker-punched me with that spell that launched me through my coffee table."

Morris pulled hard against his chains, but they connected to hooks on the floor, and there was no chance of breaking them.

In both anger and desperation, Morris yelled, "Cecil, I swear to you, if you harm a hair on my daughter's head, it will be the last thing you ever do. No amount of magic will save you from me."

Cecil pretended not to hear the threat as he maneuvered around his friend and moved towards the beverage cart. He slowly prepared himself a cocktail while humming along with the music still playing in the background. When he finished making his drink, Cecil walked back in front of his restrained friend and tried reading the emotions on the man's face. His grinding teeth were like that of a wild animal preparing to kill its prey. The deep lines on his forehead showed thoughtful contemplation, the beginnings of what might be a plan to escape. His eyes were burning with rage, but there was something else there too. Beyond the fire of anger, there was the one thing a Godmaker hoped never to show, fear. It was only a drop, the smallest possible amount, but it was enough, and Cecil seized upon it.

"What happens to your dear, sweet daughter is entirely up to you, my friend."

Cecil lingered on the word 'friend,' and it dripped out of his mouth like poison falling from the sharp fang of a venomous snake.

Trying to maintain his courageous facade, Morris replied, "Just tell me what you want so I can refuse you, and we can try to figure out what happens next."

"What do I want?" Cecil mused. "You know, after all our years of friendship, you've never once asked me that question. You aren't even really asking me now. In your self-righteous mind, you've already decided that you are the hero, and I am the villain."

Morris continued to stare straight ahead, but there was no hiding his fear now. No matter what he said or did, if he genuinely believed that his daughter's life hung in the balance then he knew he could be convinced to do anything.

"I want to be a God, Morris!" Cecil said sharply.

"Is that all?" Morris asked with heavy sarcasm. "Why on earth would you think I would refuse such a simple and reasonable request?"

Unfortunately, Morris knew Cecil's demand was not even slightly exaggerated. He wanted the Godmakers to use their power to strip away his mortal soul and replace it with the essence of eternal life.

"You know that what you ask is impossible," Morris added flatly.

"Impossible?!" Cecil yelled as he closed in on his friend. "You would think so. Your mind has always been limited. Black and white. Right and wrong. Your greatest failure is one of imagination. No, what I want is not impossible, just difficult."

"Fine. Enlighten me. How is it that you think you can become a God? You need all three Godmakers, and it has been several hundred years since the whereabouts of the third family have been known. Also, one of our three Godmakers is your estranged son, whom you haven't seen in years due to your physical abuse and emotional neglect. I highly doubt your ex-wife will be too keen on having him participate in this little endeavor, especially given the restraining order. Finally, there is the essence of power. You must possess the essence of the God you wish to supplant, the source of their power. There hasn't been a reliable record of the bolt, the trident, or the helm for almost a thousand years."

Cecil shrugged as though the problems he had just been presented were trivial details.

"As usual, you lose the forest through the trees. We don't need all three sources of power, just one, and as it happens, I am closer to finding the trident than you think. I have spent the last several years strengthening my abilities as a Water Elemental. I am ready to become the new Poseidon."

"Even if you do find the trident, what makes you so certain you will be able to wield it? You are no longer a Godmaker, and such tools are not meant for mortal men."

"Too true, my friend. There is only so much power I can attain on my own, which is why I went out of my way to acquire this."

From under his collared shirt, Cecil pulled out a necklace chain with a blue pendant attached to it that glowed and pulsed with living energy.

"That's an element stone!" Morris said in disbelief. "Those aren't even supposed to exist in our world!"

"Who says the stone is from our world?" Cecil replied playfully.

"You've gone too far this time, Cecil! You are interfering with forces beyond your control!"

"Wrong again, Morris! Everything is under my control."

Cecil dropped his calm and casual pretense. He was done pretending the man before him was anything but a hostage and a means to an end.

"It comes to this, Morris. You will make your daughter fulfill her duty as the youngest Weston, and you will help me find the missing Godmaker. Once I have been made immortal, you and your family will be safe."

"And what happens to the rest of the world when you become a God?"

Cecil's smile returned, but this time it was relaxed and genuine.

"I will use my power to restore faith in the old Gods, and I will rule, of course."

Morris pulled at his restraints, but it was hopeless to try and break free.

"And what if I refuse to help you?"

"I thought you might say something like that."

With a snap of his fingers, Cecil called forth a cyclone of ice, snow, and freezing winds that created a miniature blizzard in the middle of the room. Morris knew that something was happening in the eye of the storm, but the winds were too strong, and the snow created a thick shroud that blocked any view of the activity taking place at the center. Then, as quickly as it came, the blizzard dissipated, and, in its place, there stood one of the legendary White Knights of Winter.

The warrior wore a shining suit of armor made from platinum metal. Several pointed shards jutted out from the shoulder plates and helm, giving the armor the appearance of being covered with a hundred deadly icicles. The ornate shield was a thick wall of sculpted ice decorated with snowy mountain peaks. The knight's weapon was a large, heavy mace and chain. There was only darkness behind the two eye slits in the helm and the occasional cloud of frozen breath coming from whatever was living underneath the armor.

"I'm sure you recognize this fellow," Cecil mused casually. "The White Knights of Winter, a fierce and unbeatable band of warriors who can only be controlled by the most powerful of Water Elementals. I summoned one here to show you the measure of my resolve, but there are nine others currently closing in on your home. They have orders to either capture your daughter if you are willing to cooperate or kill her if you are not. The choice is yours, my friend."

6

Jillian watched the snow falling from her bedroom window and tried not to think about how cold she was. She guessed that about six inches had fallen so far, and there was no sign of the storm letting up. Under normal circumstances, when Jillian was cold in the middle of the night, she would just grab an extra quilt and try to get warm under the covers of her bed, but she was too nervous to lay down, so she continued to stare out her window shivering in the darkness.

When her teeth started chattering, Jillian decided she couldn't stand it any longer, and she opened her bedroom door to find two of her father's men standing in the hall. The man on the right was tall and slim with long legs that seemed to make up most of his body. Jillian thought he might be somewhat handsome if not for the vacant expression that he wore on his face. The man on the left was shorter but very muscular. He had an angry, formidable look like he had been in, and won, many physical confrontations.

"Excuse me, Gentlemen, but it is unbearably cold in my room. I was wondering if it would be possible for one of you to bring me my winter clothes?"

The two guards exchanged looks and then stared back blankly as though they didn't understand the question, but after a moment, the tall man responded, "Sorry, Miss, but the winter clothes are all shut up in the attic. Probably won't be seeing those again until, well, until winter, I would guess."

Both men laughed stupidly at the jest. Jillian faked a smile so as not to offend them.

"That would be a good point, but I'm sure you've noticed that the snow has decided to make a dramatic return."

The two men continued their laughter, appreciating that Jillian had been willing to play along with them. Now that she was in on the joke, Jillian decided that her best bet was to act like a helpless child in the hopes of stirring their pity. As she summoned a few tears and pouted her lower lip slightly, she wondered if either of the two men had children of their own and if the memory of those children would make her approach more effective.

"The thing is, my daddy left me here all alone without telling me anything about what he's doing or where he's going. I'm really scared that he's in trouble, and I just want to go to sleep so I can stop worrying about him, but I'm too cold to relax. Is there anything you can do to help me?"

Jillian immediately noticed a change take place in the tall man. His vacant expression was gone, replaced with a look of parental concern. He probably wasn't even aware that she had caught his attention, but she had, and if he had been the only man in the hall that evening, that probably would have been enough to send him climbing into the attic, but unfortunately, his colleague was not willing to take the bait.

"Oh, you're good, little girl. Isn't she good, Carl?" the short man said in a thick Irish accent.

Not sure what was happening, the tall man shook his head in agreement. The short man had a smile on his face that Jillian thought was equal parts amusement and pity.

"Look, you've got some moves. I'll give you that, but I've got a son about your age and it'd be a cold day in hell before he referred to me as 'daddy'."

Both men laughed as Jillian's face flushed with embarrassment.

"I'm sorry. I don't… I didn't mean to…"

"Save your sorry's, kid," the short man cut in. "No harm, no foul."

Then, he turned to his tall companion and said, "Carl, take this young woman down to her dad's library and build her a fire. I'll go see about getting her something warmer to wear."

Carl gave a mocking salute and replied, "Sure thing, Knox. You got it."

Jillian's new bodyguard escorted her to the Weston family library in silence. She found that she almost had to jog alongside him just to keep up with his long strides. When they arrived in the large room, he went right to work building the fire while Jillian pushed her favorite chair closer to the fireplace.

As Carl stacked wood and searched the area for a long match, Jillian sat in the chair and tried to think of something to say that might fill the uncomfortable silence. After her failed attempt at manipulation, she felt very exposed and painfully aware that she was alone with a grown man in her pajamas.

"I'm sorry if I… offended you earlier," Jillian said meekly.

"It's nothing, Miss. The cold makes us do crazy things," Carl responded with a chuckle.

Jillian wasn't sure what that meant, but she didn't know what else to say, so she just sat back quietly until the fire was roaring.

Carl and Jillian wordlessly warmed their hands next to the burning logs as Jillian continued to search for something interesting to say, but every time she tried to start a sentence, she caught sight of Carl's blank face and talked herself out of whatever she had been thinking. Jillian just started wondering if the quiet was actually worse than the cold when Knox returned with a heavy blanket and broke the terrible silence.

"Sorry, Miss, but the attic is locked up tight. I couldn't get to any of your things, but I did find this huge quilt. Between that and the fire, you should be square."

"Thank you, Mr.…."

"You can just call me, Knox."

Knox brought the quilt over to where Jillian sat and draped it over her shoulders.

"Carl, why don't you go stand guard in the hall. I'll stay here with the girl."

Carl shrugged before giving another mock salute and exiting the room, closing the large double doors behind him.

Jillian looked over at her new companion and saw that he didn't have an angry look on his face anymore. Maybe he never had because now she thought he looked more worried than anything.

"So… Mr. Knox, how is it that you came to work for my father?"

"Just Knox, Miss. Me and your dad go way back. I do a bit of muscle work for the old man from time to time. Plus, my son and I work in the stables and anywhere else your dad needs us."

Jillian's mind immediately went to her unicorn, and she wondered how much Knox knew about her dad's work.

"Dad is very proud of his stables. You and your son do excellent work keeping the horses well trained."

"Oh, sure. The horses are a piece of cake. It's the unicorn that gives us fits."

Knox shot Jillian a sly smile, revealing that he was in on the family secret.

"It's a funny thing your father does. Monsters and magic and such. I don't pretend to understand any of it."

"I'm pretty new to all of this too. My dad has been training me, but it's a lot. I would never admit this to him, but sometimes I wonder if I can handle it all."

Knox turned and knelt next to Jillian's chair.

"If you don't mind me saying, Miss, the trouble is that you are too isolated here. I've told your dad this a thousand times, but how are you supposed to be expected to save the world if you aren't even in the world? I've seen you ride a unicorn, hit a bullseye from an obscene distance, speak to visiting dignitaries in languages I've never heard of, and beat the hell out of your combat instructors. You're a perfect student, but I've never seen you be what you are, a kid. Come down to the stables, and spend some time with my son, Cain. He's arrogant and a bit of a fool, but he's also good for a laugh, and he'll show you some fun that doesn't have anything to do with your training."

With all of the advantages Jillian had been given throughout her life, she never considered what she might be missing. She knew without question that her father loved her, but he had always been closer to a teacher and mentor than a parent. He never seemed to second guess himself or question the danger of a given situation. She thought back to the night Jade was born. Would any other father in the world be willing to take the risks that he took that night? Was she a daughter to him or a prized pupil?

"You know what, Knox? That sounds great. I would love to spend some time with you and Cain. Do you think…?"

"Shhhhh. Quiet. Now." Knox stood quickly and walked over to the window. "What the hell is that?"

"What is it?" Jillian asked nervously. "What's going on?"

When Knox didn't answer, she threw off the blanket and ran over to where he stood. She looked outside at the frozen landscape but didn't see anything except the falling snow.

"There's something coming this way," Knox said menacingly. "Something evil."

Without turning away from the window, Knox drew two pistols from holsters hidden underneath his coat. "You stay right here in this room. Don't let anyone inside but me or your dad. Got it?"

Jillian nodded. "What are you going to do?"

Knox raised his weapons and replied, "Not every problem has a magical solution, Miss."

With that, he quickly walked out of the room and locked the doors behind him.

Jillian stood alone in the library, unsure of what to do next. She continued to look out the window, searching for whatever had sent Knox running from the room with his guns drawn, but she couldn't make out anything in the storm.

"They are coming," a voice whispered.

Jillian spun around to see who had spoken, but she couldn't find anyone else in the room.

"Hello? Is someone there?" Jillian tried to sound calm and assertive, but she was sure that her fear was plainly audible.

"They will be here in minutes," another phantom voice intoned. "She is not ready."

"Who will be here in minutes?!" Jillian called out as she felt panic starting to set in. She continued to search the room frantically, but the flames from the fire and the terror in her mind created shadows of monsters on the walls, surrounding her on all sides.

"She is a Godmaker!" a third voice shouted. "She must not be captured or killed!"

"Stop talking about me like I'm not here! Just tell me what's going on, or leave me alone!"

"As you wish, Godmaker," all three voices whispered in unison. "Go to your father's book and see for yourself."

Jillian hesitantly walked over to her father's desk and once again found herself face to face with the unblinking eye. She reached out towards the cover, but before she could make contact, the book flew open on its own causing Jillian to scream and jump back as the pages turned wildly.

Once the heavy text came to rest in a particular spot, Jillian waited a few moments until she was convinced that the book had found the proper page. She approached with nervous anticipation, wondering what magical creature would be revealed, only to be completely let down by the sight of two empty pages.

"I still can't read it," Jillian yelled in frustration. "All the pages are blank."

"Look again, Godmaker!" the voices replied urgently. "See the enemy that approaches."

Suddenly, the figure of a fierce knight started taking shape on the previously vacant pages. Then, another knight appeared and another after that. When the picture was complete, nine formidable-looking warriors were marching in the midst of a raging snowstorm. Some carried blades, while others favored a mace or a morning star. One knight held a large, two-handed battle-ax. Each soldier had shining white armor that was almost invisible in the snow.

"That's it," Jillian shouted. "Their armor makes them blend into the storm!"

She ran back to the window and looked out at the horizon again, but this time, she looked for shapes that didn't belong. It didn't take her long to spot the knight wielding the giant ax. Once she found him, the rest were easy enough to spot.

"They are called the White Knights of Winter," one of the ghostly voices explained. "They are a band of ten legendary warriors who are neither living nor dead. They do not eat or sleep. They do not feel pain or fatigue. Their sole purpose is to carry out the task given to them by their master, which could only be the most powerful of Water Elementals or a God of the Sea."

"Okay. Well, my dad is out dealing with a problem right now, so why would they be coming here?"

"The White Knights have not come for your father, Godmaker. They have come for you, dead or alive."

"WHAT?!" Jillian yelled as she tried to steady herself against the desk. "Why would anyone want to kill me?! I don't know anything! I can't do anything! I don't even know any spells yet!"

Jillian could feel her fear rising. None of this made any sense. She thought back to the start of the day when she begged her dad to skip to the end of her lessons. Now, she would give anything to go back to the beginning to learn one thing that might be useful in this crazy life or death situation.

"Fear not, Godmaker," all three voices said in staggered whispers. "There is one spell that can save you and your father."

"Great!" Jillian said desperately. "How do I use the spell?"

"You've truly learned nothing, Godmaker," one of the voices said with disgust. "You do not use the spell. It must become part of you."

"You must learn Prometheus' Fire," the second voice added. "It is an ancient magic of the Fire Elementals and your only hope to survive."

Jillian let out a yell of frustration and forcefully grabbed the book off the desk.

"I don't have time for these riddles! Just tell me how to save my dad."

The fireplace turned from red to blue, and a ball of living flame shot out onto the ground. A small but intense inferno burned in a tight ring on the floor.

Now, the third and most powerful of the three spirits spoke forcefully, "Step into Prometheus' Fire and allow it to burn away everything that you are. If you survive, you will emerge with the power you need to save yourself and your father. If not, Morris Weston will resume his former post of Godmaker and spend the rest of his days mourning you."

"You want me to step into that fire pit on purpose?! I can't do that! No one can do that and live!"

"If that is your answer, then you are already lost," the voices replied calmly. "With any luck, the White Knights of Winter will simply kill everyone in the house quickly and capture you rather than kill you."

"Why would they kill everyone if they are just after me?" Jillian asked startled.

"The people in this manor are tied to your family. They have all been ordered and are honor-bound to protect you with their lives. They will not shrink in the face of their duty."

Jillian thought about her new friend, Knox. He had no idea what was coming for him, and he didn't care. Based on how he ran out of the room with his guns drawn, Jillian had no doubt that he was planning to fight until his last breath. What Knox didn't know was that the fight wouldn't be a fair one, and no number of bullets were going to save him.

Without another moment's hesitation, Jillian walked over to the ring of fire and stepped inside.

7

The fire consumed Jillian in an instant. She felt the flames spread over her entire body as she tried to scream, but the heavy, black smoke filled her lungs and stole her air. All she could do was stand there and slowly turn to ash as her blood boiled and her skin melted away. Jillian closed her eyes and waited for death to take her, but it didn't happen. The pain she was experiencing was unbearable, and it felt like it had been hours since she had taken her last breath, but for some reason, she wasn't dying. She wasn't even close to death. If anything, her senses were as sharp as they had ever been, and her mind was clear.

Jillian opened her eyes to find that she was no longer standing in the Weston Family Library. In fact, she wasn't standing at all but rather floating in place. To her left, Jillian saw her burning body screaming with unimaginable pain. To her right, there was a river of clear, blue water. It shimmered with light and made a powerful rushing sound that put Jillian at ease. There was nothing but darkness in every other direction. Jillian didn't want to return to her burning body, so she willed her essence closer to the river.

The first thing Jillian saw was a fish flopping hopelessly with its last bursts of life on the shore at the water's edge. She wanted to help the poor creature, but there was nothing she could do without her body, so she watched the fish slowly stop convulsing and die. Jillian was overcome with sadness but found herself unable to cry.

She started to float away when a deep, rumbling voice called out, "Do not mourn for me. You are the one who is dying."

Jillian turned back and saw that the fish had somehow returned to the water and had grown considerably. She also noticed that the creature now somewhat resembled a grown man. Or at least, she thought it did. Every time she tried to focus her vision, the being would change from a fish to a man or a man with a fishtail or a fish with a man's head. She couldn't be certain.

Jillian had no voice in her disembodied state, so she cried out in her mind, "Who are you?"

"I am a friend who has come to help you," the man-fish replied.

"Who says that I need your help?"

The man-fish splashed his tail hard against the water. "You are the essence of the shell burning on the shore. I removed you from your body so that it will not die. Sadly, I cannot keep you like this for long, but if you would rather I just swim away, I would be happy to return you to your body so you can finish turning to ash."

Somewhere in the back of Jillian's mind was a vague memory of the voices from her dad's library telling her that she was supposed to burn to nothing, but that moment seemed like nothing more than a dream from someone else's life. The reality was she was dying slowly and painfully, and there was nothing she could do to stop it from happening.

"No, please. Don't go," Jillian thought pleadingly. "I don't want to die."

"I don't want you to die either, which is why I saved you. As it happens, I am dying too, but much more slowly than you." The man-fish flashed a sly smile. "Maybe we can help each other out."

Jillian wasn't sure why, but she didn't believe she could trust the man-fish, especially since she couldn't see its true form clearly even after staring intently for several minutes. Still, Jillian looked back at her burning body and saw the agony displayed on her face. When she returned to that body, the fire would overwhelm her again, and she would surely die.

Tentatively, Jillian asked, "What do you need me to do?"

The man-fish laughed and splashed his tail again.

"That's the best part! I don't need you to do anything. At least, not right now. You see, my brother and I each lost something we need. Right now, you're just a little girl, but one day you'll be a strong and powerful woman. When that day comes, I'll need you to help us recover what we lost."

"Fine. What do I get in return?"

"In return for your future help, I will let you bathe your body in my river."

"What good will that do me?" Jillian thought impatiently.

"This river is as old as time. It flows with all the healing properties of water magic. One quick dip, and your body will be completely protected from the fire that is killing you. You won't even feel the pain of it anymore!"

Jillian couldn't shake the nagging suspicion that there was more to the bargain than she knew, but she was running out of time and couldn't see any other alternative.

Still, she didn't want to seem too eager to play along, so she responded, "What's the catch?"

The man-fish gave a look of mocking sadness.

"Why would you think there is a catch? You need my help to save your life. I need your help to save mine. It's a square bargain. Say the word, and I will return you to your body. You run over here as fast as you can and dive into my river, and then, we're done. When my brother and I are ready, we'll find you, but it will be years before that day comes. Do we have a deal?"

Jillian took one final look at her body, writhing in pain, screaming like hell but unable to be heard or escape into the sweet release of death. She found herself wishing she had had more time to train with her father. Deep down in her soul, Jillian believed she was only as good as the lessons she had learned, and the truth was, she just didn't know enough to save herself or anyone else on her own.

She returned her focus to the man-fish and hesitantly replied, "Deal."

In the blink of an eye, all the sensations of being burned alive returned to Jillian, who cried out in endless pain. She tried to make her way towards the magic river, but the fire and smoke disoriented her. She fell several times, barely finding the strength to get back up, wanting nothing more than to stay down and wait for her life to end. With her last effort, she leaped in the direction of the river, barely falling short of the life-saving water, except for her right hand, which stretched out just enough to find sweet relief. The sensation revitalized Jillian and gave her the strength and will to pull herself towards the river inch by inch. She found slow but satisfying salvation, and when her body was fully submerged, she sat on the river bottom for several moments until all traces of the flame had been wiped from her body and mind.

The man-fish swam to where Jillian sat and circled her like a shark moving in on its prey, all the while maintaining his sly smile.

"Looks like we have a deal. Here's a little something so you don't forget."

The man-fish slapped his tail fin hard against Jillian's right arm and pinned it down against the river bottom.

Jillian could feel the searing pain of her burning flesh. She screamed and filled the water around her with the bubbles of her barely audible cries. When the man-fish removed his fin, she looked down and saw a black trident imprinted on her forearm. Knowing that she had been tricked, Jillian closed her eyes and wished for the mark to disappear. When she opened them up, the man-fish was gone, and she was once again staring at the fireplace in her family's library.

"What in the hell happened to you?" a voice called out from the doorway.

Jillian turned to find Knox reentering the room. His guns were still drawn, and he had blood running down his face from a wound she couldn't see.

"Nothing. I'm fine. What happened to you?"

"You're fine? Like hell, you're fine. Look at you! You're soaking wet and sitting in a puddle like you just stepped in from a hurricane."

Jillian looked down at her clothes and realized that Knox was right. She was soaked to the bone and freezing despite being directly in front of the fire. She grabbed the heavy blanket that Knox had brought her earlier in the evening and draped it over her shoulders.

"It's not important. What's going on out there?"

"Well, there's an army heading this way, princess. They are strong as bears, most likely unkillable, and meaner than my old man after a night out with Jack Daniels. Carl got banged up pretty bad, but I got him and my son to safety. They are hiding out in the stables, which is where we are going right now."

Jillian nodded in agreement, but before they had a chance to exit the library, there was a loud crash just outside the room. The doors to the library were large and heavy, but they were made of wood. With enough force, they would break apart, and the White Knights would most likely kill them both.

Knox holstered his guns and started pushing as much furniture as he could move in front of the library's entrance. Jillian moved to help but stopped short. The man-fish had saved her from burning to death, but she couldn't remember why she had been on fire in the first place.

"Any time you want to participate in saving our lives, just jump right in!"

Knox's yell shook Jillian out of her trance, and she ran over to help him push her father's large desk in front of the doors. They both knew that no barricade would save their lives, but they weren't ready to give up, so they kept pushing. With one final shove, the pair managed to slam the desk against the entryway, knocking several items down onto the floor with the effort. Jillian bent over to pick up everything that had fallen when she saw her father's book with the eye. Suddenly, everything came flooding back into her mind.

"Prometheus' Fire," she yelled! "That's it! I have to use Prometheus' Fire!"

Knox looked over at the young woman who was dripping water everywhere she walked. It was his job to protect her and give his life for her if it came to that. He had no way of saving either of them from what was coming, but he wasn't about to give up. He would fight until his last breath, and whether that fight lasted ten minutes or ten seconds, he would die doing whatever he could to keep her alive a little longer.

"What are you going on about?" Knox asked as he searched for more furniture to add to the barricade.

"It's a spell! I learned it, I think," Jillian said hesitantly.

There was another crash at the door, and this time, pieces of wood splintered into the room. Through the holes, Jillian got her first look at the legendary White Knights of Winter. Knox pushed his weight against the desk, doing everything he could to keep the warriors at bay, but he was only one man against a small army.

"That's great, girly. If you've got some juice, I'd love to see it right about now."

Jillian held out her hand, hoping something would happen, but nothing did. After a few more useless hand gestures, she began to panic.

"I don't... I don't know how to use it."

"Think Jillian! Think!" Knox said as he pushed his shoulder back into the desk. "What did your dad teach you about magic?"

Jillian started pacing. "I don't know! I don't know! We haven't talked about using spells yet. I don't know what I'm supposed to do!"

"Take the flame, Jillian," whispered one of the mysterious voices. "Take the flame."

The message echoed several times, and then the room fell silent again.

"What does that mean?" Jillian asked urgently. "How can I take the flame?"

Knox turned to see Jillian turning in circles while talking to the empty air above her head. "Umm. Who exactly are you talking to, love?"

Jillian ignored him and walked over to the desk. She picked up her father's book and tried to open it, but the eye was closed, and the book would not open.

"How am I supposed to take the flame?! Tell me! TELL ME!"

Another crash came into the room, and this time, Knox was thrown violently across the floor. The doors burst apart, and one of the White Knights used his morning star to destroy the desk in his path with a single blow.

Knox stood and drew his pistols.

"Excuse me, gentlemen, but this is a private party."

He opened fire on the soldiers and watched as his bullets bounced harmlessly off their armor. Knox threw his pistols aside when the clips were empty and pulled out a sawed-off shotgun from under his long coat. The force of the shotgun blast was enough to make one of the knights stumble backward a few paces, but the warrior recovered quickly and continued his assault on the room. When Know ran out of shotgun shells, he ran to a suit of armor on display. He removed the broadsword from its mount and defensively held it out in front of him.

"You want to do this old school? Fine by me!"

Knox raised the sword above his head and ran at his enemies while screaming with rage. The knight in front parried the charging man's only thrust and slammed his mace into Knox's ribs, sending him flying into the nearest wall.

"No," Jillian screamed. "Stay away from him!"

Instinctively, she ran to the fireplace and stuck her hand into the flame. To her surprise, she felt no pain, and when she removed her hand, she was holding a small orb of fire about the size of a tennis ball. Without hesitation, she threw the fireball at the White Knight closest to Knox. The force of the blow sent the knight sprawling across the floor.

For a moment, everyone turned to look at Jillian. Knox's face was a combination of intense pain and shocked amusement. He smiled up at her, his teeth stained with blood.

"Now, that's more like it. Throw another heater, girly!"

Emboldened by Knox's encouragement, Jillian turned back towards the fireplace and reached in with both hands. This time she pulled out two flaming orbs the size of softballs. She picked her targets, reached back, and rained fire. With each strike, Jillian noticed, not only were her opponents taking heavy damage, but the flames were also melting their seemingly impenetrable armor. She was about to turn and reload when one of the knights rushed at her with his two-handed ax. Jillian stood there, her body frozen with fear and unable to move. Just as the warrior moved within striking distance, Knox came charging from the other side of the room, bull-rushing the heavily armored knight. Both Knox and the White Knight fell to the floor, giving Jillian the chance to reach back into the fireplace for a new weapon. This time, she held her hands in the fire for several seconds and felt the power growing inside her. The flame felt like it was part of her body, and she absorbed it like plant roots pulling water from the ground. When she had taken in all she could and filled every inch of herself with fire, she turned back towards the scene in the room.

Knox was hurt badly and unable to continue his fight with the soldier he had brought down. The knights who had not yet been struck by Prometheus' Fire were lining up to prepare a full-on assault, but Jillian wasn't willing to give them the chance to organize their battle formation. She opened her mouth to scream, and to her surprise, a geyser of flame erupted from her body. The attack hit two of the White Knights directly, instantly evaporating them into steam and leaving only their weapons and shields behind. Jillian opened her mouth again, and this time, she held nothing back. She let loose an inferno of white-hot rage. She moved her head down the line and watched as each soldier disappeared before her eyes in a hazy mist.

The final knight was the one who had quarreled with Knox. He stood with his giant ax in hand, and Jillian could see the frozen breath rising from the helm. If the warrior was afraid to die, he didn't show it. He charged at Jillian with his weapon raised in the attack position. As the blade fell, Jillian reached out and caught the sharp edge with her bare hand. The weapon instantly dissolved into a puddle of water and iron. She casually stepped towards her foe and placed her other hand on his breastplate. After only a few seconds, the last of the legendary White Knights melted away.

Jillian looked down and saw that she held one more ball of fire, the last of her power. She focused on her father and threw the fireball out into the world and watched as it quickly disappeared over the horizon.

"Couldn't have figured out that flamethrower trick before my little tussle, huh?"

Knox tried to laugh, but the pain was too great, and he coughed up blood instead.

Jillian ran over to him. "You're hurt."

"Just a scratch, love."

Knox winced as he tried to sit up. After a few hard-fought efforts, he gave in to the pain and laid back down.

"It's a few broken ribs at best. I'd say that's more than a scratch." Jillian's eyes filled with tears. "Thank you for saving my life, Knox."

Knox flashed another bloody smile.

"Thank you for saving mine too, Jillian."

Jillian bent over and threw her arms around her friend, but he cried out in pain, so she quickly released him.

"Don't worry. My dad will be able to fix you up."

"Sure thing, girly. Will you just wait here with me until Morris gets home?"

"Of course, I will."

Jillian found the heavy blanket Knox had grabbed for her when the night began and draped it over his body. She also grabbed a nearby pillow and gently placed it under his head. The two sat together in comfortable silence and waited for Jillian's father to return home.

8

"So, what's it going to be, Morris?" Cecil could hardly contain his arrogant glee. "Are my knights bringing your daughter here to assist us, or will they be laying her lifeless body at your feet?"

"If you think you can harm my daughter and then get any help from me, you are crazier than I gave you credit for."

Morris pulled vigorously at his chains in a show of confident aggression, but both men knew the act was nothing more than a bluff.

"Such a pity. It's far past time that the girl met her dear Uncle Cecil."

The Water Elemental continued to mock his captive, savoring every moment of finally having the upper hand. Cecil had always known that he was the superior Godmaker, and now he had proven as much without a shadow of a doubt. The only thing left to do was to put his old friend in his place once and for all so that no matter how the evening turned out, the thought of revenge would be the furthest thing from his prisoner's mind.

"You know, Morris, it could be some time before your daughter arrives. I never imagined you escaping from this encounter without suffering at least a little damage. I'm not talking about anything major, just a few scars to mark the occasion. Why not just get it done before she gets here? If Jillian does manage to arrive in one piece, seeing you hurt will probably help to move things along, and everyone will be the better for it."

With that, Cecil stepped aside, and the White Knight who had not accompanied his fellow warriors moved in front of Morris, swinging his mace and chain in a slow circular motion as Cecil chuckled with delight.

"Remember, I don't want him dead, just a bit bruised and broken."

The knight nodded and began to move towards his target.

Suddenly, a bright light appeared over the horizon casting radiant beams into the room. Cecil raised a hand, halting the warrior's attack, and moved towards the window.

"What in the hell is that?"

Morris also turned towards the light and what he saw reminded him of a comet or shooting star, but it was moving much too fast, and the angle was wrong for the object to be something falling from space. If anything, the light appeared to be heading directly for the house.

"What kind of trick is this?" Cecil demanded, but before Morris could answer, the window shattered and sent the water mage flying across the room. Cecil moaned in confused agony as he lay on the glass-strewn floor for a few moments while he collected himself. When he sat up, he wiped the debris from the broken window off his jacket and looked over to find his White Knight standing perfectly still in the same spot, mace in hand and ready to attack.

"Enough of these games! Hurt him! I want to see him bleed!"

Surprisingly, the knight did not move.

"Did you hear what I said?! Strike him! DO IT NOW!"

The Water Elemental's arrogant tone had turned to one of panic. He managed to get to his feet with some difficulty and stomped over to the warrior like a child throwing a tantrum. To his horror, he saw the reason why his soldier had not attacked. A large hole had cut through the White Knight's mid-section and was growing larger by the moment. It was as though he were melting from the inside. It took only a few seconds before the once formidable knight was reduced to a puddle on the floor, leaving only his mace and chain as evidence that he had ever been there at all. Cecil looked up to find Morris standing free of his restraints and holding the fireball that had stuck the knight's killing blow.

"I should kill you right where you stand," Morris said with the same intensity as the flame in his hand. "A Godmaker does not kill another Godmaker, and you know that! What you've done...What you were planning to do… it's unforgivable."

Cecil fell to his knees, beaten and blubbering.

"Please, Morris. Don't kill me! It was all an act. I was never going to harm you or your daughter. You know that. You know that!"

Morris could barely stand to look at the man who had once been his closest friend.

"Power has destroyed you. You don't deserve the magic you have or the position you hold, but it is not within my ability to strip either from you. I can, however..."

With a flick of his wrist, Morris shot the fireball in his hand at Cecil's neck. The flame made direct contact with the water stone that Cecil had used to enhance his power. The fire burned away the stone's magic, and the bright blue exterior became nothing more than a gray rock.

"NO, MORRIS! HOW COULD YOU?! THAT ELEMENT STONE TOOK ME HALF MY ADULT LIFE TO FIND!"

Cecil began to sob hysterically while holding his once precious jewel. Through tears, he tried every spell he knew to rejuvenate the magic of the element stone, but all of his efforts were in vain.

"You're lucky I'm leaving you with your life. You don't even deserve that much, and if you ever come near me or my daughter again, that is exactly the price you will pay."

"You might as well kill me, Morris! I'll never be a God now!

With nothing left to say, Morris turned away from his old friend for the last time and walked out the door.

With Cecil's spell broken, the summer snowstorm ceased immediately, and the temperature returned to normal. Enough snow had accumulated that some areas would experience flash flooding, but it could have been much worse. The electronic company would have no issue going out to restore power to anyone who lost it, and municipal clean-up crews could begin the work of making the roads safe for travel.

When Morris arrived home, the property damage was immediately apparent. The heavy iron gate at the front entrance had been forced open and hung by nothing more than a bent metal rod. Morris drove quickly into the carport and exited his vehicle without turning off the engine or even closing the driver's side door. He hurried into the main part of the house and found nothing but destruction all around him.

Furniture was broken into irreparable pieces. Bullet holes lined several hallways. There were even a few dead guards and other members of the household. However, Morris didn't see any of those things because he didn't pause in any one place long enough to look. Now at a jog, Morris only cared about one thing, and that was the health and wellbeing of his only child. When he arrived at Jillian's room, the door was ajar but not broken. He burst into the room and called out her name, but there was no answer. Panic set in immediately, and Morris ran from room to room looking for his little girl.

"Jillian! I'm home now, my love! You can come out!"

His cries were met with nothing but silence, making Morris more and more desperate with each plea.

"Please, Jillian! Please! Come out now!"

As Morris searched for his daughter's face among the security guards who were killed during the attack, he began to notice the signs of the battle that had taken place. Nothing and no one could have possibly withstood the onslaught from nine of the White Knights. The broken furniture and lifeless bodies were proof of that, but Morris couldn't bring himself to believe that they had killed Jillian.

When Morris finally made his way to the family library, he saw that the large wooden doors had been smashed to pieces. Someone had also moved his desk in an effort to barricade the room but to no avail. Then, Morris's heart sank as he saw Jillian lying on the floor next to the fireplace in a growing pool of blood. He gasped and put a hand to his mouth. Violent, heavy sobs took hold of him at once, and the weight of his loss dropped the man to his knees. Unable to speak or scream, Morris crawled through the blood to his daughter's side. He scooped Jillian up into his arms and buried his face in her hair. Then, he let out his anguish in a long, sorrowful cry.

"Dad? Dad, what's wrong?!"

Morris pulled his face back and looked down to see his daughter's tired eyes staring up at him.

"Oh my God! Jillian! I thought I'd lost you! I thought I'd lost you forever!"

He pulled Jillian back into his chest and rocked her gently. He cried a river of confused tears made up of his grief, exhaustion, and relief.

"It's okay, Dad. Really. I'm not hurt."

"How could that be?"

Jillian turned toward the fireplace. "I used Prometheus' Fire."

Morris' eyes went wide.

"But that's… that's not possible, my love. Prometheus' Fire is a very advanced spell that few Fire Elementals are disciplined enough to attain. If my memory is correct, you must endure the living flame until your old self is burned away into nothing but ash, and then, if your spirit survives, you are reborn again."

Jillian immediately thought back to the anguish of burning alive. She remembered feeling her body being destroyed by the fire, but she wasn't strong enough to survive the process, so she made a deal with the man-fish instead, and he had given her the power she needed. Jillian was too ashamed of herself to tell her father she had failed and, instead, had taken the easy way out.

"I don't really remember any of that. All I know is we were under attack, and a ring of fire appeared. I could hear voices telling me to step inside, and somehow, I knew that was the right thing to do, so I went into the fire. When I came out, I was throwing fireballs around the room and turning those knights into puddles."

Morris continued to stare at his daughter with his mouth hanging half-open. He started three different sentences but abandoned all three when nothing but nonsense came out. When Morris finally regained his wits, he threw his arms around Jillian and hugged her tight.

"It was you," Morris said as the full realization of what had happened finally hit home. "You sent the fireball that freed me. Thank you, my love. You saved my life."

Jillian quickly looked away, uncomfortable with the praise she received because she knew she didn't deserve it.

"Even with the spell, I wouldn't have made it without Knox. He used every weapon he could find and wrestled one of the knights with his bare hands just to keep me safe. He's the real hero."

Jillian turned towards Knox, who had fallen asleep beside her. She moved over to where he lay and shook him by the arm.

"Knox, wake up. My dad is home. Tell him where you got hurt so he can fix you."

Knox's eyes remained closed, his face pale. Jillian shook the man again. When he still didn't rouse, she grabbed him by the hand and then gasped and recoiled from his icy touch. That was when she noticed the blood that had pooled beneath him.

"Knox! You have to wake up now! My dad is home, and he can fix you!"

Morris attempted to pull his daughter away from Knox's body, but she refused to leave his side.

"Knox, wake up! Please, wake up!"

"Jillian, sweetheart, I'm afraid Mr. Knox is gone."

"No, he can't be. He saved my life."

Jillian sobbed and wrapped her arms around Knox's body as she laid her head on his chest.

Morris crawled closer to his daughter and put a hand on her back.

"I will be forever grateful to Mr. Knox for the sacrifice he made for you. His death is a blood debt that can never be repaid."

"He has a son," Jillian cried out. "What's going to happen to him now?"

"Mr. Knox was Cain's only family. Now that he is gone, we must be his family. We will take the boy in and care for him as best we can."

"But he needs his dad." Jillian looked back at her father with wide, tear-filled eyes and then fell into his waiting arms. "I don't understand why this happened."

"Neither do I, my love. Neither do I."

But the truth was, Morris understood all too well why Knox had died. Innocent lives were always lost in the pursuit of power. For Cecil, the power of making and unmaking Gods wasn't enough. He needed to become a God. It was Morris's good fortune that no harm had come to him or his daughter, but Knox and Cain's bad fortune that they were caught up in the never-ending struggle of power and greed.

Jillian wrapped her arms around her father's neck and rested her head on his shoulder. Morris hummed the soothing lullaby that he had played for her on the pan flute as a baby. The melody calmed Jillian's nerves slightly, although her grief was still overwhelming. She was just starting to close her eyes when she felt a searing pain radiating from her forearm. She was horrified to find the black trident mark that the man-fish had left as a symbol of their pact pulsing on her skin. She drew in a sharp breath and fell away from her father.

The sudden movement startled Morris. He noticed Jillian looking down at her arm, but there was nothing there. "What's wrong, my love?"

Jillian searched for the mark, but it had faded. She quickly composed herself and replied, "Nothing. I'm just really sad and exhausted. Do you think I can go to bed now?"

"Of course, Jillian. You have been through enough for one night. Sweet dreams, my love."

Jillian kissed her father lightly on the cheek and stood to exit the room. She peered over her shoulder before leaving and saw her dad pouring himself a drink from his beverage cart. She guessed that it would probably be the first of many, but he had been through a lot, and she wasn't about to try and deprive him of the one thing that might help him relax a little. When Jillian was back in her room, she looked around and noticed everything was the same. The battle had not reached her private space, and she was grateful. That was when she saw something on her bed that hadn't been there before. It was a folded blanket with a note on top that read:

Girly,

Found this extra blanket in case you get cold while you sleep. I'll be standing guard outside your room until your father gets back, so you don't have to worry about a thing. Sleep well.

Knox

Jillian dropped the note to the floor as her emotions overtook her once again. She felt guilty that Knox had died protecting her and terrified of the black trident mark on her arm and the favor she would have to do for the man-fish someday. Most of all, Jillian was ashamed that she wasn't the hero her father thought she was and that she didn't have the courage to tell him that she had failed. Physically and emotionally exhausted, Jillian laid down on her bed, scooped the blanket up in her arms, and cried herself to sleep.

PART 2
CHARLIE WESTON EVERETT

9

Jillian scanned the radio for anything that would help to keep her awake for the last few miles of her drive home. It had been another long day working with her father, and all she wanted was to slip into a scalding hot bath and forget how much her muscles ached. Jillian caught a glimpse of herself in the rear-view mirror and barely recognized her reflection. Her strawberry blond hair was coated with dust and half-heartedly pulled into a messy bun. Her usually sparkling blue eyes looked more of a dull gray, and the bags under them revealed how tired she was. When she finally pulled into her driveway, Jillian let out a loud sigh of relief and painstakingly turned off the car's engine and began to gather her things. The walk from her car to the front door felt torturously long, and Jillian felt the pain in her feet with every step. Flats would have been a better choice than the heels she was wearing, but she had no idea when she started her day that she would end up sprinting through the woods chasing after an angry forest nymph that could disguise itself as a common flower. Jillian made a mental note to keep a pair of running shoes in her trunk so this type of thing wouldn't happen to her again.

The first thing Jillian noticed when she walked inside was random lights turned on throughout the house. This was one of her bigger pet peeves, but she was too tired to care, so she collapsed on the bench in her home's entryway and buried her face in her hands.

"Our son is waiting for you."

Jillian turned her head to see her husband standing in the kitchen doorway with a smile on his face. She smiled back as she removed her shoes and rubbed her throbbing feet.

"It's way past his bedtime, Pat."

Patrick stretched his arms towards his wife, signaling that he wanted a hug. Jillian attempted to look annoyed, but she couldn't resist her husband's boyish charm. He had a certain goodness in him, a light that filled her with happiness and hope. Their son, Charlie, had inherited that same light, and she was no more able to resist his charms than her husband's. Jillian fell into Patrick's arms and laughed as he lifted her off the ground and spun her around a few times.

"In my defense, I put the boy to bed on time, but I can't make him go to sleep. He lives for your stories." Patrick's playful expression turned serious as he added, "They are just stories, aren't they?"

This was a question that Patrick asked often and in many different ways. Ever since Charlie had been a toddler, Jillian had taken to telling him stories about her work to prepare him for the unusual world into which he had been born. While exciting and full of adventure, the stories she told her son were also riddled with danger. Patrick had insisted that the worst parts be left out and that happy endings always be the natural conclusion. He worried about Charlie finding out too much about his destiny too soon. It was clear to Jillian that her husband was not altogether comfortable with the idea of their son following in the Weston family line of work. Still, as much as he worried, he was also very supportive, and he promised not to interfere with Charlie's eventual training.

"Patrick, I know you worry, but Charlie needs to know the truth, and telling him about all the things that I do through made-up bedtime stories is the perfect way for him to begin to learn without explicitly telling him, which we both decided he is not ready for."

Patrick nodded in agreement, but Jillian could tell he was holding something back.

"I know what you're thinking," Jillian said slyly.

"No, you don't!" Patrick replied with a grin. "You have many special abilities, but mind-reading isn't one of them."

Jillian closed her eyes and touched her index fingers to her forehead, pretending to read her husband's thoughts. Patrick gave a fake laugh and reached for his wife's hands. She gripped his fingers and opened her eyes to meet his gaze.

"We've been in love long enough for me to know what you're thinking without any help from my 'special abilities'. You're thinking, 'What if Charlie wants to be a policeman or a doctor or a lawyer?'"

Patrick turned away, but Jillian quickly grabbed his chin and refocused him.

"My love, if I've told you once, I've told you a thousand times, Charlie is free to choose his future. We will be proud of him and love him and support him no matter what he decides to do with his life, but he needs to know that working in my world is an option. And should he decide not to pursue the Weston legacy, then he at least needs to know enough to pass along the vital information to his children someday so they can make the same choice."

"I just can't help but think that your dad is the one pushing you to introduce Charlie into the family business."

"That's not true, Patrick. Dad doesn't even know that I'm telling Charlie these stories. If the choice were up to him, he would have Charlie in the field already." Patrick opened his mouth to say something, but Jillian interrupted, "But it's not up to him. We are Charlie's parents, and we get to decide how and when Charlie will learn the whole truth."

Patrick let out a long sigh and kissed his wife with deep affection.

"You're right. I know you're right. It's not even that I don't want Charlie to choose that life. It's exciting and important work. I just worry about him. I worry about both of you."

"I know you do. That's why I love you so much. You're the best husband and father, and somehow, you always know the right thing to do. You have this unshakeable sense of morality that I can't even begin to understand."

Patrick shook his head. "It's not unshakeable, Jill. It's not." Patrick kissed his wife again, then gestured towards the stairs that led up to

Charlie's bedroom. "Your audience awaits. What is tonight's adventure about?"

Jillian smiled and started slowly climbing up the steps. Without turning back to her husband, she casually replied, "I'm not sure yet. I might tell Charlie about my mother."

Patrick raced up the stairs to catch up to his wife.

"Your mother?! Jill, I don't know if that's such a good idea. It's not like we can take a family vacation to see her, and isn't she like the Chief of her tribe?"

"She isn't a Chief. Her people don't have that kind of power structure. She is just an honored storyteller. She keeps the oral history of her people alive. And I know we can't go visit her, but that doesn't mean I don't want Charlie to at least have an idea of who she is and where she has been his entire life."

Patrick tried to relax the worried expression on his face but was unable to do so. In a semi-panicked tone, he replied, "It's not who she is that worries me; it's where she is that could be a problem."

Jillian relented. "Fine. I guess you're right. But I'm telling him when he's older!"

Patrick nodded vigorously and stepped aside so his wife could continue up the steps. When she was almost at the top, she yelled to Patrick, "Since you couldn't get our son to bed, will you at least draw me a hot bath? Like, really hot. Dragon's breath hot."

Patrick bowed deeply and replied in a mocking tone, "Anything for you, your majesty."

Jillian snickered at her husband's remark and continued quietly towards Charlie's room in the hopes that he had fallen asleep, but no such luck. She could hear him quietly playing with his toys, and there was also a light shining underneath the door, which meant he was using his reading flashlight for his game. Jillian opened the door slowly, and she heard her son scramble into his bed. When she entered, she found Charlie breathing heavily with his eyes closed tight and the flashlight still shining somewhere on his bedroom floor.

"Who exactly do you think you're fooling, Charles?"

Without opening his eyes, Charlie smiled his father's smile and laughed softly. Jillian rolled her eyes as she moved to sit on the edge of his bed.

"It's pretty late, you know. Maybe it would be better if we skipped the story for tonight."

Charlie ended his half-hearted charade and sat up at once.

"No, mom! We can't skip story time! It's my favorite!"

Jillian took a moment to pretend like she was considering her options. She studied her son's face and marveled at the light of perfect innocence shining through him, making him glow. All mothers see the goodness in their children, but this was different. Charlie was something special.

Even though Jillian had been telling the truth when she told Patrick that Charlie could choose to be anything he wanted, she knew that he was destined to be important to the Weston family legacy. When given a choice, he would take up his mother and grandfather's line of work, and the stories she told him were the beginning of his training. They were his introduction into an entirely unknown world of magic that only a special few ever really understood, but a Weston had been safeguarding that magic since the dawn of civilization, and Charlie was next in line.

"Fine! I will tell you a story, but no questions and no interruptions. It's late, and you should already be sleeping."

Charlie nodded his approval and propped himself up to give his mother his full attention.

"Have I ever told you about my time with the fire beasts?"

Charlie's bright blue eyes widened as he slowly shook his head.

"They are magnificent and amazingly powerful creatures called the Ignidore. You may not realize this, Charlie, but many of the animals you know also exist on other worlds in different shapes and forms. Your grandfather and I have spent a great deal of time studying and naming those animals, and the Ignidore are my favorite group."

Charlie's mouth hung open with excitement and disbelief. "Wow! What kind of animals do they have?!"

"Well, I always loved the Embear, a creature that looks and acts just like the bears here in our world except it is made up entirely of orange and red flames. Embears also produce cute little cubs made up of blue flame, and they eat special berries that grow naturally in their world." Jillian couldn't help but relish in her son's awestruck expression and continued, "I almost ate one of their berries once by accident because I didn't know what they were! I took one off a bush, and it felt like a regular raspberry in my hand. I was about to pop it in my mouth, but luckily, Grandpa Weston grabbed it right out of the air. The berry burst into a small ball of flame right in his hand."

"OH MY GOSH! Good thing Grandpa was there to save you!"

Jillian nodded in agreement and continued, "But the most powerful of all the Ignidore is Incinidore, the legendary fire dragon. He is the protector of the fire realm. I was never lucky enough to see him in person, but Grandpa Weston claims that he once saw Incinidore protecting the fire region from attack."

Charlie looked both sad and confused. "Why would anyone want to hurt the animals?"

Jillian took her son's hand and explained, "My sweet boy, no matter where you go, there are good people, and there are bad people, and you can't always tell the difference by what they say. You have to watch out for what they do, and then you'll know for sure who they are in their heart."

Charlie smiled and leaped out from his covers to give his mother a hug. Jillian squeezed her son tight and kissed his cheek, and she rocked him in her arms.

"Now, it is time to go to sleep."

Charlie groaned but didn't put up much of a fight, signaling that he was ready for bed whether he was willing to admit it or not. Jillian laid her son down gently and went through the usual ritual of lining up his favorite stuffed animals: a dragon, a frog, a panda, and a sloth, in that order. Then, she sang his favorite nighttime song, "Take Me Out to the Ballgame." Finally, Jillian kissed her son on the forehead and wished him sweet dreams.

After sitting with him in darkness for a few moments, Jillian stood to leave the room, but before she could reach the door, Charlie asked, "Mom, who are the Gods?"

Jillian wasn't sure she understood her son's question. "What do you mean, Charlie?"

The young boy sat up a little in his bed and answered, "Dylan told me at school about how there used to be all kinds of Gods that lived in the world with people, but now they are all gone. Where did they go? Are they up in heaven?"

Jillian realized that her son was confusing mythology with theology.

"The idea of a single God in heaven is a matter of opinion and personal faith. The Gods that Dylan is talking about are Zeus, Anubis, Odin…"

"What about Thor?" the boy yelled out excitedly. "He's my favorite Avenger!"

Jillian nodded in agreement. "Thor is perfect. Most people believe that these Gods were just made up stories used to help people understand how the world worked."

"So, the Gods were good then?" Charlie asked.

Jillian's face grew serious, and she shook her head.

"According to the stories, some of the Gods were kind to the people who worshiped them, but others were cruel and heartless beings. The evil Gods took the power they were granted and used it to control and manipulate other people and other Gods. A few Gods became obsessed with their power and never stopped looking for ways to increase their influence over all of humanity."

Charlie gripped his covers and pulled them up around his face in fear of his mother's ominous warning. Jillian could see that she had gone a little too far, and she thought about the promise she had made her husband to keep things as light as possible when educating their son about certain truths.

With that in mind, Jillian scaled things back by saying, "You don't have to be afraid of the Gods, Charlie."

The young boy pulled his covers down just far enough to ask, "Why not?"

"Well, for starters, they have been gone for many years. No one has seen or heard from them in centuries, which is why most people believe they are myths and legends. The second reason is that even with all of their power, ultimately, they need us more than we need them. Without our worship and our permission for them to exist, they have no weapons to use against us."

Charlie's face and posture relaxed, and Jillian could tell she had succeeded in reassuring him.

"So, you could just walk up to a God and take his powers?" Charlie asked playfully.

"I can't, but you might be able to." Jillian knew she was getting dangerously close to the Godmaker conversation and that her son was far from ready to hear about it, so she added, "Because you're such a tough guy!"

Then, she reached out and tickled her son as he laughed and flailed to escape her attack. After a few moments of play fighting, Jillian settled her son back onto his pillow and kissed him goodnight again.

She quietly slipped out of the room and began closing the door when she heard Charlie's voice call out, "Mom, will the Gods ever come back?"

Jillian poked her head back into the room and replied, "No, Charlie. The Gods are gone, and they aren't coming back."

With that, Charlie rolled over and went to sleep. Jillian closed the door to her son's room and pressed her back against the frame, praying that she had not just lied to her boy. She looked down at her forearm, waiting to see if the black trident would re-emerge, but it never did. It had been almost fifteen years since the night she had made her devil's bargain with the man-fish, but she knew the day was coming when she would be called upon to fulfill her end of the deal. It was only a matter of time.

10

Charlie continued to receive his informal training through his mother's stories for several years. He grew up hearing tales of creatures from other worlds, beasts of myth, and legends about Gods and heroes from many different cultures. As Charlie got older, Jillian could be more specific about some of the things she had done, but she never let on that her stories were true. As a result, Charlie grew up with a love of various mythologies and legends. He had a deep appreciation for a whole world that he believed was only part of his imagination. But with each passing year, Charlie got closer and closer to the truth that the stories were a training manual for a job he was destined to do.

By the time Charlie reached his pre-teen years, he found that he had outgrown his mother telling him bedtime stories. Instead, he preferred to read books of his choosing on similar topics, such as Arthurian legend and various notable demigods. While this hobby wasn't one shared by many of his classmates, Charlie managed to connect to his peers in other ways and had no problem making friends.

Even though Charlie wasn't the tallest kid in his class, he developed an athletic build, which was accentuated by his preference for wearing gym shorts, tee shirts, and sneakers to school every day despite what everyone else was wearing. Charlie also had a knack for fitting in with nearly every social group, giving everyone he spoke to the impression that he valued what they had to say. The biggest thing that set Charlie apart though was that he was a genuine, down-to-earth, nice guy who had a reputation for being honest and unusually kind for a teenager. Everybody liked him.

***

With their son entering his adolescence, Jillian informed her husband that the time had come to tell Charlie the truth about what she did for a living so that he could make his choice and take his place within the Weston family legacy.

"So how does this work exactly? Does he just blow out the candles, and we hand him a dragon egg?"

Patrick could see that his attempt at humor fell flat as he watched Jillian roll her eyes at his remark.

"We've been over this, Pat. In fact, we went over it before we got engaged, before we got married, and before Charlie was born. We have also been over it several times in between. The Godmaker is told on their thirteenth birthday at the exact time of their birth. It's why my dad woke me up at 2:48 AM to give me Jade and why we will be telling Charlie about everything after dinner at 6:42 PM. This is a big day for Charlie and the whole family."

"The Weston family, you mean," Patrick snapped back with more venom than he meant.

"No, not the Weston family. Our family. Charlie will be great at this, but he is going to need you as much as he'll need me to reach his full potential. In this house and out in the world, he'll be Charlie Everett. He will only be Charlie Weston when we are training at my dad's or if the world needs him, God forbid."

"Charlie hasn't been to Weston Manor since he was a little boy. He's going to wonder what's going on when we randomly tell him he'll be going there every weekend from now on."

"By that time, we will have already told him everything he needs to know to make his decision, so it won't be a big surprise that he needs to go there for training. Besides, he has been asking us to visit his grandfather at Weston Manor for years, and we've never been able to give him a straight answer about why he has never been allowed to visit. It will be nice to put an end to this lie."

"I guess. Kind of like burying Santa all over again," Patrick said with a shrug. "You only had one parent guiding you through all this stuff, so what makes you think I'll even be any help to Charlie?"

Jillian gently rested her hand on her husband's shoulder and replied, "That's exactly why I know how much he'll need you."

Patrick smiled and threw up his arms in defeat.

"Okay. Okay. But your dad better not be thinking of giving us any weird pets as Charlie's birthday present. I don't want to try and explain to the neighbors why I'm walking a three-headed lion every morning."

Jillian moved toward Patrick like she was going to attack him when her cell phone rang. Patrick used the distraction to his advantage and fled from the room laughing.

Jillian giggled and yelled after him playfully, "Yeah, you better run!"

When she looked down at her phone, Jillian saw a text from a number she didn't recognize. When she opened the message, it read, "It's time." Before she had a chance to contemplate the meaning of the words, Jillian felt a burning sensation on her forearm that she had not felt in over twenty years. Instinctively, she rolled up her sleeve and ran her arm under the cold water from the kitchen sink, but it didn't help dampen the pain. Then, to Jillian's horror, the black trident appeared. She gasped and fell backward, knocking over a fruit bowl and a flower vase. The crash brought Patrick running back into the room.

"Oh my God. What happened? Are you okay?"

Patrick walked over to his wife and tried to help her up from the ground, but she shrugged him off.

Jillian quickly rolled her sleeve down over her wet skin and replied, "I'm...I'm fine. I was just washing something, and I thought I saw a bug. I got scared and fell back."

Patrick looked back at his wife skeptically. "Since when are you afraid of bugs?"

Anger flared in Jillian's eyes, and she shot back defensively, "I don't know, Pat. It was a big bug, okay? I have to go out for a bit."

"What?! What do you mean you have to go out? It's Charlie's birthday, and we have to do the whole magic thing."

Jillian looked away and shifted uncomfortably.

"Yeah, I'm having second thoughts about that. Maybe telling him today isn't such a good idea after all."

"But you just said…"

"I know what I said, Pat," Jillian yelled at her husband. "I won't be gone long. We'll talk about this more when I get home. Just tell Charlie I'll be back soon."

Patrick crossed his arms defiantly and stared at his wife, waiting for her to tell him the truth.

When she continued to stare back at him in silence, he let out a deep breath and replied, "Fine. I guess I'll clean this up, and you can go do whatever you have to do all of a sudden."

"Thanks," Jillian replied flatly as she grabbed her purse off the dining room table and walked out the front door.

It was 7:02 PM when Jillian finally returned home. Patrick could see unmistakable exhaustion on his wife's face, and it looked like she may have been crying. He wanted nothing more than to go to her and ask if she was all right but couldn't bring himself to do it. He was still too angry at her for lying to him and storming out of the house, completely missing Charlie's birthday. 6:42 PM had come and gone without so much as a text message, so Patrick had decided to light the candles and apologize to his son on his mother's behalf. There was nothing else to do. With no idea of where Jillian had gone or when she might come back, he simply moved the day forward as best he could on his own.

Jillian walked over to the dining room table and plopped down into a seat next to Charlie. With tremendous effort, she managed a halfhearted smile.

"Did you save me any cake?"

Charlie looked to his dad for some sign of what to say or do, but Patrick just continued staring at his wife in disbelief.

Charlie turned back to his mom and replied, "You missed my birthday."

A tear rolled down Jillian's cheek as she nodded.

"Where were you?" Charlie asked innocently.

"I'm sorry, sweetheart. I had to work."

Jillian's voice trembled as more tears streamed down her face.

Charlie looked down at the half-eaten piece of cake in front of him.

"Was it so important that you couldn't be here for my birthday?"

Jillian nodded as she let out an audible sob. Charlie got up from his seat and threw his arms around his mother. She squeezed him tight and cried heavily into his shoulder.

"It's okay, mom. It's fine."

"I'm so sorry, Charlie. I'm so sorry."

Jillian repeated her apology over and over again. Charlie continued to reassure her, but his understanding only caused her more pain. In some ways, she wanted him to be angry and upset with her because she knew she deserved it, but that just wasn't who Charlie was.

"Charlie, why don't you go to your room and call Dylan?" Patrick cut in. "I'm sure she would like to wish you a happy birthday too."

Charlie gave his mom one last squeeze and kissed her on the cheek. Then, he ran out of the room and went upstairs to call his best friend.

When Patrick heard his son's door shut, he looked over at his wife, who was still crying into her hands.

"What the hell is going on, Jillian? I want the truth, and I want it now. Does this have something to do with all the Godmaker stuff? Is Charlie in danger?"

Jillian looked up at her husband with desperate, tear-soaked eyes.

"I'm sorry, Pat. I'm sorry for everything. I'm sorry I lied to you. I'm so sorry I missed Charlie's birthday. I'll never forgive myself."

Patrick could see the hurt on his wife's face. He knew she was reaching out, begging for understanding and forgiveness. He wasn't ready to give her that. Not yet. But he knew she was genuinely sorry, so he softened his tone.

"Just tell me what happened today. I think I deserve at least that much."

Jillian reached out and grabbed Patrick's hand. To her surprise, he didn't pull away.

She took a few deep breaths and replied, "I can't tell you everything." Patrick started to pull his hand away, but Jillian squeezed him tight and continued, "It's for your own safety! I promise! Charlie's too!"

Patrick contemplated his wife's words for a moment and then relaxed back in his chair, signaling Jillian to continue.

"When I was about Charlie's age, this terrible thing happened. My dad never told me all the details, but do you remember the summer snowstorm when we were kids?"

"That was you?" Patrick asked with amazement.

Jillian shook her head.

"No, we didn't cause the storm, but we were the ones who stopped it. These knights were literally breaking down my door to capture me or kill me; I'm not sure which. I didn't know any magic yet to defend myself, but I heard these voices telling me to step into a ring of fire that appeared on the ground. I didn't have a better option, so I stepped in.

Patrick's eyes went wide with fear and surprise. "What happened?"

"I burned." Jillian's face twisted with remembered pain. "It hurt more than anything I have ever experienced. I could feel my life slipping away, and there was nothing I could do about it. Then, suddenly, the pain stopped. I'm not sure what happened next, but somehow, I had gotten outside my body. The only thing I could see was a river, so I moved towards it, and I met this giant fish person there."

"A giant fish person?" Patrick asked skeptically.

"I don't know. I don't remember if I ever saw him for what he truly was, but he offered to save me from burning. He told me he could save my life if I helped him with something. I didn't want to die, and I didn't know what else to do, so I agreed to the deal. When I opened my eyes again, I was back in my father's library, and I had the power to throw fireballs that were strong enough to kill the knights attacking me. A few hours later, my dad came home, and that was the end of it."

Patrick rubbed his forehead, something he tended to do when he was stressed.

"Okay...That's a lot to take in. So, you, a thirteen-year-old girl, were under siege by a band of knights who wanted to kill you. Having no ability to fight off your attackers, a voice in your head told you to step into a ring of fire, which you did, naturally. Your body started to burn when a giant fish person offered to save you in exchange for a favor. You agreed, and the next thing you knew, you were shooting fireballs across the room and taking people out left and right. Does that pretty much summarize the story you just told me?"

Jillian furrowed her brow.

"You have a frustrating habit of making everything I say sound crazy when we talk about stuff like this."

Patrick burst out laughing.

"Oh, I'm sorry! I just doubt this is what the Chong's are talking about next door."

Jillian's face became a scowl, and Patrick knew that his attitude was not helping the already tense situation.

"I'm sorry. Look, I know you're telling me the truth. It's just hard to digest stories like that sometimes. I think it's safe to say, we had very different childhoods."

Jillian let out a laugh despite herself and nodded her understanding.

Patrick grinned as he felt his frustration beginning to melt away. He thought back to how much easier the dynamic was with his wife before Charlie was born. Jillian had never lied to him or tried to protect him from the truth, and he accepted the inherently dangerous nature of her work. Hell, he admired her for it, but now that all the danger was being laid at his son's feet, every decision seemed much more difficult, and Patrick didn't always see eye-to-eye with his adventurous wife.

Cautiously, Patrick continued to probe Jillian for more information.

"I still don't understand what your story about the fish guy has to do with Charlie's birthday."

"It's about the favor I promised to do. When I made the deal, the man-fish told me that the day would come when he would need my help to find something for him and his brother, then he stamped a black trident mark on my arm and sent me on my way. I haven't seen the mark since that night...until today."

"So, your debt has been called in," Patrick said with a sigh. "I'm betting the situation must be pretty serious if whoever waited twenty years to contact you. Well, let's get your dad on the phone and see what we should do."

Patrick attempted to pull his phone out of his pocket, but Jillian grabbed his hand hard.

"No! My dad can't know about this!"

"Why can't he know?"

"I never told him about the deal or how I managed to save myself that night. Someone close to me died, and he was already blaming himself for the loss. I didn't want this weighing on him too. I still don't."

Patrick let his phone fall back into his pocket.

"Fine. Then, what are we supposed to do?"

"You don't have to do anything. I'm going to handle this situation myself. I'll find whatever it is they need me to find, and then it will be over. No mentioning anything to Charlie or my dad, okay?"

Patrick nodded hesitantly. "What are we doing about telling Charlie all the other stuff?"

"All that has to wait until I'm done with this. He doesn't know anything about it, so it's not like he'll be disappointed. Once I'm confident my problem is solved, we'll figure out a different time to tell Charlie about the Weston family."

Jillian paused and locked eyes with her husband.

Tearfully, she added, "I really am sorry, Pat."

Patrick took his wife's hand and kissed it gently.

"I forgive you, especially since you so selflessly volunteered to do all the dishes."

Jillian groaned and replied, "You wash, and I'll dry. Deal?"

Jillian leaned forward and kissed her husband on the lips. The two ate cake together and laughed like nothing had ever been wrong.

11

Despite Jillian's assurances to her husband that she would have no problem honoring her commitment to the man-fish, it quickly became apparent that the task set before her was not one that would be easily accomplished. As the days passed, Jillian came home later and later. She was constantly exhausted and irritable. Nothing, not even the boyish charms of her husband and son, could cheer her up. Whenever either of the men would ask if she was okay, she would simply reply that she was fine and walk away. On more than one occasion, Patrick found his wife crying in a closet or bathroom. He did everything he could to try and console her, but Jillian continued to withhold the details of her problem, so there was little he could do to help.

Eventually, Jillian's state deteriorated enough for Patrick to disregard her wishes and call her father for assistance. To Patrick's surprise, Morris claimed that it had been weeks since Jillian had checked in with him, and she wasn't returning any of his phone calls. Both men decided that it was time to intervene and find out exactly what was going on. After the call, Patrick went in search of his wife, but she found him first.

"Hey there, hot stuff," she called out to him.

Patrick was shocked to see Jillian smiling because she had rarely done so since Charlie's birthday.

"Hey, Jill. Umm. I just got off the phone with your dad. We thought that maybe it was time for the three of us to talk. He is going to come over tomorrow night."

Jillian frowned playfully.

"Can it wait? I thought we could have a date night tomorrow."

"I don't know, Jill," Patrick replied, unsure of what to make of his wife's proposal. "You can't deny that something has been wrong with you lately, and your dad says you haven't been working with him for almost a month. I know you've been preoccupied with the whole unfulfilled promise thing, but none of this is like you at all."

Jillian dropped her playful act and moved toward her husband.

"Patrick, I'm sorry. For everything. I know things have been weird since Charlie's birthday. I've been holding on to so much. I just want to keep you and Charlie safe."

Patrick could see the tears forming in his wife's eyes, and he reached out to pull her close. Jillian pressed her face into Patrick's chest and began to cry.

"What is it, Jill? Tell me what's going on."

Jillian wiped her eyes and looked up at her husband with a genuine smile.

"It doesn't matter anymore. It's over now. I'm finally done with all of it."

"What do you mean, you're done with all of it?" Patrick asked in disbelief. "All of what?"

"Just what I said. I'm done with this work, at least for now. I need a break. I think it's time for me to reevaluate some things."

Patrick could feel the relief wash over him. Because of his marriage to Jillian, the most extraordinary woman he had ever met, he was made privy to all the secrets of the universe and was amazed and impressed by everything he had seen with his own eyes. But unlike his wife and her father, Patrick always saw more danger than wonder. Whatever it was Jillian had to do to fulfill her promise had forced her to know that danger as well, and now, he could finally stop worrying.

Unfortunately, Patrick's euphoria was cut short when Jillian added, "I think now might be the perfect time to step back from my fieldwork and take on the role of Charlie's primary trainer."

"Wait. What? We are still telling Charlie?"

Jillian looked surprised. "Of course, we are still telling Charlie. It's his destiny."

Patrick could feel the frustration rising in his chest.

"But Jill, I thought you just said that it was time to reevaluate some things?"

"Yes, it's time for me to reevaluate MY work. Nothing has changed for Charlie. He is the next Weston in line."

Patrick felt his heart break into a million pieces of disappointment.

"Whatever it is you just went through... You want that for our son?"

Now, it was Jillian's turn to do the consoling.

"Patrick, you know better than most what's out there. Yes, the dangers are real, but the danger of doing nothing puts everyone at far greater risk, not just for those of us who know, but for everyone. Charlie needs to know the truth."

Patrick pressed his palms into his eyes and rubbed hard until everything went black.

He continued for several moments before saying, "It's not easy, Jill. It's not easy being married to someone whose destiny is so much bigger than your own."

"Is that what you think? Is that how you feel? That you are so insignificant to your son and me?"

Jillian pulled Patrick's hands away from his face.

"Look at me right now. I could not do this without you. Charlie will not be able to do this without you. You ground us. You give us strength and courage. The world is about to open up to our son, and he will still need you to teach him how to be a good man. He is going to look to you to remind him who he is. Charlie may work in my world, but he has your heart."

Two small tears rolled down Patrick's cheek. He wiped them away quickly and asked, "Where do you want to go for our date?"

Jillian smiled and resumed her flirtatious demeanor.

"I don't know, babe. Surprise me."

She gave her husband a wink and walked flirtatiously out of the room.

Before Patrick had a chance to chase after her, though, Jillian poked her head back in and added, "Please, call my dad and cancel your intervention for tomorrow night. I don't want him spoiling our fun."

Patrick nodded enthusiastically as he pulled out his phone.

Jillian blew her husband a kiss and disappeared from view. As Patrick began to dial his father-in-law, he could hear her call out to him playfully, "When you're done, come and find me if you can."

12

The dismissal bell rang, and the usual chaos ensued in the hallways of Albion Middle School as Charlie left his last class of the day with a smile on his face and a carefree attitude in his heart. As he approached his locker to drop off his books and grab his jacket, Charlie could see one of his classmates out of the corner of his eye. The boy's name was Sydney Sedah, and Charlie didn't know much about him except that he was kind of small for his age, carried an art notebook with him everywhere he went, and he gave off a weak and defenseless vibe that was like a lightning rod for the worst kids in school.

Even though Sydney seemed like a nice enough kid, he and Charlie weren't friends. They weren't even really acquaintances. Barely a day passed when Sydney wasn't being harassed for one reason or another, and even though Charlie wanted to do something to help his classmate, he didn't know how to intervene without making himself a target. So, Charlie did what everyone else did and turned a blind eye to the abuse. It wasn't until the latest incident with Christian Relic that Charlie was pushed past the point of apathy and into the path of the school's most notorious bully.

***

As an infant, Christian had been surrendered by his biological parents at an emergency room in Atlanta, Georgia. No identifying information was left behind, so the baby was immediately put into the foster care system. A devout preacher of a small-town congregation and his infertile wife immediately jumped at the chance to adopt the child, and, after several home visits, a mountain of paperwork, and a few court appearances, the baby was adopted into the Relic household and immediately baptized with the name, Christian.

The first few years of Christian's life were picturesque. With the baby they had spent years praying for, Reverend and Mrs. Relic adored their son and gave him all the love and attention a young boy could ever hope to receive. Every Sunday, Mrs. Relic and her new baby would sit in the front pew of their church and watch Reverend Relic spread the word of God to an appreciative and attentive crowd. At the end of each service, the little family would greet each person at the door, and everyone remarked on the quality of the sermon and the beauty of the baby.

Then, as Christian became a toddler, everything changed as a rumor circulated through the small town that Reverend Relic had been inappropriately involved with one of his teenage parishioners. While never proven, the girl's family was quick to defame the Reverend and began a movement calling for his immediate removal from the church. In the end, Reverend Relic was investigated but never charged with a crime despite circumstantial evidence that he had conducted a brief sexual liaison with an underage minor.

Unable to survive the rumor mill, the Reverend promptly resigned his post and moved his family from their home in Georgia to Albion, Connecticut, in an effort to escape past transgressions. Unable to preach and living in poverty, Mr. Relic found himself taking solace in two things: alcohol and a flamboyant southern televangelist constantly preaching on a free public-access channel.

At first, the Relic family would watch the televangelist and pray together that their luck would change. For a short time, Mr. and Mrs. Relic believed that their new circumstances would only be temporary and that they would be delivered from their misery in time, but after months of unemployment, Mr. Relic quit looking for a job, and Mrs. Relic mostly stayed in bed and slept.

By the time Christian turned five, his father had all but given up on God except when Christian needed to be punished. In those moments, he would turn the televangelist on and crank up the volume as high as it would go. Then, Mr. Relic would remove his belt and beat his son repeatedly while crying and shouting out barely intelligible lines of scripture and the occasional amen. At first, Christian struggled against the abuse. After each thrashing, the young boy would watch the charismatic televangelist in the hope of improving himself in his father's eyes, but after years of maltreatment, he began internalizing the pain, making it part of him, twisting him into a barely recognizable person.

When Christian turned 10, he started taking on the personality traits of the only role model he had: the larger-than-life preacher on television. At first, Christian contained himself to sermons in his empty bedroom. He emulated the televangelist's thick southern accent and practiced his own style of wild arm movements and body language. As Christian grew more confident, he started aggressively speaking about God directly to his peers. None of his classmates knew what to do when he started with one of his religious rants, but they soon discovered that laughing at him would result in a brutal physical altercation. After many suspensions, Christian realized that brute force would not take him as far as charm and carefully selected targets. He could always resort to violence if needed, but he preferred to be the center of attention for what he had to say rather than whom he could beat in a fight.

By the age of 13, Christian burned with a fire kept white-hot by years of physical abuse. He was a little taller and stronger than most of his peers and a lot meaner than all the other bullies in Albion Middle School combined. Thanks to the countless hours he had spent studying the televangelist, he was a gifted speaker, and he had a certain kind of charisma generally reserved for supervillains. Anyone who didn't know Christian well would probably describe him as handsome. He had dirty blond hair that he kept perfectly combed at all times and intense green eyes that seemed to glow when he spoke. He always wore ill-fitting suits or, if the day was particularly hot, a buttoned-up vest and tie donated by the Salvation Army. His smile could shift from friendly to deadly mid-sentence, and he was very outgoing with students and teachers in a cocky, arrogant kind of way. If he wasn't so angry and vicious by nature, Christian could have been an effective class leader, but any time a classmate would try to befriend him, the relationship would inevitably end with an argument or a fistfight.

***

Christian bullied Sydney every chance he got by pushing him down during the school day, knocking his food tray out of his hands, and calling him names like "Sadney." On the day of the incident with Charlie, Christian had singled out Sydney for what he called "deviant behavior," a phrase often used by the televangelist when discussing sin. Christian had adopted the expression as a way of calling out anyone who had wronged him, offended him, or was the slightest bit different from everyone else. While Sydney did his best to keep a low profile, he just couldn't escape Christian's wrath. On this particular day, Sydney had tripped in the art room and almost spilled red paint on Christian's black pants. After careful inspection, no damage had been done to either of the boys' clothing, but the near miss was enough to fire up Christian's rage.

After classes were dismissed and students had gathered their jackets and backpacks from their lockers, they all began flooding outside and moving towards their respective bus stops or to their parent's car for pick up. It just so happened that Charlie's bus stop was right next to Sydney's, and he saw his visibly nervous peer praying that his bus would arrive before Christian could find him and torture him outside the supervision of the school's adults. Unfortunately, fate was not kind to Sydney that day, and Christian found his prey.

As was Christian's custom, he began to shout to anyone who would listen about the so-called crimes of the victim he had chosen for that day.

He held out his arms in a mocking, cross-like gesture and yelled, "My friends, we have a deviant among us!" He pointed one of his arms at Sydney and continued, "This sad, pathetic excuse for a boy has no place here. He has no friends. He has no skills. He has no talent. In short, he has nothing to contribute to this world."

A distant voice yelled for Christian to shut up, but more kids began crowding around to see what would happen. Christian's particular gift was that he knew how to work a crowd. Even if he didn't exactly win over his classmates with his bullying, he was able to talk them into silent, passive consent in return for the promise of putting on a show. Christian's actions and his style were just outlandish and cartoonish enough that no one knew what to do, so everyone just stood there and watched the public beatings and humiliations take place. Some kids felt ashamed afterward that they didn't do anything to stop the attack. Most kids didn't know how to feel or talk about it, so they just pretended like nothing happened and went on with their lives.

Like Sydney, Christian wasn't really on Charlie's radar. Charlie had heard disturbing things about the school bully, but he had never witnessed an attack with his own eyes. Like many of the adults who heard about Christian's violently flamboyant nature, Charlie assumed that much of what had been whispered was greatly exaggerated. No one was that crazy, except in the movies. But now Charlie had a front-row seat to Christian's insane ranting, and it was clear that nothing had been overstated. If anything, the rumors downplayed the bully's true power because even though Christian's tone was mocking and his face held a devilish smile, there was no way to describe the rage and anger in his eyes.

"I hold this boy guilty in the eyes of the Lord for his deviant ways, and I cast him out, so help me, God."

With that, Christian moved towards Sydney and pushed him down on the ground hard. The impact of the fall made Sydney drop his art book. Christian quickly snatched the book off the ground and flipped through the pages.

Sydney was too scared to stand, but he yelled, "Give me back my book, Christian! I never did anything to you!"

Christian laughed and responded, "That's right, Sadney. And you never will."

Then, he looked Sydney right in the eyes and tore out the first page. Sydney screamed in horror and devastation as he watched his art, his life's work, be torn from its book and crumpled into a ball of garbage. Christian tossed the wadded paper into Sydney's face and turned back towards the stunned crowd. He relished in their fear and disbelief.

As he scanned the faces of the onlookers, drinking in their weakness, he thought, "This is real power. This is God's strength."

Again, Christian opened the art book, and he held the next page between his thumb and forefinger. He made a show of his intentions by exaggerating every movement with his hands and overexpressing every moment of joy with his face.

He began slowly tearing out the page when a voice called out from behind him, "That's enough, Christian. Give Sydney his book back."

Christian turned to see Charlie helping Sydney to his feet.

Charlie had been at the edge of the gathered crowd talking with his best friend, Dylan, while everyone else was watching the brutal scene. Dylan had been Charlie's best friend since they were in pre-school, and since she didn't have any siblings, she liked many of the same things that Charlie liked, which meant that she grew up playing pirates and tackle football instead of some of the other games that girls in their class played. Dylan didn't mind, though. Fun was fun, and she always had a blast with Charlie.

"Besides," she would think, "Who says girls can't play tackle football, anyways? I'm better than Charlie most days."

On the day of the incident, Dylan had been telling an amusing story about something that had happened to her during gym class when she saw that Charlie was no longer paying her any attention. He was still looking at her and nodding, but the fight had stolen his focus, so Dylan reached out and grabbed Charlie's chin abruptly.

"What did I just say?" she demanded.

Charlie shrugged. He looked uncomfortable, like the sound of Sydney being tortured was causing him physical pain.

Dylan sighed and hugged her friend.

Before breaking the embrace, she whispered in his ear, "Be careful."

And with Dylan's blessing, Charlie was gone.

Christian took a moment to think about his next move before he said, "The Lord has no issue with you, Charlie. This is between me and him."

"Not anymore," Charlie replied as he took a step forward. "Now, it's between me and you. So, you've got two choices. You can give Sydney his book back and leave him alone, or we can see if God will fight your battles for you."

Christian smiled nervously. No one had ever stood up to him before, and even though he had never lost a fight, the kids he beat up were always smaller than him. That's when he decided to do something dirty.

Christian spun back to the crowd and yelled, "The Lord has a forgiving heart. I will let this boy go for now, but he has been warned."

Christian turned back towards Charlie and Sydney and tossed the book at Charlie's feet.

"Here ya go, great protector," Christian taunted.

Charlie bent down to pick up the book and felt a sudden terrible pain as Christian thrust his knee directly into Charlie's chest. The force of the blow left Charlie breathless as he fell to his knees. Dylan gasped and screamed for her best friend. The other kids who had gathered to watch the confrontation were now screaming, "FIGHT!" Christian was happily playing to the crowd, convinced he had already struck the decisive blow.

To his surprise, Charlie got up, dusted off his gym shorts, and said, "I would have thought God's wrath would have more muscle behind it."

Charlie moved toward his opponent with force, and Christian was so caught off guard by the suddenness of the attack that he tripped over his own feet and fell to the ground hard when he tried to step back from the advance. Unable to catch his balance, Christian hit his face on a rock and chipped his tooth from the impact. His mouth began to bleed, and he cried out in pain.

Charlie stood over his bloody opponent, who lay in a heap on the ground. He knew what he was supposed to do next: throw the finishing punch. But Charlie didn't do that. Instead, he extended a hand to Christian to help him up. As far as Charlie was concerned, the fight was over. There was no need to carry a grudge past that moment, and he was content to let the whole thing end there, but Christian didn't take Charlie's hand. He was too embarrassed and in a tremendous amount of pain.

At that moment, all the darkness inside the bully gathered into one all-encompassing, all-consuming idea: revenge. Christian turned from his classmates and scrambled away as fast as possible, a permanent mark of hate and shame imprinted on his soul with Charlie Everett's name associated with the humiliation.

Just like that, Charlie won the fight without throwing a single punch. He had also shown himself to be the bigger man and revealed Christian as a coward. The crowd of children immediately began to disperse. Some kids laughed and pointed at Christian as he ran away crying, but most of them ambled towards their bus stop, confused about what they had just seen. Dylan ran to her best friend to make sure he was okay, but before she could get to him, Charlie put up one finger to signal that he was fine and needed a minute alone. Dylan understood that he would come to her when he was ready, so she nodded and went to wait for Charlie back at their bus stop.

Charlie picked up Sydney's art book and walked over to his classmate.

"Are you okay?" Charlie asked.

Sydney nodded as he wiped the dirt off his faded jeans and batman t-shirt. When he had finished cleaning himself off, Charlie returned the notebook, and Sydney quietly mumbled, "Thanks, Charlie."

"Don't mention it, Syd."

Then, Charlie turned and walked back to his bus stop.

Dylan didn't say anything to Charlie when he returned. She didn't ask if he was okay or say she was proud of him. Instead, Dylan did what she always did when Charlie impressed her. She punched him in the shoulder. Hard.

"Ow! One fight isn't enough?!"

Charlie rubbed his shoulder and looked over at his smiling friend. He hated that she could punch him whenever she wanted and then smile, and suddenly, he wouldn't be mad anymore, but that's just the way it was. After five minutes of waiting and rubbing his bruised shoulder, Charlie and Dylan's bus came, and they got in line to board. Just as Charlie was next to get on the bus, he heard a voice call out to him. It was Sydney.

"I want you to have this," the small boy said.

Sydney handed Charlie a crumpled-up piece of paper.

Charlie recognized it as the page Christian had torn out of the art book. He didn't know what to say, so he just held the wadded-up ball in the palm of his hand and stared at it.

"Anyways, thanks for everything, Charlie," Sydney mumbled, breaking the awkward silence. "See you tomorrow?"

Charlie nodded, put the paper in his jacket pocket, and climbed onto the bus. After Charlie found his seat next to Dylan, he unfurled the paper Sydney had given him. It was the cover art for some kind of superhero named, Ultra-Man. The hero was flying above a city skyline in his purple and green spandex costume, complete with a silver cape and the letter "U" in bold purple lettering on his chest.

At the bottom of the illustration was an inscription, "Dear Charlie, thanks for showing me that heroes really do exist. Your friend, Sydney."

Dylan wrapped her arm around Charlie's and put her head on his shoulder.

"That was really stupid, you know?"

Charlie shrugged. "Yeah, I know."

They both laughed and rode the rest of the way home in silence.

When Charlie arrived home, he ran inside, excited to tell his parents about the action at school.

To his disappointment, he found the house empty with a note taped to the refrigerator that said, "Charlie, your dad and I are out for a date night. We will be home late. Eat the leftovers in the fridge. We'll tuck you in when we get home. Love, Mom and Dad."

Charlie sighed and pulled the leftovers out of the refrigerator. The rest of the evening was pretty uneventful. Charlie ate dinner, did his homework, and watched television for thirty minutes longer than he was supposed to, but with his parents out late, he was willing to risk it. He put himself to bed at 10:07 PM and waited for his parents to come home so he could tell them all about his fight with Christian. At 10:48 PM, his parents still weren't home, and Charlie was getting too tired to keep his eyes open. He decided to rest for a few minutes to get a little bit of his energy back, but the short rest quickly turned into a deep sleep, and Charlie drifted away into a replay of his confrontation with Christian.

Charlie was woken from his sleep by a kiss on his forehead. Even though the room was completely dark, he knew his mother was sitting next to him.

Groggily, Charlie sat up and said, "Mom… what time is it?"

She put a gentle hand on her son's shoulder and laid him back down on the bed.

"It's late, Charlie. I'm sorry to wake you, but I hadn't seen my boy all day, and I needed to sneak a kiss."

Charlie smiled and said, "I love you, Mom."

Charlie's mom ran her fingers through her son's hair and hummed a quiet tune. The sensation completely relaxed him, and he could feel himself drifting back to sleep.

After a few minutes of hair stroking, Charlie felt his mother rise from his bed and heard her say, "I love you too. More than you know. Sleep well."

Charlie closed his eyes again as his mother moved towards the door but suddenly, he remembered the story he wanted to tell her.

"Mom, wait! You'll never believe what happened today! I saved this kid named Sydney from Christian Relic and…."

"I believe it, Charlie," Jillian interrupted. "You're a good person through and through, and I want to hear all about it tomorrow, but right now, you need your sleep."

Charlie begrudgingly agreed and laid his head back down on the pillow. He told himself that he would reenact the whole story for his mom in the morning. Except that never happened. Charlie never got the chance to tell his mother the details of his heroic actions because that was the last time anyone saw Jillian Weston Everett.

13

The local police looked for Charlie's mother for two weeks before the FBI took over the case. Every professional involved in the search came away with the same head-scratching conclusion that Jillian Everett had vanished without leaving a single clue. There was no cell phone to trace, no license plate to run, and no credit cards to track because all her belongings were right where she always left them. None of her clothes were missing, and she had not taken a single dollar from her bank accounts.

The local and regional news outlets ran the story of Jillian's disappearance for about two weeks. At first, it was the major headline, with considerable air time given to photos of the Everett family, people talking about where they had last seen Jillian, and how she was a wonderful person who couldn't possibly have any enemies. After about a month, the updates on the case became a secondary headline with brief clips of press conferences with Albion's Chief of Police. Another month after that, the sensation of the story dried up. The news outlets set up a spot on the homepages of their respective websites for people to report any tips or clues, and that was the end of any active reporting on Jillian Everett's sudden disappearance.

Charlie was devastated by the loss. At first, he couldn't believe it was real, convinced that his mother would show up in some strange place and that the disappearance would just be some kind of misunderstanding.

Then, after a few months of holding out hope that she would be found, she was. Her body was discovered in a dumpster by a popular young musician named Jeff Kerrington, who had been taking a smoke break behind the restaurant where he was playing a show. He told the police that the body was so badly disfigured that he didn't even recognize the remains as human at first. When he finally realized what he had found, Mr. Kerrington ran for help as quickly as he could.

On the day of the discovery, the Chief of Police arrived at the Everett household with Patrick waiting for him on the front porch.

"Good evening, Mr. Everett. Wanna head inside so we can talk?"

Chief Buxton saw that the man's eyes were red and puffy, a clear sign he had recently been crying. When the Chief had called earlier in the day to say that he would be stopping by, the phone call ended abruptly. He guessed that Mr. Everett already suspected the news he was going to receive, or maybe he didn't know and was just too afraid to have any conversation that might diminish his hope for a happy ending.

"I don't want Charlie to hear," Patrick managed to say with a quivering voice.

The Chief let out a sigh. "There's no point in dragging this out. We found a body behind Mi Casa, that Mexican spot on Listorti Street."

Patrick doubled over like he might be sick, but he stood again after several deep breaths. "Maybe it's someone else. Can I see…," he paused. "Can I see the body?"

"Normally, that's exactly what we would do next, but it doesn't make much sense in this case. Even if it is your wife, I don't think you'd be able to recognize her. I don't want to get into the details, but whoever this person was got hurt pretty bad."

That was more than Patrick could take. He fell to his knees and began to sob uncontrollably.

The Chief looked around uncomfortably and dropped to one knee beside the crying man. "Look, we need to run some tests to find out if the body we found belongs to Jillian. To do those tests, I need your consent. This might be the only way to know for sure, one way or the other."

Patrick continued to cry out in pain like he hadn't even heard the Chief's request. For his part, Chief Buxton lightly patted the heartbroken man on the shoulder and occasionally murmured half-hearted words of comfort.

After what felt like a lifetime to the Chief, Patrick finally lifted his head and replied, "Do whatever you need to do."

That was all the old cop needed to hear.

"One of my Sergeants will be in touch with the results."

With that, the Chief rose and returned to his car. He lingered in the driveway for a moment, watching Mr. Everett. The poor man didn't seem to have the strength to stand up. Then, Chief Buxton spotted the face of a young boy staring at him through the upstairs window. The Chief waved, but the boy didn't wave back. He wanted to say something that would make both the father and son feel better about losing someone close to them, but he had never been very good at that sort of thing. What he could do was figure out if the dead woman was Jillian Everett. If she wasn't, he could give them back a little bit of hope. If she was, he could at least give them closure.

A week later, the test results confirmed the worst. Jillian Everett was dead. The news hit Patrick and Charlie hard but in very different ways. Patrick completely shut down and responded almost as though he had barely known Jillian at all. At the funeral, the eulogy he gave for his wife was shockingly brief and devoid of any of the feelings you would expect a grieving husband to express. His behavior offended many guests, especially when he berated Morris Weston for no reason and forced him to leave his own daughter's memorial service even though he had paid for the entire event. Charlie felt the loss in a more traditional sense. At first, he couldn't believe that the test results were real, and he started doing his own investigation into the body that had been found behind the Mexican restaurant. When his inquiries stalled, Charlie began praying to all the Gods he had ever read about to use their power to bring his mom back to life. When that didn't work, he fell into a deep depression and stayed there well past the funeral.

Charlie tried looking to his dad for comfort, but the broken man was utterly changed and unable to console his son. He was too angry, and for some reason that Charlie didn't understand, that anger was aimed at his Grandpa Morris. Charlie would watch his father shuffle from room to room after the funeral, with no particular purpose other than staying mobile and upright. The man was barely alive himself, crippled by overwhelming grief and regret.

The only time Charlie saw any life in his father at all was when Charlie's grandfather would call and ask to see his grandson. In those moments, Patrick would scream and shout and curse, saying things like, "I will not let you take my son too, Morris!" Charlie didn't know what that meant, but he was too afraid to ask.

Over the next few months, the only person Charlie could turn to was Dylan. She was Charlie's rock, and he leaned on her heavily for a long time. Instead of just seeing each other at school every day, they started texting and calling each other constantly. She would walk with him between classes and sit with him at lunch. After the school year ended, Dylan's parents met with Charlie's dad to offer their help and support. With Patrick being emotionally crippled by the loss of his wife, the adults agreed that Charlie needed Dylan's help to get him through his grief. After much pleading from Dylan on her and Charlie's behalf, it was decided that she would be allowed to ride her bike to Charlie's house several nights a week to sleep over so that he wouldn't have to be alone. The rule was that she was supposed to sleep in a guest bed that had been set up on the other side of the room, but she rarely did, choosing instead to lay right next to her best friend. He liked to put his head on her shoulder while she ran her hands through his hair like his mother used to do. Some nights they talked. Some nights they cried. Mostly, they just lay together, and Charlie felt safe. The already close friends became even closer, and Charlie didn't know what he would do if Dylan weren't there to save him.

Dylan wasn't the only friend to come through for Charlie, though. Word spread quickly through the community about Jillian's disappearance, and after the first week of searching with no luck, Charlie came home from school one day to find the first full issue of

Sydney's comic book, *Ultra-Man,* waiting for him in his mailbox. He smiled for the first time since his mom's disappearance while running his fingers over the hand-drawn cover. He took the comic book up to his room and allowed himself to take his mind off everything by getting lost in the compelling story and detailed artwork. Ultra-Man's alter ego was a small, shy kid named Kyle McClammer. In the first few pages, Kyle finds a magic hat that contains the essence of every element on earth. Simply by putting on the hat and wishing for the power to do good, Kyle is transformed into Ultra-Man, whose powers are nearly limitless as long as they are being used to help people. Any bit of corruption or evil instantly removes Ultra-Man's abilities and banishes the wearer of the magic hat from ever accessing them again.

Charlie was so impressed by the comic book that he decided to dig out his class directory to find Sydney's phone number and thank him for the gift. The phone rang a few times before he heard someone pick up the line, but no one spoke.

After a few seconds of waiting, Charlie said, "Hey Sydney, it's Charlie. I just wanted to thank you for the Ultra-Man comic. It's really good. I can't believe you made that yourself."

There was a long pause, and Charlie wondered for a moment if he had been disconnected, but then Sydney replied, "If you ever need a sidekick, I will make myself available."

"Ummm. Okay," Charlie stammered, not sure what to say in response to his classmate's proposal. "Thanks."

"See you tomorrow, Charlie."

And with that, the conversation ended. Charlie pulled his phone away from his face and just looked at it in disbelief.

"That is one weird kid, but I like him."

Then, Charlie picked up the issue of Ultra-Man and reread the entire thing.

From that point on, Charlie received a new issue of Ultra-Man in his mailbox every month. Each new issue was better than the last, and Charlie would always call Sydney after reading the whole thing twice to thank him. Sydney would always respond by saying something strange about being Charlie's sidekick and end the conversation abruptly. It was their little routine, and Charlie enjoyed it.

Even though Sydney and Charlie never got together to hang out, Charlie would find Sydney in school and ask him things about Ultra-Man. Eventually, other kids started to overhear the two boys talking about the comic, and one classmate, Amy Berner, said she could help Sydney make high-quality copies of each issue so that more people could read it. Sydney was reluctant at first, but after a little convincing from Charlie, Sydney and Amy began working together on every edition. It wasn't long before all the kids in school were reading about Ultra-Man's heroic exploits, but no matter how popular the comic got, Charlie always had his issue first, and it was never a copy, always the original.

After about a year of grief and avoidance, enough of the pain and sadness had dulled that Charlie and his dad found they could co-exist in a new routine that felt tolerable. Neither of the men would describe their lives as particularly happy, but it was a definite improvement over the state of depression they had been stuck in before. Unfortunately, the bond between father and son had all but died with Jillian. Patrick just couldn't bring himself to be vulnerable with his son. It was too hard, so they both settled for mutual respect befitting a father and teenager and never tried for anything more than that.

Over time, and with a considerable amount of begging, Patrick finally allowed Charlie to visit his grandfather periodically in public places, although the two men continued their mysterious feud with one another.

Despite all the unhappy changes, Charlie managed to survive because he had Dylan. She provided him with all the love and support he needed that he wasn't getting at home, and slowly but surely, she helped to rebuild him into someone close to the person he had been before his mother's disappearance. The trouble was that Charlie's classmates no longer knew how to treat him. He had been the victim of a great tragedy, unlike anything any of them could imagine. As a result, everyone became polite and overly kind, treating him like a piece of glass that might break. Even Christian backed off and left Charlie alone.

Only Dylan and Sydney stayed the same, refusing to let their best friend become a pariah, and they did such a great job that Charlie barely noticed that everyone else kept a safe distance.

14

The soft, welcoming sound of birds chirping roused Charlie from his sleep. When he opened his eyes, he was greeted by a picturesque Saturday morning in spring. He sat up just enough to see outside his window, and he could feel the warmth of the sun on his face.

Outside, Ms. Cordner was walking a dog that was a little too big for her, and she struggled to keep pace with it as the dog frantically searched for the perfect spot to relieve itself. Mrs. Kudelchuk was busy mowing her lawn, and the Garcia family was piling into a minivan parked in the driveway a few houses up the street. Charlie opened his window, and he could feel the heat from the bright morning entering his room, accompanied by a slight breeze. Everything was perfect.

Charlie jumped out of bed with excitement. He didn't exactly have plans, but he was looking forward to reading the latest issue of Ultra-Man, which Sydney never failed to deliver on the second Saturday of each month. He was also excited to be spending the entire afternoon hanging out with Dylan. It had been almost a year since Charlie's mother had disappeared, and Dylan didn't sleep over as often as she used to, but whenever she did come over, she and Charlie would still lay in bed together, talking and laughing as though nothing was wrong. Lately, their conversations revolved around Sydney and trying to figure out a way to convince him to hang out with them outside of school. Thanks to Charlie, Sydney had gained some respect from his peers for his talents, and everyone loved reading Ultra-Man, but Dylan had noticed that Sydney was still alone a lot, and she suggested that they find a way to make him part of their little group. Charlie liked the idea, not only because he wanted Sydney to have friends but also because he genuinely liked Sydney's strange, quirky personality.

Charlie searched his room for the first clean clothes he could find. For all of his good traits, tidiness and organization tended to fall by the wayside, and he sometimes struggled to find things quickly. He settled on a pair of gym shorts that passed the sniff test and a vintage Third Eye Blind t-shirt that had belonged to his father. Next, Charlie ran to the bathroom, splashed cold water on his face, and brushed his teeth. He intentionally kept his hair short enough so that he rarely needed a comb, and after just a few minutes of basic hygiene and self-maintenance, Charlie was ready to start his day. He sprinted down the steps towards his front door and flung it open. The whole wide world was waiting for him, but right as Charlie went to take his first step outside, he heard his dad's voice call out to him from the kitchen.

"Charlie, hold on a second. I need to talk to you."

Charlie exhaled, and his body deflated like a balloon. For a second, he thought about pretending like he didn't hear his father's command, but he thought better of it, not wanting to incur any unnecessary wrath, and slowly shuffled towards the kitchen.

The first thing Charlie noticed was that his dad was wearing a suit. That was not good news. The only time his dad wore suits was when he had to go into the office, and when he went to the office on the weekend, his dad insisted on making sure Charlie had adult supervision. Before Patrick even got a chance to speak, Charlie began protesting what was about to happen.

"No! No! NO! Dad, please don't do this. I'll do anything. Chores, homework, ANYTHING!"

Patrick didn't look up from his phone but still responded, "You should be doing all of those things anyways."

Charlie's dad started moving around the kitchen, gathering all of the things he would need for the day, and Charlie followed him around like a lost puppy and continued to argue his case.

"Dad, this is crazy. I'm almost fourteen years old. I can take care of myself. You used to leave me home alone all the time when Mom was here."

That comment stopped Patrick in his tracks. Mentioning his mother was a low blow, and Charlie wasn't usually so bold about bringing her up in casual conversation, but this was an emergency. His weekend was being threatened, and he had to act quickly and decisively if he was going to change his father's mind. The only problem was that playing the "mom" card had unpredictable consequences. Sometimes, just the mention of her sent his father into an unyielding rage. If Charlie had summoned that beast, he wasn't just going to lose his Saturday but his Sunday as well. Other times though, mentioning her made Charlie's dad completely passive, and he would cave on everything just to avoid the conversation.

After pressing a final button on his phone, Patrick looked at his son and said, "You're right. You're growing up. You're a responsible kid, and you never cause any trouble. I don't think you need a babysitter anymore."

Charlie let out an excited yell and started pumping his fists in the air. He was right in the middle of a victory dance that featured finger guns and side-to-side hip movements when his father grabbed him by the shoulder and proceeded to burst his son's euphoric bubble.

"Your grandfather wants to spend the day with you, Charlie. He's been asking me for weeks, and before this conversation, I thought having you spend the day with him at his house would be a perfect way to kill two birds with one stone. After this, we can figure out the new rules for you being left alone when I'm not here, but today I need you to help me keep a promise to your grandpa."

Charlie holstered his finger guns, feeling the pain of bitter disappointment. It had been years since Charlie had been allowed to visit his grandfather at Weston Manor, and he genuinely liked Grandpa Morris. The old man looked and acted like a retired James Bond. He wore nice suits and walked with a polished wooden cane that had a dragon's head on the top. Everything he said had an air of dignified importance, but there was also a calm, nonchalant presence he brought to any conversation. He acted as though he could solve all the world's problems in an hour over a good scotch.

When he was with Charlie, though, Morris Weston could also be funny and weird. He had a bunch of crazy, made-up stories, and

Charlie loved hearing about his grandfather's adventures because of how animated and alive the old man was while telling them. No matter how ridiculous the story got, Morris never broke character. He knew how to keep his audience on the edge of their seat, and usually, Charlie would be excited for an opportunity to spend the day with him at his huge mansion. But today just wasn't a good day to be stuck inside talking about the impossible or hearing about what life was like when Grandpa Weston was young. After Charlie had a second to think about the situation though, he decided that this moment was still a big win for him. After all, his normally overprotective father had acknowledged that he was growing up and no longer needed the same level of adult supervision. In the end, Charlie decided to accept his fate with only a minimal amount of whining and complaining. After all, he had to mourn a little bit for his lost Saturday.

Charlie pulled out his phone to text Dylan the bad news.

"Change of plans. My dad is making me spend the day with my grandfather."

"You suck, Charlie! We were supposed to show up at Sydney's house today and surprise him!"

"Ugh! I know! It's not my fault!"

"Whatever... I'll just go there by myself and make Sydney my new best friend."

Charlie was surprised at how much reading that message hurt his feelings. He replied with an angry face emoji.

"You know I'm only joking, Charlie. Don't get all crazy on me. I'll come over tonight, and you can tell me about the weird stories your grandpa tells you."

Charlie laughed and was relieved that he had reclaimed his spot as Dylan's best friend even though he had never really lost it.

"Sounds good. I'll see you tonight. Try to be a little quieter coming through my window this time. It's been a while since you slept over, and I'm not sure if my dad is cool with it anymore."

"Well, clean up your room, so I don't trip over the crap you leave everywhere."

Charlie laughed again and sent a winking emoji before putting his phone back in his pocket.

After gathering all his things for the day, Charlie walked out to the car with his dad just in time to see Sydney putting the next edition of Ultra-Man in their mailbox.

"Excuse me," Patrick yelled out. "We don't want any solicitors."

The sudden rebuke made Sydney go completely still with one hand on the door of the mailbox and the other clutching his comic book.

Charlie could see that Sydney was frozen like a deer staring in the headlights of a car, so he ran to the rescue.

"It's okay, Dad. Sydney is a friend from school. He's the one who gives me that comic book that I read."

Patrick gave the young man a wave and replied, "Sorry about that, Sydney. Nice work on the comic. I haven't read it, but the artwork is really good."

Patrick waited a moment for a response but quickly realized that there wasn't one coming, so he proceeded to climb into his car and start the engine.

Charlie went over to the mailbox and did his best to calm Sydney down.

"Sorry about that. My dad didn't mean to scare you. Is that the new Ultra-Man?"

Sydney looked down at his shaking hand holding the comic book.

"Yeah… It's a good one. Ultra-Man gets a sidekick. Ultra-Boy."

Charlie gently grabbed the comic and replied, "Sweet! Sounds awesome. Every good hero needs a sidekick, right?"

Sydney nodded and was about to speak, but Charlie interrupted, "I know, Syd. If I ever need a sidekick, your services are available."

"That's correct," Sydney replied.

Charlie rolled his eyes and slapped his friend on the shoulder.

"Don't worry, Syd. I don't think the world will ever be so desperate for a hero that I become the best option."

Sydney didn't laugh or smile.

"Maybe you can't save the world, but you can save the day. You saved mine once, so what's the difference?"

Charlie was about to respond when his dad honked the horn, signaling to Charlie that it was time to leave.

"Sorry, Syd. We'll have to pick this up another time. Thanks for the comic, though. I'll read it later tonight with Dylan."

Charlie saw Sydney blush at the mention of Dylan's name, and he wondered if his new friend might have a thing for his old friend. He felt a small stab of jealousy but quickly shook off the feeling and climbed into his dad's car.

The pair silently made their way to Grandpa Weston's house. Usually, Charlie and his father had no problem finding things to talk about, but today Charlie couldn't help but notice all the people doing things outside and wished that he was out there with them, enjoying the perfect spring day. Charlie's dad was unusually quiet too. Whenever there was a lull in the conversation, Patrick always broke the silence with a joke or a fun fact or some other conversation starter, but today, something was different. He seemed fidgety and uncomfortable, like his suit didn't fit him correctly or someone had messed with the settings on his seat. Something was going on, and if Charlie hadn't been in a funk of his own, he would have said something, but as it was, they made the entire ten-minute drive together in miserable silence.

Charlie and his father turned down a side street on the other side of town, a well-known area for wealthy people. Charlie marveled at the enormous houses with all of their unique features. Many of the homes had beautiful stained-glass windows, while others had entire walls made out of glass to let in as much natural light as possible. Charlie's favorite house was made to look like a castle from the Middle Ages. It was built entirely of stone and had a keep at the very top where Charlie spotted an old man sitting in a lawn chair and reading the newspaper.

At the end of the road, they came to a gate that featured the same dragon head that sat on top of his grandfather's cane. The gate opened automatically as the car approached, and they made their way down the long, winding driveway towards Grandpa Weston's large, secluded estate. Along the route, Charlie saw several fountains that got bigger as they got closer to the house. The detail and ornateness of each fountain increased as well, with each one featuring a mythical creature like a minotaur or phoenix. Charlie wanted to ask his dad to pull over to look at them more closely, but he knew his dad was in a rush, so he remained silent and attempted to take everything in quickly as they drove past.

The landscaping featured shrubs and bushes that had been trimmed to match the design of the nearest fountain. There were also flowers of varying shapes, colors, and sizes. Charlie didn't know the names of any of the plants he saw, but he thought they were beautiful. He considered asking his grandfather if he could take one home to give to Dylan, but just the idea of giving her a flower made him feel embarrassed, so instead, he took a picture and sent it to her with the caption, "Pretty beautiful, right?"

She responded, "Wow. Is your grandfather a gardener or something?"

That was when Charlie realized, maybe for the first time, that he had no idea what Grandpa Weston did for a living. He knew that his grandfather was in his late seventies and was most likely retired from work. Still, whatever he had spent his life doing, he must have done very well because the only thing larger than the very large driveway was his massive house in the middle of a well-manicured lawn.

The mansion itself was old and featured some extravagant architectural choices, such as large watchtowers, an observatory, a stable, an iron gate, and craziest of all, a drawbridge with an actual moat. Despite having a good relationship with Grandpa Weston, Charlie had only been to his home once or twice when he was young. He tried to remember what the house was like on the inside, but the only thing he remembered at all was an old book with an eye on it. Since Jillian had disappeared, Charlie had been prone to nightmares about his mom, and that book was always in them. He shook the idea out of his mind and returned his focus to the gigantic house.

"This place is huge! It looks just like a real castle. Dad, what does Grandpa Weston do?"

Patrick continued staring blankly out the front window as they made their way towards the drawbridge.

"What does Grandpa do for a living?" Charlie repeated.

Again, there was no response. Charlie turned to ask his question for the third time, but before he could speak, he noticed that his dad was sweating profusely even though the air conditioning was running. For a second, Charlie feared his dad might be having a heart attack.

Charlie gently grabbed his father's arm and whispered, "Dad...."

The slight contact was enough to shake the dazed-looking man out of his trance.

"I think he used to work with animals," Patrick replied as he exhaled a deep breath.

The words fell out so unconvincingly that Charlie wasn't sure he believed them, but he didn't know how to ask his dad what was wrong, so he decided to let it go.

Then, without warning, Patrick stopped the car, turned to his son, and said, "We're here."

15

Even though the drawbridge was down, Patrick stopped the car just short of the crossing. He rolled down the driver's side window and pressed a button on an intercom next to the road.

"Charles, my boy!" a voice from the speaker on the intercom boomed. "Welcome back to Weston Manor!"

Charlie was immediately excited by the tone of his grandfather's voice and shouted back, "Hey Grandpa! What are we going to do today?!"

The voice on the other end of the intercom laughed and replied, "We are going to have an adventure! What else?!"

"Hello, Morris," Patrick interjected. "Are we okay to cross the drawbridge?"

There was an awkward pause before the voice responded, "Is that you, Patrick? You sound strange."

"Yes, it's me. I'm just in a bit of a hurry to get to the office. Can we cross the bridge?"

Another long pause followed. Finally, the voice said, "Of course you can cross the bridge… If you remember the password."

Charlie's dad closed his eyes and let his head crash into the top of the steering wheel. He mumbled a few words under his breath and sighed heavily.

"Please don't do this, Morris," Patrick moaned with his eyes still closed. "You know I hate this stuff."

With a slight laugh, Morris replied, "I'm sorry, Patrick, but those are the rules. If you want to cross the bridge, you must speak the password."

Patrick looked at his watch and then over to his son. Charlie wasn't sure what was going on or why his dad didn't just drive over the bridge since it was already down, but for whatever reason, they remained parked.

Finally, Patrick straightened his tie, took a deep breath, and said wearily, "Enter as friends, leave as family," and without another word, he put the car into drive and crossed the bridge as quickly as possible.

Once the car passed through the iron gate, Charlie found himself in a courtyard filled with the same beautiful flowers and large fountains that he had seen on the road leading up to the house. Patrick pulled his car right up to the door on the far edge of the courtyard. He parked the vehicle and then turned the engine off altogether.

Charlie started to unbuckle his seatbelt so he could leave and start exploring when his dad said, "Your grandpa lives a different kind of life than us. I don't know what you're going to hear or see in there, but I do know that it's time for you to hear it."

Charlie had no idea what that meant, and he looked back at his dad's serious face with confusion and fear.

"Dad, what are you talking about?"

"I don't have all the answers, Charlie," Patrick continued with a slight tremor in his voice. "I've done my best without your mom, but there are some things I don't know. There are some things I don't want to know. What I do know is that your mother loved you more than anything in this world. She would want you to know the truth no matter how I felt about it."

Charlie shifted uncomfortably in his seat.

"Dad, you are seriously freaking me out."

Patrick put his hand on his son's shoulder.

"I'm sorry. Just know that I love you, and when I pick you up later tonight, we can talk about whatever you want. You're going to have questions, and I will do my best to answer them."

Patrick pulled his son towards him and into a long hug. It was the warmest embrace Charlie had gotten from his father in almost a year, so he pushed his nervousness out of his mind and enjoyed the moment.

When the hug was over, Patrick returned to his seat and said, "I hope you have a fun day with your grandpa."

Charlie wasn't sure what to say at this point, so he just responded, "Thanks… I'll try."

Then, he climbed out of the car and nervously watched his dad drive back over the bridge and down the long driveway.

Charlie started to relax a little once his dad was out of sight. He had no idea what was going on, but he was beginning to suspect that this was going to be more than a casual visit. Whenever Charlie and his grandfather had spent time together in the past, it was always someplace fun that Charlie picked out. Before that moment, it had never occurred to him to ask why he had never been allowed to go to Weston Manor.

"So, why now?" Charlie wondered. *"What's so special about today?"*

Charlie strolled through the courtyard while he thought about everything his dad had been saying in the car.

"What did he mean about mom wanting me to know the truth? The truth about what? Is she still alive? Is she here for some reason?"

Charlie shook the thoughts out of his mind. There was no way his mom would be hiding out here for a year without contacting him.

"No," Charlie thought. *"Mom isn't here, but whatever today is or is supposed to be, has something to do with her. I know it."*

After a few more minutes of thoughtful wandering, Charlie found himself staring at an incredibly lifelike statue of a dragon carved out of stone. He admired the detail of the scales on the dragon's body, its massive wingspan, and the sharp spikes on the tail. Charlie quickly looked around the courtyard to see if there were any guards or groundskeepers close by. When he didn't see anyone, he made an impulsive decision to climb on the statue's back and pretend that he was soaring through the clouds. Much to Charlie's irrational disappointment, when he finally managed to get himself in position, the dragon did not magically come to life.

Charlie did notice, though, that the statue was unusually warm. He had expected to feel cold, smooth stone on his hands and body, but the dragon's scales were rough, and the torso felt like it was radiating heat. Even stranger, Charlie could have sworn a sound was coming from inside the statue.

Thump, Thump.

He pressed his ear against the stone and closed his eyes.

Thump, Thump. Thump, Thump.

After a couple of minutes of concentration, Charlie locked in on the faint noise, a slow, steady drumming.

Thump, Thump. Thump. Thump. Thump, Thump.

No, not a drum...

THUMP, THUMP! THUMP, THUMP! THUMP, THUMP!

A heartbeat!

"Oh my God! Oh my God! This thing is… Oh my God!"

Charlie quickly climbed down from the statue just as a voice boomed into the courtyard.

"Fancy a ride, Charles? I'm afraid this dragon is quite out of the question. Statues make very poor aviators."

"Grandpa, it's alive!" Charlie yelled to the open air. "It's warm, and I heard its heart, and we have to do something! There's a real dragon in there!"

Not a moment after the words escaped his lips; Charlie felt a warm rush of embarrassment pass through him. He whirled around, and sure enough, the statue was perfectly still. Charlie put his hand on the torso, expecting to feel the heat, but the dragon was cold, smooth, and lifeless.

"What was that, my boy? I'm afraid the microphone didn't quite pick up what you said."

"Nothing," Charlie said meekly. "I just said that it's a really cool statue."

"Yes, Charles. I agree. It's one of my favorites. Now, if you would be so kind, come through the large wooden door on the other side of the courtyard and join me. We have a lot to do today."

Charlie made his way to the door and knocked a few times, but no one answered, so he grabbed the large handle in the shape of a dragon's head and pulled as hard as he could. The door was very heavy, and it took all of Charlie's strength to open it enough to squeeze through. Once inside, he stared down a long, narrow hallway that was lit by actual torches.

"This is so weird," Charlie said to himself.

It took a minute for Charlie's eyes to adjust to the low light, but once they did, he started following the torches down the hall. As he walked, he felt a chill run through his body, not sure if he was cold or just nervous.

There was another door at the end of the long hallway, but this one was a standard size. Charlie turned the doorknob and pushed into a room that was unlike anything he had ever seen. The first thing he noticed was a black, grand piano playing by itself without any music for the instrument to follow. Before Charlie had a chance to investigate further, he heard his grandfather's jubilant voice.

"Charles, my dear boy! It's been too long. How are you?"

Charlie ran over to his grandfather and gave him a big hug.

"I'm good, Grandpa. This house is amazing!"

"Well, Charles, when you get to be as old as I am, you find that you have a whole life's worth of junk that you have collected from different places and different times. It just so happens that some of my junk is a little more interesting than the ordinary."

Charlie could see that his grandfather was not exaggerating. There was a whole life's worth of things in the giant room, and some of it was very unusual. He found that he liked the crazy and colorful artwork on the walls. There were also some interesting sculptures that were professionally lit and displayed. Each time Charlie stopped to admire a different painting or trinket, his grandfather would act as a museum curator and begin telling him every known fact about the particular piece.

Charlie loved listening to his grandfather speak passionately about everything because even though the old man was prone to embellishing his stories, that was exactly what made them exciting. Morris was in the middle of a lively tale about how he had fought some kind of trained, adolescent polar bear when Charlie caught the reflection of the sun shining off of something in one corner of the room. While his grandfather busily reenacted his wrestling match, Charlie moved towards the bright light and found that the reflection had come from the suits of armor worn by two knights posed in attacking positions. Between the warriors was an extravagant marble pillar, which stood about four feet tall, on top of which was a black velvet pillow with some kind of red ball resting on it.

Charlie could still hear his grandfather speaking to him in the back of his mind, but something about the red ball was calling to him. For the second time that day, Charlie could hear the slow, steady rhythm of a heartbeat, and the sound put him in a trance that compelled him to keep moving forward. Somewhere in the distance, his grandfather's voice continued getting louder, but Charlie couldn't stop himself. He stretched out his hands towards the magical red ball, and just as he was about to grab it, he felt his grandfather pull him by the back of his shirt and yank him to the ground. The force of the fall shook Charlie out of his daze.

"Ouch! What the heck, Grandpa? Why did you just tackle me?"

"I'm sorry, my boy," Morris said as he helped his grandson up from the ground. "I tried to yell at you from across the room, but it was like you couldn't hear me. I don't move as quickly as I used to, and I was barely able to get to you before you touched the egg."

"That's an egg?" Charlie asked as he brushed himself off. "An egg for what?"

Before Morris could answer, Charlie regarded the display again, but this time for a different reason.

"Wait a second. The knights moved. They were attacking each other before, but now they look like they are about to fight…me."

When Charlie had first seen the display, the knight in the silver armor with the dark blue shield was lunging his sword towards the knight with the black armor. The black-armored knight used his shield to block the oncoming attack and had his sword ready to deliver a counter thrust. Now, both knights were facing Charlie directly and had their swords raised above their heads.

Morris put his arm around his grandson and led him towards one of the black leather couches positioned around the stone fire pit in the middle of the room. Charlie looked back over his shoulder at the knights and noticed that they each had a dragon painted on their respective shields. The silver knight's dragon was ice blue, and the black knight's dragon was the same red color as the egg.

"Charles, did your father tell you anything about why I wanted you to come here today?"

Charlie remembered the strange conversation he had with his dad in the car, but he wasn't sure what to say about it, so he just shook his head.

"I'm not surprised. You might have noticed that your father and I are not on the best of terms. Don't get me wrong; I like your dad. He's a good man, and he has done his best with you since your mother…," the old man's voice trailed off.

"Since she died?" Charlie asked.

Charlie saw his grandfather wince and realized that even though he would always love his mom and would miss her throughout his life, he had found an acceptance that probably wasn't available to his grandfather, who had known her from the minute she was born through adulthood.

"I'm sorry, Grandpa. I didn't mean to upset you."

"No, Charles. I should be the one apologizing to you. I didn't want these secrets between us, but your father thought it best to wait until you had a proper amount of time to grieve. Maybe he was right. There is no way to know."

Charlie started to get the same nervous and uneasy feeling in his stomach that he had when he was talking to his dad in the car.

"Grandpa, what are you talking about?"

"The truth, Charles! I'm talking about the truth! When your mother disappeared, everyone looked, and no one could find her until that business with the body in the dumpster, and this whole time we have allowed you to believe that she is dead, but it isn't so. The truth is, she is alive, and we are going to find her."

The words crashed down on Charlie like a tidal wave of raw emotion. After a few moments of trying to process what his grandfather had said, he realized that he had forgotten to breathe and started coughing while trying to get air back into his body.

"What do you mean Mom is alive?!" Charlie choked out as he continued gasping.

Morris took a moment to return himself to his calm and poised demeanor so that both he and his grandson would not be hysterical at the same time.

"Charles, I know this is a bit of a shock…."

"A bit of a shock?" Charlie yelled. "I'm sorry, grandpa, but that's crap, and you know it."

Charlie wanted to get his breathing under control so he could stand up and pace around the room, but he was afraid that he would end up getting light-headed and pass out into the fire pit.

"I need to know everything, and I need to know it now! Where is Mom? Does Dad know she's alive? Where has she been for the last year?!"

Charlie's grandfather stood up from the couch and made his way toward a beverage cart. He used a pair of tongs to remove a single ice cube from a gold-plated bucket and placed the cube into a small, ornate glass. The clinking sound of the ice seemed deafening in the quiet room. Finally, Morris poured a reddish, brown liquid into the glass until it was half full. He looked down for a long moment, closed his eyes, threw his head back, and consumed the entire drink in one large swallow.

The elder gentleman remained still with his eyes closed. He looked peaceful, like his body was in the room, but his mind was on a sandy beach on an island in the Pacific Ocean. When his wit returned, Morris took a deep breath and told his grandson everything he had been holding back for the past year.

"Charles, your mother and I are Cryptozoologists, which means we study and help protect animals that are thought to be mythical or imaginary. The animals we protect are incredibly rare and beautiful, but they are also powerful and potentially dangerous, which is why their existence is a well-kept secret to most of the world. Unfortunately, keeping these creatures hidden from society is impossible because most of them are wild, and they appear and disappear as they please. Still, the Cryptozoology community, your mother and I included, have gone to great lengths to either hide them or work their existence into mythology so that people aren't actively out hunting them."

Charlie waited for a moment to see if there was more, but Morris had finished his speech and was busy preparing a second pour of whatever he had downed a moment earlier.

The room started spinning, and Charlie felt like he might be sick. Morris took a step towards his grandson, but Charlie quickly put up his hand, signaling the old man to stay back.

"Grandpa, this really isn't funny. I appreciate everything you are trying to do for me. I think in some really dumb way, you are trying to help me move on, but I'm not a little kid anymore. You can't just tell me one of your crazy, made-up stories and expect me to believe that everything is going to be okay. Mom is gone! She isn't coming back! I've made my peace with that, so you don't need to pretend like she is still going to come home for my sake because that just isn't going to happen."

Morris approached Charlie slowly and sat down beside his grandson.

"Charles, my poor boy, I wish this were all a crazy story or a bad dream. I want to wake up as badly as you do, and let me be perfectly clear; your mother is not going to magically reappear. Wherever she might be is most certainly not a good place, but she is somewhere on this earth, which means there is a chance we can find her and bring her home."

Charlie stood angrily and marched back in the direction of the display of the two knights.

"I don't believe you! I don't believe any of it!"

Morris remained seated to give Charlie some space and replied, "I know this is a lot to take in, Charles, but try to think back. Your mother and I have been telling you stories all your life about places we've been and creatures we've encountered, and they haven't all been fairy tales either. You know the strengths and weaknesses of all the myths, Gods, and legends of almost every culture known to man. You have unknowingly been preparing for this moment your entire life."

Charlie didn't know what to think or believe. His head was a tornado of memories and information, but he couldn't settle his mind on anything in particular. Then, he caught sight of something on the black knight's shield.

"That's a red dragon. Mom told me a story once about a dragon like that. She said it existed in another world and that you had seen it. What was the dragon's name?"

Charlie looked intensely at his grandfather as the old man stood from the couch and approached the display.

When Morris was standing directly in front of his grandson, he replied, "The dragon is made entirely of fire, and his name is Incinidore. He is the protector of the fire creatures known as the Ignidore."

Charlie stumbled backward, almost falling to the ground. He attempted to speak, but no words came out.

Morris turned from his grandson to the display and continued, "Charles, though these two gentlemen may appear to be enemies in combat, the truth is, they are brothers in arms, legendary knights sworn to protect all that is innocent and preserve goodness at any cost. These soldiers are not robotic. They are flesh and blood men of another world, or at least, they were at one point. Their bodies have long since passed away, but their spirits remain to continue fulfilling their knightly duty. When you arrived, they had been sparring with each other. They froze in position when you entered the room. The silver knight with the blue dragon on his shield is named Brock. He is from the Order of the Blue Horizon, a group of battle veterans and magicians who summon their strength from the purity and revitalizing power of water. His companion in the black armor is named Addison. He comes from the Order of the Red Star, a band of warriors who draw their courage and determination from the living flame. Together, they have one goal, one purpose for their constant training and the sacrifice of their spirits' peace, and that is to protect this dragon egg. It is one of only a dozen known to be in existence. The deep red color means that the dragon inside will be the embodiment of the living flame. This magical creature will be responsible for keeping the remaining acolytes of the Order of the Red Star alive so that their traditions and their magic can continue to live on for many generations to come. I expect that this egg will hatch someday, but probably not in my lifetime. It will be up to you to care for it, at which point Brock and Addison will leave and work together to find a new egg to protect until it is ready to hatch."

"Wow! My own dragon!" Charlie replied sarcastically. "I'll take him with me to Hogwarts next year."

Morris frowned.

"Ugh. Hogwarts. We asked her to write one little story about a troll so that we could bolster them in the modern mythology a little bit, and what do we get? A story about a magic boy and a magic school. The troll barely even features in the first book. Now, I'm a muggle; you're a muggle; everyone is a blasted muggle. There are no magical people, only magical things."

"I like the Harry Potter books," Charlie replied, unsure of what else to say.

Morris shrugged his shoulders.

"Yes. Everyone does, including me. I guess that kind of talent simply can't be contained."

"So, what are you saying, Grandpa?" Charlie asked with skeptical amazement. "This is a real dragon egg?"

"Correct," Morris replied matter of factly.

"And the piano is playing by itself because of...?"

"Magic."

"And these knights move because of…?"

"Also magic," the old man answered again.

"My dad couldn't cross the drawbridge without saying the password because…?"

Morris smiled and finished his grandson's sentence.

"I have lots and lots of magic. Well, I don't have magic, per se. No one has magic. It's a bit of a lost art form. Real magic comes in two parts, the spell and the conduit for that spell. Without both of those things, there is no magic at all."

Charlie's grandfather moved towards a lamp in the corner of the room and continued, "For example, let's say my desired outcome is to light up this room. The lamp is my magical conduit, and electricity is the spell. Without electricity, I cannot turn on the lamp. Without the lamp, the electricity has nothing to power, and the room remains dark. The spell and the conduit must work together to produce light. Simple magical conduits are relatively commonplace if you know where to look and are willing to pay the price for them. I have spent my life and a large fortune collecting various trinkets and items capable of channeling all kinds of simple magic. I mostly use those items for comfort, such as the self-playing piano over there. The spells for that kind of magic are easy to learn and safe to use, but the real magic spells, the kind of spells that save or destroy the world, you could die a thousand deaths just trying to learn one of those, and even if you do learn it, you still have to find the proper conduit for it, which is equally dangerous."

Morris raised his glass to take another drink, but quickly added, "Also, I have a giant sea serpent that swims in my moat. He is trained to attack anyone who tries to cross the bridge without the password. You can never be too careful, Charles."

Charlie turned back towards the display again.

"These knights protect the dragon egg. You pulled me to the ground because if I had touched the egg… they would have killed me."

"My dear boy, nothing and no one here is going to kill you," Morris said reassuringly. "You are my blood, which means you are protected as long as you are on my property. Your father… not so much. I like him, but that's just not the way the spell works."

This day was not going the way Charlie had imagined at all. In one conversation, magic had become real, a dragon egg was sitting on a pillow right next to him, and a giant sea serpent was waiting in the moat to swallow his dad.

Charlie knew that he had to try and focus on accepting everything he had just learned. Otherwise, he was going to lose his mind and end up in a padded room. After a few moments of quiet reflection, he settled on the topic that mattered to him the most and asked, "What does all of this have to do with Mom?"

Charlie's grandfather smiled and replied, "Come take a walk with me."

16

Morris led his grandson back towards the fire pit in the middle of the room. Without a word, the old man used the end of his cane to press a hidden button on one of the stones, and an elevator came down from the ceiling while a panel from the floor covered the flames. The door to the elevator opened, and Charlie, who had given up on trying to make sense of all the craziness he had just been told, followed his grandfather inside without question.

There were several buttons on the elevator wall, but they weren't marked by a floor number. Instead, they denoted a location on the property. A red light marked the passenger's current location. The button you pressed as your destination would light up green.

Charlie scanned the panel and saw a button for the observatory, a separate button for each of the eight bedrooms, a button for the pool house, one for the library, and dozens of other controls that would lead passengers almost anywhere on the grounds. Finally, Charlie's grandfather pressed the button labeled "Stables." As the doors closed, Charlie couldn't help but wonder how an elevator could move the two of them to a location outside the house.

"I know what you're thinking," said Charlie's grandfather, "but this is no ordinary elevator. Did you ever see *Charlie and the Chocolate Factory*, with the elevator that could go in any direction?"

Charlie nodded his head, and Morris continued, "Well, I invented that concept. Of course, the movie elevator wasn't real, but I gave them the idea based on my elevator here. We can move anywhere on the property through this system. Come to think of it, the boy in that movie was also named Charlie. How amusing."

Charlie smiled and gave a nervous laugh, but only because he didn't know what else to do. He thought back to the scene in the movie that his grandfather had referenced. He couldn't remember for sure, but he had some vague memory of the elevator crashing through a roof and going airborne. Charlie gripped the handrail tighter and prepared himself for a possible flight.

As they traveled, Charlie timidly asked, "Does this work by magic?"

Charlie's grandfather pondered the question before answering, "All science seems like magic to those who do not understand, and all magic seems like science for those who do understand."

Charlie had no idea what that meant, but he was already confused enough, so he decided not to ask for an explanation.

When the elevator doors opened, Charlie and his grandfather were in the stables, a quarter of a mile from the house. Charlie stepped out of the elevator and into a long row of horse stalls. The boy and his grandfather moved casually through the row, and Charlie frequently paused to visit each occupant.

"These horses are amazing," Charlie said as they came to the end of the row.

Charlie's grandfather smiled and, as he led Charlie to the final stall, he replied, "Yes, these are some of the finest horses in the world. Purebred Spanish stallions. They are beautiful and remarkably fast, but none of them hold a candle to this girl."

Morris pointed at the animal in the last enclosure, and Charlie couldn't believe his eyes.

"Oh…my…God. It's a… It has a… Is this real life?!"

Up to this point, Charlie was pretty sure he believed everything his grandfather had told him. He had seen the dragon egg and the moving knights with his own eyes, but this was different. The animal standing before him was about the same size as the other horses but much stronger looking. Its mane and tail flowed with streaks of silver, and its green-tipped horn looked sharp enough to pierce through anything that stood in its way. Charlie couldn't help but think that the creature was not supposed to exist, and yet, there it stood, a beautiful, perfect, white shining beacon of pure goodness. It was a real unicorn.

Morris watched his grandson take in the full beauty and power of the mythical beast and thought, *"It never gets old. The feeling of being in the presence of these amazing creatures never fades. Even after spending my entire life protecting them and being around them, I still look upon their raw power and unparalleled beauty with the same awe as my grandson, who is seeing it all for the first time."*

"Charles, this is Jade," Morris said as he rested a hand on Charlie's shoulder. "She was your mother's unicorn, and now, she's yours."

Charlie's eyes immediately began to fill with tears.

"I'm sorry, Grandpa. I love her. I don't know why I'm crying."

"I miss your mother every single day," Morris said softly. "Some of my happiest memories are of watching her ride Jade. I wish she were here to tell you all of these things. I wish she were here to be your mother. As happy as I am to be here with you and serve as your guide into this new world, I can't help but feel sad that I am the one here to share this with you for the first time, and she is not. I can't promise that we'll be able to get her back, but I can promise that we will try everything in our power to find her together."

For a moment, Charlie felt better, and he started to smile. After all, if it were possible for him to be standing beside his mother's unicorn, maybe it would be possible to bring her back from wherever she was hiding. Maybe there was hope after all.

Unfortunately, the joy in Charlie's heart didn't last long and quickly gave way to fear and doubt. At least with the way things were, there was closure. What happened was horrible, and it changed him forever, but he was finally picking up the pieces and moving on with his life. The idea of believing that he might see his mom again was just too hard. He had already held on to that fantasy for too long, and he couldn't do it again, especially if there was a chance of losing her a second time.

"This doesn't make any sense. What does this have to do with Mom 'disappearing'?" Charlie used air quotes to indicate that he didn't fully believe that his mom might still be alive.

"Charles, the work we do…."

"No, I don't think so," Charlie interrupted. "We don't do any work. You do work. I haven't agreed to anything."

"Fine," Morris continued calmly. "The work I do is inherently dangerous. For starters, most of the animals we encounter are potentially deadly. Take Jade, for example. She's beautiful and majestic and at least twice as fast as any horse in the world, but…."

"Anything she stabs with her horn will turn to stone," Charlie finished.

"Well done, Charles. That's correct. Also, unicorns have a unique healing property. Their blood can cure almost any wound or illness. Of course, it can't bring a person back to life, but it can certainly save someone from death."

"I still don't see the problem. Are you telling me that Mom was eaten by a dragon or something?"

Morris moved past Charlie and opened Jade's stall door. Then, he led his grandson and the unicorn over to the large stable gate and flung it open. As soon as Jade viewed the large expanse of the field before her, she took off like white lightning.

As the old man and his grandson watched the unicorn sprint across the open field, Morris said, "The trouble is, Charles, we aren't the only people who know of the existence of unicorns and all of the other mythological creatures in the world. Some have dedicated their lives to studying and protecting these animals, but others are trying to profit from their existence. Imagine the price a vial of unicorn's blood could fetch on the black market. Many hunters would love to capture and kill a unicorn to cut off its horn and create a dagger that can turn things into stone. Some want the horn simply for display purposes."

Charlie's face twisted in anger and disgust. "That's horrible," he said. "Who would do that?"

"Unfortunately, Charles, it is more common than you think, which is why I believe your mother was kidnapped. You see, she is an expert in field research. She knows as much about these creatures as I do, but she's forty years younger and more than capable of helping some nefarious collectors capture the rarest, most powerful magical conduits in the world." Morris could see the stunned look on his grandson's face and quickly added, "I'm not saying she's one of the bad guys, Charles. I'm just saying that I think she's being forced to help people whose motives may not be for the greater good, and if she thought she was protecting her family, it's possible that she didn't even put up much of a fight. Your mother loved you more than anything, and she would have done anything to protect you. Now, she is the one who needs protection, and that is where you come in, my boy. I have all the knowledge we need to save your mother and continue protecting the magical creatures of the world, but I just don't have the physical tools anymore. As difficult and humbling as it can be to face your limitations, no magic protects a person from time and its effect on the body. The man I once was is long gone, and I need you to become my apprentice so you can do the things that I can't. Together, I know we can save her."

Charlie leaned against the stable door and tried to process everything his grandfather had told him, especially the parts about his mom.

Where was she? Was she safe or even alive? Could he really do anything to get her back?

"Do you want to ride her?" Morris called out from the middle of the field.

Charlie looked around, confused. Somehow, his grandfather had managed to make his way over to Jade while he had been lost in thought.

"Do you want to ride her, Charles?" Morris yelled again.

Charlie felt a wave of excitement rush through his body.

"Hell yes, I want to ride her," he yelled as he sprinted to his grandfather's side.

Morris frowned. "Language Charles. Jade is a unicorn, not a mechanical bull."

"Sorry, Grandpa," Charlie said impatiently. "So, what do I do?"

Charlie's grandfather laughed and said, "This is no horse, my boy. You don't do anything but sit there and try to hold on. Jade will take care of the rest. I think you will find that if you speak to her gently, she will understand what you say. If you listen carefully, you might just understand her as well."

Charlie wasn't sure what that meant, but he didn't care. After the weirdest day of his life, he was ready to reap the benefits of all the shocking news that had been laid in his lap.

Charlie had just put one foot in his grandfather's hands so he could get a boost onto Jade's back when he heard, "CHARLES EVERETT! DON'T EVEN THINK ABOUT IT!"

Charlie turned around and saw his dad sprinting towards them.

"Get away from that beast!" Patrick yelled again. "It's dangerous."

"Good afternoon, Patrick," Morris said calmly with a slight smile. "I wasn't expecting you so soon. I see you remembered to use the password. Otherwise, we wouldn't be suffering from this interruption."

Patrick was fuming.

"I must have been crazy to leave my son with you," he shot back. "We had a deal, Morris. I agreed that Charlie should know the truth about his mom, but you promised you would leave out all of the Cryptozoology stuff."

Morris straightened his posture as much as possible and retorted, "I'm sorry, Patrick, but there is just no way to explain Jillian's absence without revealing the truth in its entirety. It's time. It is long past time."

"That is not your decision to make."

"You're right! It's Charles'. He is old enough to decide for himself."

With that, the two men looked over at Charlie, who was still standing next to the unicorn. Charlie knew that both men were expecting him to speak up and choose one side or another, but he didn't want to do that. How could they expect him to make that choice? How could they put him in this position?

The more Charlie thought about it, the angrier he got until he worked up the courage and strength to step towards his elders and say, "Both of you lied to me. You've been lying to me for over a year. I know you had your reasons, but it doesn't change what you did. A lie to protect me is still a lie, and before I decide anything, the first thing I need to figure out is how and when I can forgive you. Both of you."

Charlie pushed between the two men and started walking towards the car when he heard his grandfather call out, "Charles, wait."

Charlie stopped walking, but he didn't turn around.

"Charles, I'm sorry. I should never have let you believe that your mother died. Asking you to help me fix this… It's not your responsibility."

"I think it's fair to say that I've made some mistakes handling this whole situation," Patrick added. "I wasn't there for you after your mom disappeared, and I will regret that for the rest of my life, but I decided to spare my son the false hope that might just make his life unbearable. Maybe I was wrong, but I would do anything to protect you from that pain or disappointment. I'm sorry."

"I understand why you did what you did," Charlie said without turning around. "But I don't know if I can forgive you. Not yet."

Charlie walked back to the car with his dad trailing by a few steps. Neither of them spoke. When both of them were inside the vehicle, Patrick handed his son something covered in gift wrap and a bow.

"This is a birthday present from your grandfather. He knows it's coming up next week and that you may not see each other between now and then."

Charlie took the gift and wordlessly folded his arms around it. He wasn't in the mood for presents and didn't care about his birthday. It was just another day in his life when he wished his mom would be there and she wouldn't. Charlie thought about telling his dad to forget about his birthday, but instead, he just tightened his arms around his grandfather's gift and stared out the window. When Patrick realized that his son was not going to open the present, he started the car and drove towards the bridge. When they reached the moat, he mumbled the password, "Enter as friends, leave as family."

"You don't have to say it when I'm in the car," Charlie said sullenly. "Nothing here can hurt me."

"What do you mean?" Patrick asked.

Charlie continued to stare out the window and sighed, "Never mind.

17

Charlie woke suddenly from another light sleep filled with strange dreams. It had been nearly three weeks since the trip to Weston Manor, and the visit had somehow hampered his ability to sleep through the night. Pain radiated from Charlie's temples, and he groaned with the exhausting realization that he had failed to get more than a few hours of sleep. He looked over at his calendar hanging on his wall and saw the birthday crown Dylan had drawn in permanent marker on April 27. Charlie remembered asking her not to write anything about his birthday, but she responded by punching him on the shoulder and doing it anyway. He let out a heavy sigh and rolled away from the calendar, so he didn't have to see it.

In addition to the mysterious dreams that consumed Charlie's mind at night, a million anxious thoughts raced through his head during the day. He felt perpetually torn between the hope he was trying to suppress about his mother, the anger he still felt towards his dad and grandfather, and the excitement of exploring a whole new world of mythical creatures. The trouble was, he couldn't compartmentalize any of his thoughts. Everything was just sitting on the surface, screaming for attention. His feelings overwhelmed him and made him feel sick with anxiety and helplessness. As a result, Charlie drifted through school like a zombie and barely slept more than a few hours every night.

Charlie wanted to share all of his news with Dylan, but he didn't even know how to start the conversation. How do you tell someone that your grandfather owns a dragon egg or that you almost got to ride a unicorn? How do you explain that your mom, who you thought had been dead for the last year, might be alive? Charlie knew that telling Dylan the truth would change their relationship forever and not necessarily for the better. She was the only stable thing in his life, and he wasn't willing to risk losing her for anything.

Charlie had barely spoken to his father since being picked up at Weston Manor, and he hadn't reached out to his grandfather at all. He had mostly forgiven them but wasn't ready to have the serious conversations coming his way. Charlie had a lot of questions but wasn't sure he could handle the answers, so he decided not to ask.

Overwhelmed by his emotions, Charlie continued to lay in bed and stare up at the ceiling. He started thinking about the weird dreams he had been having. They weren't exactly scary, just confusing. He always woke up feeling restless, like there was something he needed to do. His brain was subconsciously trying to tell him something important; he just couldn't figure out what it was.

***

Charlie was back at his grandfather's house, watching Jade as she ran through an open field. Suddenly, a blinding light appeared over the horizon. Charlie puts up his hands to shield his eyes, but the light was too powerful and continued to overwhelm him. He called out for his dad and grandfather, but no one answered. Half blind, Charlie stumbled through the field, trying to feel for Jade or anything familiar, but quickly realized that he was utterly alone. After what felt like an eternity of being lost in darkness, the light gradually went out, and Charlie's senses returned to him slowly. When he opened his eyes again, expecting to find the source of the beacon, he instead saw a mysterious person in a long, red cloak standing twenty yards away. The person in the red cloak started moving towards Charlie, his face completely concealed by an oversized hood that managed to contort itself perfectly with each step so that no identifying features of the owner could be seen. When the unidentifiable person was standing mere feet away, he extended his arms and offered Charlie an old book. Despite everything, Charlie felt no reluctance towards the stranger and took the book willingly.

On the cover of the dusty volume was a living, blinking eyeball staring Charlie right in the face. Charlie was surprised to find that he wasn't afraid to look back at it. In fact, a calm, comforting feeling came over him as he held the book in his hands and gazed into the somewhat familiar eye. Instinctively, he gripped the cover of the book with his fingers and turned to the first page. Just as he was about to begin reading, an obnoxious buzzing sound rang in his ears and jolted him awake.

***

Charlie hadn't even realized that he had drifted back to sleep until his phone buzzed with an alert that meant a new text message had come through. It was from Dylan.

"HAPPY BIRTHDAY, CHARLIE! Feeling 14 yet?!"

Charlie desperately wanted to see Dylan and tell her the truth about everything but wasn't sure if she could handle it. It dawned on him that his situation with Dylan was forcing him to make the same choice his dad and grandfather had to make; tell the truth and risk a mental and emotional meltdown or lie to protect the person you love.

Charlie wasn't sure what to do, but he knew that he wanted to see his best friend, so we wrote back, "Hey. Thanks. To be honest, I'm not really feeling it this year. Maybe you could come over and show me how to be 14 since you've had a month to practice."

"Ugh! I can't come over today!" Dylan texted back. "My grandpa is in town for some reason, and my parents aren't letting me leave. I tried begging but no luck."

Charlie was more than a little disappointed, but he didn't want to take his frustrations out on his friend, so he responded, "That's cool. Tomorrow?"

"You know it! I'll come over after lunch. Dylan out!"

Charlie laughed. Dylan could always make him laugh. Ever since they were little, she knew what to say to make him feel better.

Charlie got up slowly, determined to do something worthwhile when he heard a voice quietly call his name. He looked around the room but didn't see anyone, so he continued shuffling around, aimlessly preparing for his day. Then, while brushing his teeth, Charlie heard the voice speak to him again.

This time, he called back, "Hello? Dad, did you call me?"

From downstairs, Patrick answered, "What did you say, Son?"

Charlie stopped brushing so he could listen closely, and the voice, which was only as loud as a whisper, spoke his name a third time.

Patrick yelled again from the bottom of the stairs, "Charlie, are you okay?"

Charlie didn't answer and instead said in a low whisper of his own, "Who's there? I'm warning you; I have powerful magic."

"There are no magical people, only magical things," the voice whispered back.

Charlie dropped his toothbrush and sprinted out of the bathroom, but right when he turned the corner to go downstairs, he ran into his dad and fell to the floor.

"Charlie! Are you okay?"

Charlie looked back over his shoulder like someone or something might be chasing him, but there was nothing there.

"Yeah, Dad. I'm fine," Charlie lied. "I was just going downstairs to get a snack and didn't expect you to be at the top of the steps."

"You were going downstairs to get a snack in your underwear?"

Charlie looked down at himself and realized he was still in his boxers.

"Also, you have toothpaste all over your face. What's going on?"

Charlie rubbed the back of his hand against his mouth, which wiped away some of the toothpaste but mostly just smeared it around his face.

"Sorry, Dad. Just really hungry, I guess."

Patrick looked at his son suspiciously before standing aside and saying, "Alright, well, enjoy your snack."

Charlie nodded and proceeded to jog down the stairs. Before he reached the bottom, though, his dad called out, "By the way, your friend Sydney is in the kitchen."

Charlie stopped dead in his tracks.

"Geez, Dad. A little heads up would have been nice."

"It's not my fault you decided to go downstairs half-naked!" Patrick joked. "Put some clothes on!"

Charlie rolled his eyes and called out over the banister, "Hey Sydney. I'll be right down. Just have to get dressed really quick."

Charlie waited a moment for a response but quickly realized there wasn't one coming, so he turned back up the stairs towards his bedroom. Once Charlie got within five steps of his door, he began to tiptoe as quietly as possible. He didn't hear the mysterious voice and didn't want the voice to hear him. It took about five minutes for him to move three feet, and when he finally made it to his room, he summoned all his courage, flung the door open, and charged inside like he was running headfirst into a war.

After Charlie managed to get his breathing under control, he stood in the middle of a quiet, undisturbed room, feeling like an idiot. Clearly, all the weird dreams and restless nights had messed with his head. He laughed at himself, got dressed, and went downstairs to see his friend.

"Happy birthday, Charlie," Sydney said as casually as he could though still clearly rehearsed.

"Thanks, Syd. How did you know it was my birthday?"

"Dylan told me at school yesterday. She is very kind."

Charlie nodded as he poured himself a bowl of cereal.

"Yes, she is very kind," Charlie agreed. "So, what brings you by? I don't think you've ever even stepped foot on my driveway, let alone inside the actual house. Dylan and I thought we might have to kidnap you or something."

Charlie took a bite of cereal as Sydney responded dryly, "I wanted to talk to you about the disturbing dreams you've been having."

Charlie spit out most of his milk and almost started choking on the cereal.

"How the hell do you know about those?! Were you the person whispering to me in my bathroom?!"

"You're hearing voices now too? Probably not a good sign."

Charlie grabbed Sydney by the arm and dragged him upstairs. Once inside his room, Charlie locked the door and then turned to question his friend.

"What do you know?" Charlie demanded.

Sydney was visibly nervous and upset. He tried speaking, but no words came out.

"Hey man, I'm sorry I freaked out on you," Charlie said, feeling guilty for how he reacted. "It's just that I haven't been sleeping well because of those dreams, and I haven't told anyone about them, not even Dylan. So how do you know?"

Sydney composed himself by taking a few deep breaths and making strange, flowing hand movements. Then, he responded, "I've been having the dreams as well. Actually, that's not true. I'm watching you in your dream, if that makes sense. It's like I'm standing right behind you in your mind, but you can't see me. I can see everything you see, though. I think. There's a unicorn, a bright light, and some person who gives you a weird book. Pretty crazy stuff, but very cool."

Charlie looked at his friend with a mixture of stunned disbelief and incredible relief.

"Oh my God. You really can see my dreams. How is this possible?"

Sydney was glad that his friend was mostly happy with the news that someone else could see his dreams. Charlie was the one person that Sydney didn't want to disappoint. He didn't know how to express it in words, but Charlie was his hero and not just because of what happened with Christian. Charlie was Sydney's hero because he treated everyone with kindness and respect and convinced other kids in the school to do the same. Life had gotten a lot better for Sydney since everyone stopped picking on him. In fact, most of the kids in school told him how much they loved reading Ultra-Man and that they thought his work was really good. His classmates wanted to talk about Ultra-Man with him all the time, and Sydney often found the long conversations difficult. Still, he tried his best to accommodate them because having people like you and wanting to talk to you is a way better problem than having them hate you and actively trying to make your life miserable.

"I don't know how it's possible," Sydney replied, "But I have been seeing your dreams for the past week. Today was the first day I could come over to talk with you about it."

Sydney paused for a few moments to give Charlie an opportunity to say something but quickly became impatient and added, "What do the voices say to you?"

"Oh, God. Do you hear them too?" Charlie asked desperately.

Sydney shook his head.

"No, I don't hear any voices. I can only see your dreams."

Charlie plopped down on his bed and yelled into his mattress. He wanted to tell Sydney the truth so he could unload at least some of his burden and have someone to talk to, but the fact remained that he had just started spending time with Sydney and wasn't sure if he was someone who could handle a secret this huge.

Sensing Charlie's hesitation, Sydney decided to interject on his own behalf, "Charlie, anything you tell me will never be repeated. I owe you everything, and I've been telling you from the start that I am here to help you. You can trust me."

Charlie wasn't sure how, but he knew that Sydney could be trusted. He had seen all of the crazy dreams for himself and still chose to come forward to find out more about what they meant. Charlie took that as a sign that Sydney could handle the truth, so he took a deep breath and prepared to bare his soul to his friend.

"Okay, Sydney, here's the thing," Charlie began. "The thing is… bad things are going on in the world. I mean, things are happening that people don't know anything about." Charlie began and ended this way two or three more times before burying his face in his hands. He was trying too hard to sugarcoat the truth to make the situation more palatable, but there was no way around the unicorn in the room, so he decided the only way to say it was just to say it.

"I am part of a long line of Cryptozoologists who have dedicated their lives to the protection of mythical creatures. The unicorn you saw in my dream is real. Her name is Jade. My grandfather is going to teach me everything he knows, including stuff about magic and dragons. Also, he thinks bad people have kidnapped my mom so that she can help them steal magical artifacts that will give them power and money. I have no idea what my dream means, but I am pretty sure it is somehow connected with my mom's disappearance and might be a clue about how I can find her."

Charlie exhaled the remainder of the air in his lungs and looked at his stoic friend.

At first, he expected Sydney to run from the room screaming. Then, he thought Sydney might burst out laughing. But Sydney didn't do either of those things. Instead, he adjusted his glasses and calmly asked, "So what do we do next?"

Charlie was floored by his friend's unbelievable nonchalance about everything he had just learned.

"Did you not hear all the crazy, ridiculous, impossible stuff I just told you?! My grandpa has a dragon egg! He has magical stuff everywhere in his house! I rode a unicorn! Well, I almost rode her, but still!"

This time Sydney took off his glasses and began cleaning them with his Batman shirt. While inspecting the freshly cleaned lens, he asked, "Charlie, are you crazy?"

"I don't think so," Charlie responded hesitantly.

Sydney returned his glasses to his face.

"I don't think so either, and you aren't a liar. Everyone knows you are an honest, upright person, so why wouldn't I believe you? Yes, the things you have presented me with are unusual, but I have no problem believing them because you believe them. So, I ask you again, what do we do next?"

Charlie opened his mouth to begin protesting again, but he stopped himself. Sydney didn't need to be convinced or tricked. He had carefully listened to everything he had been told and made the conscious decision to believe his friend, something that Charlie needed more than ever.

"Thanks, Syd. You have no idea how good it feels to be able to talk about all of this with someone."

"I told you I was available for sidekick duty," Sydney replied.

Charlie laughed at his super-serious friend. "I don't want a sidekick, Syd, just a friend."

Sydney flashed a quick but genuine smile and then returned to his usual, thoughtful gaze.

Charlie smiled back, and a wave of relief washed over him. No matter what happened next, he wouldn't be alone, and that made a huge difference.

"I assume you will be telling Dylan all of this when you see her."

Sydney's statement abruptly halted Charlie's moment of sweet relief. "What makes you say that?"

"She is your best friend," Sydney replied, looking puzzled and a little uneasy. "Why would you tell me all of this stuff and not her?"

"I never would have told you either if you weren't able to see my dreams. Dylan is different. She's… I don't think…."

"You are in love with her," Sydney said flatly.

"Yeah. I mean, no! I'm not in love with her, but we have a different kind of friendship. If I tell her all of this, she will think that I'm crazy, and I don't want her to think that I'm crazy."

"You aren't crazy, Charlie. I know you're not, and you know you're not. I won't say anything, but you should tell Dylan the truth if she is the friend you say she is."

And without another word, Sydney got up and left.

Charlie thought about running after Sydney but decided against it when he saw the birthday crown drawn on his calendar.

"She is the only person who really cares about me," Charlie thought. *"I can't lose her."*

Charlie sat around for a few minutes, hoping that Dylan would call or text him, but she never did. He wanted to see her but didn't want to seem pathetic, so he put his phone in his pocket and went to the bathroom to splash some cold water on his face. As he looked at himself in the mirror, Charlie felt the frustration of knowing that he wouldn't be able to talk to her about anything real when he did see her. Instead, he would have to lie, and that made his heart hurt. He had never lied to Dylan about anything, but the only way to protect her was to keep her away from the truth. His mom had known the truth, and someone had taken her for it. He wouldn't let that happen to his best friend.

When Charlie returned to his room, he glanced at his bed and saw something impossible. The unopened birthday present from his grandfather was propped up on a pillow, looking like it was waiting for him to open it. Charlie had stuffed the gift in his top desk drawer the day he received it and hadn't moved it once. He hadn't even looked at it. Now, the shining paper and red bow were on full display and seemingly begging for Charlie's attention.

Charlie angrily swiped the present off his pillow and watched it fall to the floor and bounce into his closet. He wasn't sure what it was or how it mysteriously made its way to his bed, but he couldn't handle any more surprises. Charlie flipped off his lamp and again found himself staring at the ceiling, waiting to slip back into the dream with the unicorn, the mysterious person in the red hood, and the blinding light.

18

Dylan arrived at Charlie's house early the next afternoon. When Charlie saw her bike coming up the street, he ran out into the road to meet her. He didn't even wait for her to say hello. He just grabbed her off the bike and wrapped his arms around her.

After a couple of minutes, Dylan asked, "Umm, Charlie… You realize you are still hugging me, right?"

Charlie nodded.

"Well, are you going to let me go?"

Charlie shook his head.

Dylan pretended to get annoyed, but the truth was that she liked Charlie's long hug. Actually, she loved his long hug but was too self-conscious to let herself be that vulnerable with him. They had been best friends for as long as either of them could remember, but it was only recently that Dylan had started to wonder what that friendship meant to her. She knew without a doubt that she loved Charlie, but she was beginning to have new feelings mixed in with years of friendship and wasn't sure what to do about them. That uncertainty made her a little more aware of the things she did and said around him. Dylan wondered if Charlie was having the same sort of problem but was too embarrassed to ask.

Dylan saw Sydney sitting on Charlie's lawn in the background and called out to him for help.

"Can you get him off me, please?"

Sydney shook his head. "No, I don't believe I can."

Eventually, Charlie ended his marathon hug. As he and Dylan separated, Charlie's hand slid down and found Dylan's. He gripped it instinctively, and she grabbed it back. It felt natural to both of them, and neither wanted to let the other go, so they stood in the middle of the street hand-in-hand, just looking at each other. Dylan was a little taller than Charlie, but he didn't care. She was slender but also strong, and he liked how she could look incredibly girly one minute and just like one of the guys the next. Then, Charlie noticed that Dylan was wearing her long, brown hair down. He wasn't sure when he decided that he loved it when she wore her hair down, but it was his favorite thing about her, along with her brown eyes, her perfect smile, and the dimples she got on her cheeks when she laughed.

"You guys are making me regret my decision to come here," Sydney said, ruining the moment.

Dylan laughed nervously, and Charlie blushed as he stammered out an apology.

"Sorry, Syd. We're just goofing around to make you uncomfortable."

"Good job. It's working," Sydney replied while adjusting his glasses.

Dylan was a little hurt by Charlie's response to Sydney. She was perfectly comfortable holding his hand. They had held hands before. Why should this be any different?

Dylan quickly let go, and Charlie looked at her, but before he had a chance to protest, she said, "Joke's over, right?"

Charlie looked like he might offer something in his defense but wilted and said nothing. Instead, he picked up Dylan's bike and walked it toward his front yard.

"So, what did you boys do yesterday for Charlie's birthday?" Dylan asked.

Charlie and Sydney looked at each other nervously.

"I didn't realize it was a trick question," Dylan added, sensing their hesitation.

Sydney could see that Charlie was forming a lie in his mind, so he decided to speak first to save Charlie from himself.

"I came over briefly and wished him a happy birthday. We spent a little time in his room, and then I left."

Charlie nodded with relief. Everything Sydney said was true, just with a few small bits of information left out.

"Yeah, it wasn't much of a birthday. I saw Syd for a bit, went to dinner with my dad, and then went to sleep early. Pretty boring day."

Dylan rolled her eyes.

"Wow, Charlie. I'm surprised you even managed to get up this morning after such a wild time. Come on, Sydney! We have to help Charlie live a little."

Sydney shrugged and responded, "Charlie probably lives more than we think."

"How mysterious," Dylan teased.

The three friends continued to banter with each other for a few minutes before they began the discussion about what they should do for the rest of the day. Dylan wanted to go on some kind of adventure to make up for Charlie's boring birthday. Charlie pretended he was up for anything, but after another night of restless sleep, he was more tired than he wanted to admit.

Again, Sydney attempted to come to Charlie's aid and suggested they go to the library and play board games. Even though Charlie had never played any of the games at the library, he pretended like he thought it was a great idea. When both boys looked over at Dylan for her approval, she was lying in the grass and pretending to be asleep.

After a few more minutes of arguing, the trio settled on riding their bikes to a nearby pond where they could go swimming, but before they had a chance to get away, a giant dog wandered into Charlie's front yard.

At first, the three teenagers watched the huge dog and wondered where it came from, but after a few minutes of staring, Dylan said, "I bet there's a reward for finding it."

Charlie's eyes lit up at the suggestion that the three of them could earn a little money for returning a dog that had come right to them, but he was also a little nervous about approaching a strange animal that he had never seen before.

"What if it bites?" Sydney asked.

"Come on, man," Dylan shouted. "The dog is wearing a pink collar with a bow on it. How mean could it be? Besides, it's free money."

Charlie thought about all their options. Teenagers needed money for things, and he wasn't interested in getting a job mowing lawns. On the other hand, putting a pink collar on a dangerous animal doesn't make it any less dangerous. Charlie was one of the strongest kids in his class, and Dylan was one of the fastest, but a scared dog would easily outrun them both. An angry dog could rip them to pieces.

In the end, Dylan decided for all of them by standing up and slowly moving towards the strange animal. Following her lead, Charlie and Sydney got up and took opposing positions so that they could come at it from all sides. Charlie decided that even though he was willing to go along with his friend's plan, he wouldn't be the one to make the first move, so he gave Dylan a silent nod indicating that she should reach out and try to bond with their visitor. Dylan rolled her eyes at Charlie in disgust, and she reached out her slightly shaking hand.

In his mind, Sydney was screaming in panic, but to his credit, he didn't run, complain or refuse to participate because he wanted to feel like he belonged. Even though he was terrified about what might happen, Sydney was having fun just going with the flow and taking advantage of opportunities as they presented themselves. This type of spontaneity was way outside his comfort zone, but with his friends there to push him, he was willing to go along for the ride.

As Dylan inched closer and closer, the dog lazily turned its head toward her. There was no growling or barking or baring of teeth, just an enormous, disinterested-looking animal that still managed to scare all three of them with its massive size.

Then, finally, the moment of truth came. Dylan had a look in her eyes like she was nearly finished diffusing a bomb. A single bead of sweat ran down her forehead and hung on the end of her nose with all the weight and anticipation of the moment. As the droplet fell to the ground, Dylan's hand landed on the dog's head. Before she even had a chance to let out a sigh of relief, the dog put its enormous paws onto her shoulders, pinned her to the ground, and started giving her the tongue bath of her life. The boys burst out laughing.

"GUYS! HELP ME!" Dylan screamed.

Dylan was trapped underneath the gigantic dog and completely covered in drool and slobber from its huge, pink tongue. Sydney thought it was hilarious. He laughed so hard that he could barely breathe. Charlie made half-hearted attempts at lifting the dog off of Dylan but quickly realized that he wasn't strong enough to do anything, so he joined Sydney in laughter as he sputtered out apologies.

After a few minutes, the dog let Dylan get up from the ground. She stood with a stunned, horrified look on her face. She wanted to wipe all the drool off her body, but her hands were also covered in the dog's saliva, and her shirt was soaked in it. After what seemed like forever, Dylan angrily turned to her male companions.

"Well, that sucked. I'm going to go home, burn my clothes, take a shower, and cry for a bit. You two watch the dog until I get back."

Charlie stopped laughing.

"What are we supposed to do with it?"

Dylan didn't look back as she walked toward her bike. Instead, she just jumped on, and as she began peddling away, she shouted, "Don't let it get away, or you'll pay for my new shirt with your share of the reward money."

Sydney turned to Charlie and said, "If we lose the dog, there won't be any reward money. What she said doesn't make sense."

"This is no time for logic, Syd. We have an animal to guard."

Charlie and Sydney looked over at the beast sitting on the lawn beside them. Even though his fear was gone, Charlie was still nervous that he would end up with the same fate as his friend. So, to be on the safe side, he decided not to pet the dog at all.

After about ten minutes of waiting, Sydney asked permission to go inside to use the bathroom and call his mom. Charlie told him he didn't have to ask permission, but the thought of going inside someone's home without asking made Sydney extremely uncomfortable. Still, Sydney nodded his agreement and went inside.

"You wouldn't believe the crazy week I've been having," Charlie said to no one in particular.

The dog turned its giant head as if it wanted Charlie to continue with his story. Charlie looked around for a moment, and when he saw they were alone, he decided to pour his heart out to his canine companion. He talked about his mom, his grandfather's magic, cryptozoology, the unicorn, and how he didn't know what he should do next.

By the time Dylan returned, the dog's head was resting comfortably in Charlie's lap.

"You've got to be kidding!" Dylan yelled. "I get the most disgusting bath of all time, and I come back to find you hanging out with the enemy?!"

Charlie laughed. "It's not our enemy, Dylan. It's just a dog, and I like her."

Dylan felt a small sting of jealousy. She didn't know what to do with the feeling, so she did the only thing she could think of and punched Charlie in the arm.

"Ouch! What the hell?"

"You deserve it, and you know it!"

"Don't worry, Dylan. You'll always be my best girl," Charlie said reassuringly as he rubbed his sore arm.

Dylan could feel her face getting warm, so she turned away and said, "Come on, boys. It's time to get that reward."

Charlie looked down at the dog in his lap. He didn't want to give her up now. They had bonded. He had confided in her and told her his fears and his doubts. Charlie knew that Sydney would never give his secrets to anyone, but it felt good to have someone to talk to who couldn't talk back. The dog was just there to listen, and in return, all she needed was a little petting and a soft place to put her head. Charlie glanced up at Dylan, who was already on her bike. There was no turning back now. He knew his best friend too well, and once she set her mind to something, that was it. There was no way he would be able to convince her to forget about the reward. Even if he could, it wasn't like he could just keep a dog that didn't belong to him. She had a pink bow on, which meant that she belonged to someone and the owner was probably worried.

Charlie reluctantly stood up, and the dog stood beside him. For the next several hours, Charlie, Dylan, Sydney, and the dog went from house to house in their neighborhood. Everyone fell in love with the giant animal immediately, but no one knew where it came from. When all the neighbors refused to claim ownership of the dog, they went house to house in the next neighborhood but still didn't have any luck. No one had ever seen the dog before, and there weren't even any posters on telephone poles or street signs.

When the afternoon started to progress into the evening, Dylan, Sydney, and Charlie decided to give up their search for the day and go back to Charlie's house. When they arrived, Charlie saw that his dad's car was parked in its usual spot, but he didn't recognize a second car parked on the street.

"Whose car is that?" Dylan asked, but before Charlie had a chance to answer, his father and grandfather opened the front door and walked outside.

Despite what had happened, Charlie was happy to see them both together. He didn't want to stay mad at either of them anymore for protecting him from the truth, especially now that he was in the same situation with Dylan and was making the same choice they had made.

"Grandpa!" Charlie shouted as he ran over to give his grandfather a hug. "What are you doing here?"

"Well, Charles, your father and I have been talking, and we both realized that we owe you a long-overdue apology."

Charlie wanted to hear what his father and grandfather had to say, but he wasn't ready for Dylan to know everything, so he quickly grabbed her by the hand and brought her forward for an introduction.

"Grandpa, this is my best friend, Dylan."

Charlie's grandfather reached out his hand to shake the girl's and said, "Dylan! What a wonderful name! And who might you be, young man?"

Sydney looked down at the ground and mumbled something in response.

"This is Sydney, Grandpa. He's our new friend. He is a pretty amazing artist."

Morris' expression changed to a look of keen interest.

"An artist?! I love art. Sydney, you will have to show me some of your work sometime."

Sydney nodded but said nothing in response.

"I see you found your birthday present," Patrick said as he gestured to the dog standing in the middle of the group.

Charlie's eyes grew wide. "My birthday present?! Are you serious?!"

Patrick put his arm around his son.

"You bet. This dog is a present from your grandfather and me. We know you can handle the responsibility."

Dylan put her face in her hands and exhaustedly asked, "So we spent the whole day looking for the owner of a dog who belonged to you the entire time?"

No one spoke. Dylan turned and punched Charlie in the arm again.

"You owe me a new shirt," she said.

Charlie laughed, but he also winced a little. He was going to have a bruise for sure.

Before Charlie had a chance to say anything in his defense, Dylan quickly kissed him on the cheek and said, "I've got to head home for dinner. I'll text you later. Happy Birthday, Charlie."

Sydney took that opportunity to get away from the discomfort of meeting and speaking with new people.

"Wait up, Dylan! I'll ride home with you!"

Charlie watched his friends ride down the street, and he felt a full, happy feeling in his heart. He loved spending time with Dylan and Sydney, and even though the day was wasted, it didn't feel like a waste. He still had fun, and he was feeling like his old self.

"Now, there is a lovely girl, Charles," Morris said, breaking the silence. "Well done, my boy."

Charlie blushed and quickly changed the subject.

"Okay, guys. Spill it. What is this animal really?" Charlie asked skeptically.

"What do you mean, Charles?"

"You own a unicorn and a dragon egg and a giant serpent that swims in your moat. God knows what else you have, and this so-called 'dog' is huge, so I want to know what it really is."

Patrick knelt and started petting the newest member of the family.

"Her name is Zag, and she is a mastiff, which is a large breed of dog."

"Zag is just like every other kind of dog except for one difference," Morris added. "She will live as long as you do."

Charlie looked down at Zag, and Zag looked back up at Charlie.

"You mean she will live longer than other dogs?"

"No, Charles. I mean that Zag will live the exact number of years, months, weeks, days, minutes, and seconds you live. Your last moment on this earth will also be Zag's. She will be your faithful companion throughout your entire life."

Charlie wasn't sure why, but his eyes began to fill with tears.

Patrick wrapped his arms around his son and whispered in his ear, "I'm sorry for all of it, Charlie. I should have told you the truth. I was scared and alone, and I know that doesn't excuse any of it, but I felt a strong need to protect you."

Now, Charlie was sobbing openly. He couldn't help it. The hug, combined with the exact words he needed to hear, was too much for his heart to take.

"I blamed your grandfather for what happened to Mom, and that wasn't fair," Patrick continued. "I knew about the work she did, and it never bothered me. In fact, I loved it. I was scared for her at first because the types of things she faced were unbelievable, but your mom was an unbelievable person. I would never have asked her to stop because what she did was important, and she loved doing it. Now, it's time for you to make a choice. After talking with your grandfather last night on the phone, I have decided that I will not push you to follow in your mother's footsteps, but I'm not going to stop you either. I know it's dangerous, and you may not be able to save Mom, but if there is even a chance she might still be out there in the world, maybe the three of us can find a way to bring her home."

Charlie felt a wave of relief wash over him. He hadn't realized it until then, but his dad's blessing was the key to unlocking his confidence. Charlie finally had the clarity he had been missing, and even though he wasn't sure exactly how he would do it, he knew what needed to be done.

19

Charlie shot out of bed thirty minutes before his alarm went off with pure adrenaline coursing through his body. For the first time in over a week, he hadn't dreamt about the blinding light or the red hooded figure, and the uninterrupted night of sleep had recharged his battery. More than that, though, he couldn't wait to begin training with his grandfather.

A week had passed since Charlie's birthday. Everyone agreed that he should take that time to think about if he was ready to commit to the responsibility and inherent dangers that came with learning about the profession that had gotten his mother kidnapped. So, Charlie took the week and thought about all his options carefully. He really didn't like the idea of lying to Dylan, and he also knew that working with his grandfather was no guarantee that he would be able to save his mom. The truth was, she might never be found, and Charlie had to accept that. But, on the other hand, if there was any hope of rescuing her, this training was the only way Charlie could acquire the skills and knowledge he would need to bring her home.

Charlie's mind was a mix of nervousness and excitement as he haphazardly flew across his room, grabbing clothes, notebooks, shoes, his laptop, and other supplies. He shoved as much stuff as he could into his backpack and then got dressed quickly and ran downstairs to grab a bagel and a glass of juice before hopping on his bike to head off to his grandfather's house for an introductory lesson about dragons.

Zag was waiting for Charlie at the bottom of the steps. Usually, she slept in Charlie's room, but it seemed that she was as anxious to start the day as he was. Despite Zag's size, she was a gentle, sweet dog. She loved being in Charlie's company, and she followed him everywhere. Charlie was happy to have a loyal companion by his side, especially with uncertain times ahead.

Charlie ran into the kitchen and quickly gathered his breakfast to go, barely noticing his father sitting at the dining room table.

"Good morning to you too, Son."

Charlie paused for a moment with a bagel in one hand, a water bottle filled with orange juice in the other hand, and a mouth full of apple slices. He tried to speak, but tiny bits of apple flew out of his mouth.

"Well, that's nice," Patrick said as he rolled his eyes. "I get it. You're excited, but don't forget that just because I don't know any spells or own any cool magical objects doesn't mean I have nothing to teach you. Lesson one: Be nice to your dad!"

Charlie swallowed the apple in his mouth and smiled.

"Sorry, Dad. I'm just really excited to get started. We're going to learn about dragons today!"

Charlie's dad stood up and walked over to his son.

He set his coffee cup down on the kitchen counter and said, "Charlie, you're going to be great at this. I know it. You will do amazing things, but you aren't going to do those things because of the magic you learn or the mystical items you find. You are going to succeed because of who you are. Charlie Weston Everett is kind, thoughtful, loyal, adventurous, and brave. Don't let what you learn or the power you achieve change the person you are."

Charlie put down his bagel and water bottle and hugged his dad.

"The only reason I think I can do this is because you think I can. I won't stop being Charlie."

Patrick gave his son one last squeeze and said, "Well, what are you waiting for?! Go learn about dragons. Take notes so you can tell me all about it later."

Charlie smiled and grabbed the remainder of his breakfast. He was halfway out the door when his dad called out to him. Charlie poked his head back inside.

"What's up, Dad?"

"Have fun riding the unicorn, but do me a favor, and don't ride any dragons just yet."

Charlie laughed and shouted back, "No promises, Dad!"

With that, he slammed the door and was on his bike headed for Weston Manor.

For the first half of the ride, everything was perfect. Charlie peddled down the sidewalk at a leisurely pace, and Zag padded along beside him. As the duo made their way, Charlie allowed himself to fantasize about wearing shining suits of armor, brandishing a sword, and riding a dragon into battle.

Charlie was right in the middle of wondering if there had ever been a warrior Cryptozoologist when something cold struck his face. The sensation was jarring enough to shake him out of his daydream and bring his attention back to the real world.

The first thing Charlie noticed was that he was soaked. He wondered if he had accidentally ridden his bike through the path of a sprinkler, but when he looked around, he saw that it was raining. By the looks of how wet everything was, it had been raining for at least a few minutes.

Charlie pedaled his bike under a large tree to shelter from the storm and pulled out his phone to check the weather forecast.

"That's weird. It's not supposed to rain today."

Zag was too busy licking the droplets off her nose with her enormous tongue to give Charlie much in the way of affirmation.

"What do you think we should do, Zag? Go home or keep going to Grandpa's?"

This time Zag looked up at Charlie and nuzzled her head under her master's hand. Based on his surroundings, Charlie figured he was about halfway between his house and Grandpa Weston's. If he went home, he could play video games and maybe hang out with Dylan and watch a movie, but if he went to Weston Manor, he could still learn about dragons, even if the rain meant he couldn't ride Jade. In the end, it was an easy choice.

Charlie hopped back onto his bike and yelled, "Come on, Zag! A little rain can't stop us."

Zag jumped up to obediently follow her best friend, but before Charlie could get moving again, something hard hit the back of his bike helmet.

"You're dead, Charlie," a voice yelled.

Charlie spun around to see Christian standing in the rain about 10 yards away.

"Our poor, downtrodden hero. How the angels weep for you," Christian said in a mocking tone with his arms raised towards the sky.

"What do you want, Christian?"

Christian began walking towards Charlie with swagger in his step and evil in his eyes. When he was only a few feet away, Zag stood up to her full size and began growling with dangerous intensity. Christian ceased his progress but did not look startled by Zag's presence.

"So, you lost your mother and replaced her with this. That's kind of pathetic, Charlie."

Charlie could feel the anger rising in him.

"Don't talk about my mom, Christian, or I'll finish the fight we started last year."

Christian chuckled as he straightened his tie.

"Oh, you mean that little scrap where you sucker punched me? I hardly remember it. Are you still dwelling on that, Charlie? Seems like you have some anger issues."

"You're the one with the issue, Christian," Charlie yelled as he stepped forward. "You're a bully, and no matter what you do or try to do to my friends or anyone in our school, I'll stop you."

Charlie turned to walk back toward his bike when he heard Christian call out, "Why would I want to hurt anyone? I'm actually pretty sweet on your little lady friend, Dylan."

That was it. Christian had found the weak spot. With one comment, Charlie's composure was gone. His good sense had evaporated. Charlie turned back towards his foe with white-hot anger, but somehow, Christian had quietly managed to close the distance between them and buried the brass knuckles he was wearing deep into Charlie's rib cage. All the air left Charlie's body, and he began to collapse, but Christian caught him by the arm before he could hit the ground and propped him up as a shield from the giant dog who was growling and ready to pounce.

"Tell your mutt to run up the street. I have no intention of being ripped apart by that beast."

Charlie started to speak, but Christian punched him again before any sound could come out. Charlie's knees buckled from the pain, but Christian continued to hold him up.

"Tell your mutt to leave," Christian demanded.

Charlie breathlessly choked out, "Go on, Zag. I'll be fine. Just go."

Zag reluctantly padded up the street about twenty yards, but she never took her eyes off her owner. When she had gone as far as she was willing to go, she lay down on the sidewalk and waited for the whole ordeal to end.

"Alone at last," Christian taunted. "I have no delusions about being able to outrun that dog once I let you go, so it would be in your best interest to keep her close because I will kill it, and you know I will. Do you understand me, Charlie? If that dog gets anywhere near me, I will kill it and bury its body right next to yours."

Charlie nodded his understanding, and Christian let his victim fall to the sidewalk.

While Charlie lay there motionless, Christian walked a wide circle around his fallen rival.

"Now, everyone will see who really won the fight." Christian bent over and put his face inches from Charlie's. "I'm going to walk away now, Charlie. I'm going to stroll back up the sidewalk and whistle a little tune while I do it because I am done with you. You are dirt under my feet, and I want you to remember what happened here the next time you're feeling brave."

Christian stood and planted one more kick into Charlie's abdomen. Then, he laughed, slicked back his hair, and yelled out, "So much for the great Charlie Everett!"

And just like he had promised, Christian strolled up the sidewalk, whistling as he went.

Zag immediately returned to her owner and sat beside him protectively. Charlie remained on the sidewalk for a few minutes to gather as much air as possible before attempting to stand. Every part of him hurt. Charlie wanted to burst into tears, but he was afraid that doing so would only cause him more pain, so instead, he walked over to his bike, picked it up, and limped the rest of the way to Weston Manor.

By the time Charlie made it to his grandfather's house, he was completely soaked and exhausted. He parked his bike next to the large door with the dragon's head on the handle and was barely able to pull the enormous door open in his weakened condition, but somehow, he found the strength and continued.

When Charlie entered the parlor, he saw his grandfather sitting on one of the black sofas surrounding the indoor fire pit. The sound of the door opening either startled the old man or woke him up from a deep sleep because he jumped off the couch and turned towards the noise with a terrified expression.

"Charles? What on earth are you doing here?"

Charlie closed the door behind him and started dripping rain and blood onto a large mat. He remained there as he weakly responded, "It's Sunday. I came to learn about dragons."

"It's pouring rain. How did you get here?" Morris demanded.

The sharp tone of the question made Charlie feel a little nervous.

"I rode my bike here, Grandpa. What's wrong?"

The old man narrowed his eyes as though he were looking for something familiar in a complete stranger. All the while, Charlie was still soaking wet, in a tremendous amount of pain, and freezing cold. He wanted to limp over to the fire pit to warm up, but he was afraid to make any sudden moves. Zag must have sensed the tension in the room because she barked loudly and pawed at Charlie's waist, causing him to yell out in pain and nearly collapse to the ground.

Charlie's near fall helped Morris come to his senses, and he sprang into action.

"Charles, my boy," Morris said apologetically. "I am so sorry. Look at you. You're soaking wet and…covered in blood? What happened?!"

Morris moved quickly towards the parlor's bathroom. He emerged with two large towels and a plush robe. Charlie took the first towel and went to dry off Zag but was met with intense pain while bending over. The ache in his body forced Charlie to drop the towel to the ground, and Morris had to step in and support his grandson before he fell to the floor.

To accommodate her master's limitations, Zag shook off as much water as possible and moved into the room towards the fire pit. To her delight, a large dog bed had been prepared for her. She circled the bed three times and then laid down and made herself comfortable.

Meanwhile, Charlie used the second towel to dry himself off as his grandfather helped support his weight.

As Charlie ran the towel through his hair, he said, "Grandpa, what just happened? You looked like you had no idea who I was."

Morris helped maneuver Charlie to one of the black couches near the fire and replied, "Forgive me, my boy. You caught an old man dozing. I was having a very vivid dream, and when I woke up, you had appeared unexpectedly. But enough about me, Charles. What on earth happened to you?"

Charlie slipped off his wet shoes and laid down on the couch in the most comfortable position he could manage.

"I ran into someone from school," Charlie said through clenched teeth. "It isn't exactly someone who likes me very much."

"A boy in your class did this to you?" Morris gasped. "No, Charles. This cannot stand. I demand this boy's name immediately. Then, we will see who has the nerve to put his hands on my grandson! I will…"

"Grandpa, stop," Charlie shouted. "It's over. I don't want to fight with him anymore, and we have more important things to talk about today anyway. I just want to lay here and forget about it."

Morris stood near the door of his parlor, holding a sword in his right hand and his rain jacket in his left. He paused at the door and tried to allow reason to sink in.

"I suppose attacking a young boy with a knight's blade would be frowned upon."

Charlie nodded emphatically. "We can't exactly save Mom if you go to jail."

 The old man smiled and returned his jacket to the coat rack and his sword to the display.

"Wait here, Charles. I have something that should help."

With that, Morris flew out of the parlor, and Charlie was left alone with his injuries.

He took a moment and tried to take stock of what hurt the worst, but he couldn't decide. Everything in his midsection felt like it was on fire. He was confident that his ribs were at least bruised, if not broken. He would have a hard time explaining all of this to his dad, who would insist on bringing him to the hospital. Charlie mused that a hospital might not be a bad idea, and he thought about suggesting as much to his grandfather when the old man returned to the room.

"This will do the trick, Charles."

Charlie tried to sit up to see what his grandfather was talking about, but the pain was too intense, and he flopped back down on the couch.

"Don't sit up! Don't sit up! Lie flat, and let me do the rest."

Charlie did as he was told and stared at the ceiling as his grandfather carefully lifted the boy's shirt and surveyed the damage.

"Oh boy. These ribs are most definitely cracked. It's no wonder you are in such great pain."

Without saying another word, the old man began rubbing a thick cream onto Charlie's wounds. Charlie immediately felt intense heat in the places where his grandfather applied the ointment. He tried to lift his head to see what was happening, but the pain was too great, and he let out a scream.

"I know, my boy. The worse the injury, the worse the burning sensation, but it will be over in a few more moments."

"I feel like I'm on fire," Charlie yelled.

"You are, in a sense. This medicine is a mixture of unicorn saliva, which has healing effects, and phoenix ash, which has regenerative properties, but it's the phoenix ash that makes the wound burn."

Just as Morris had promised, the pain ceased a couple of minutes after the cream's application, and Charlie couldn't believe how much better he felt. It was like a miracle. He sat up slowly, expecting to feel agony, but instead, there was only mild discomfort.

"Am I healed?" Charlie asked.

"Not entirely," his grandfather replied. "You will need to drink this every day for the next week for those ribs to go back to perfect working order."

Charlie reached out and took a vial of purple liquid from his grandfather's hand. The smell coming from the bottle was so repulsive that he nearly dropped the potion on the floor.

"I have to drink this? What the hell is it?" Charlie asked.

Morris looked at the vial and responded, "It's medicine, Charles, but trust me, the less you know, the better."

Charlie tucked the bottle into his pocket and made his way toward the bathroom to get out of his wet clothes and into the soft robe that his grandfather had brought him.

When Charlie returned and joined his grandfather on the couch, Morris said, "So you made it all the way here in the pouring rain on your bike. You are your mother's son."

That made Charlie smile.

"This storm came out of nowhere," Charlie mused. "I checked my phone on the way here, and there was no rain in the forecast for today. Not a single drop."

Morris laughed as he sipped on something from his beverage cart.

"Yes, Charles, this storm certainly is unexpected." The old man's voice trailed off, and Charlie noticed that his grandfather was staring at the rain with a faraway look in his eyes.

"So, should we get started?" Charlie asked, breaking his grandfather's concentration.

Again, Morris looked momentarily disoriented but quickly recovered and said, "Yes, of course. Today we are going to discuss the origin of dragons and how that origin relates to caring for and raising a baby dragon, as you will be expected to do when our egg hatches."

For the next hour, Charlie and his grandfather talked about the many different kinds of dragons. He took notes and asked insightful questions. He was delighted to learn that, although rare, dragons were far from extinct. They were simply well-hidden and well-trained. Unlike unicorns, dragons no longer existed in the wild. It was too dangerous for an untamed dragon to roam the world. Its actions would be too unpredictable, and therefore, its existence would be too difficult to conceal. So instead, a group of respected Cryptozoologists bred, trained, and cared for the remaining dragons in various locations around the globe.

Charlie learned that his grandfather's sea serpent was a breed of water dragon. Morris explained that the serpent guarding his home was black, approximately two hundred feet in length and ten feet wide. It had a silver mane that ran from the top of its head to the tip of its tail. The sea dragon also possessed wing-like appendages that helped it steer through the water in the same way a fish would use its fins.

Morris also noted the absence of a horn on the crest of the serpent's head, as only the female of the species possesses a horn.

Charlie was entranced throughout the entire lesson. After a while, he stopped taking notes and eagerly listened to every word his grandfather had to say. Charlie also noticed that every few minutes, his grandfather would start staring out into the rain again with a blank expression on his face. It was almost like his body was there, but his mind was somewhere else. When Charlie asked a question, his grandfather would snap out of his daydream, but it was clear that the old man was distracted by the storm that had come so unexpectedly.

20

When Charlie's alarm woke him at 6:15 AM on Monday, he was surprised to see that he had twelve text messages waiting for him, one from Sydney and eleven from Dylan.

Sydney's text had come in at 5:32 AM. It read, "Are you okay?"

Charlie didn't remember having any weird dreams about the person in the red hood or the blinding light, so he wasn't sure why Sydney would think something was wrong. Then, Charlie noticed the empty vial of medicine that his grandfather had given him. He wondered if Sydney had somehow found out about his fight with Christian. It was doubtful that Christian would bother reaching out to Sydney just to gloat, but he couldn't think of any other reason his friend would be concerned. Charlie hesitantly put his hand on his ribs and was surprised to find that he didn't feel any pain. Besides barely being able to choke down the disgusting purple liquid, the medicine worked fast.

Charlie typed back, "Yeah, I'm fine. What's up?"

He was about to hit send when another message came in from Dylan.

"ARE YOU REALLY JUST GOING TO IGNORE ME?!?!"

Charlie opened the string of unseen messages from his best friend and was shocked to find that the first text was a photo of him lying on the ground in the rain, covered in his own blood. The caption of the photo read, "The Great Charlie Everett!" Charlie hadn't even noticed that Christian had taken a photo of him. He had been in too much pain and could barely even breathe, let alone stop Christian from taking that picture. Charlie continued to read the rest of the text messages that had been coming in non-stop since 5:45 AM when Dylan got up for school.

IS THIS REALLY YOU?!

OMG! CHARLIE! ARE YOU OKAY?

WHAT HAPPENED?!

WHY AREN'T YOU ANSWERING ME?!!!!!!

ARE YOU IN THE HOSPITAL?!?!

I'M COMING OVER!!!!!

YOU BETTER BE DEAD, OR I'M GOING TO KILL YOU!!!!

SYDNEY SAYS THAT HE ISN'T SURE IF IT'S YOU....

IT IS YOU! I KNOW THAT SHIRT!

CHARLIE!!!!!!! TELL ME YOU'RE OKAY!!!!

I'M COMING OVER FOR REAL!

Charlie was about to start writing a text back when a knock on his window made him jump and throw his phone across the room. It was Dylan. She was wearing a blue rain jacket over her pajamas. She hadn't even gotten ready for school yet. Charlie rushed over to the window to let his friend inside before she got completely drenched from the unexpected storm that had started the day before. Dylan quickly climbed through the window and threw her arms around him.

"Please tell me you're okay," Dylan pleaded between sobs. "Please, Charlie. Just tell me you're okay."

Charlie put his hands on the sides of Dylan's head and reassured her.

"I'm fine, Dylan. Trust me. I'm totally fine."

Dylan continued to cry as she took out her phone. She held up the photo that she had received.

"Is this really you?"

Charlie looked away and nodded. Dylan began sobbing again, so Charlie took his friend's hand and put it under his shirt. "Feel my body, Dylan. There's nothing broken or even bruised. He just knocked the wind out of me. That's all."

Dylan looked down at her hand on Charlie's chest. She traced the lines of his rib cage with her fingers and wondered if Charlie had any sense of how badly she wanted to kiss him, not in a passionate, romantic sort of way but in a reassuring, loving way. Dylan wanted him to know that she loved him and would always love him and that his pain was her pain, but before she could even finish her thought, Charlie leaned in and kissed her gently on the cheek. Dylan closed her eyes and finally allowed herself to feel everything she had been feeling for Charlie. Then, after a moment, the kiss ended, and Dylan opened her eyes again.

"What was that for?" she asked.

"You're always there for me. Always. Even when I don't even ask. I love you, Dylan."

Tears of joy and exhaustion started falling gently down Dylan's cheek. This time, she had no desire to hide her feelings behind frustration or nervousness. Instead, she wrapped her arms around her best friend and replied, "I love you too, Charlie."

The two teens stood in the middle of the room, holding each other. Charlie was thrilled to be with Dylan so openly and vulnerably for a change, but he was also a little confused. He wanted to ask what this meant for their friendship and if her love for him was like a brother or a boyfriend, but he also didn't want to ruin the moment. Plus, Charlie wasn't even sure what his exact feelings were. He hadn't planned on kissing Dylan. It just sort of happened. She was crying for him, and he felt terrible because she felt terrible. It was like her pain was his pain, and he wanted to make it go away. He wanted her to know that he was okay so that she could be okay. But years and years of friendship clouded the issue, and Charlie wasn't sure exactly what he saw happening between them.

Before Charlie had a chance to do anything, a knock came on his door.

Dylan immediately made a break for the window, and Charlie yelled out, "One second, dad. Just getting dressed. I'll meet you downstairs for breakfast."

Before Charlie had a chance to lock his bedroom door, Patrick entered the room.

"Woah! Dad! How about a little privacy?"

"Woah! Charlie! How about a little honesty?" Patrick responded sarcastically.

Patrick moved past his son and looked around the room. After a few seconds of searching, Dylan was found hiding in a closet. She stumbled out and took her place next to Charlie. Both teens waited nervously for the yelling to start. Then, instinctively, they grabbed each other's hands and stood together as one.

"Well, I guess I will be driving you to school today, Dylan."

The two teens looked at each other with complete shock and disbelief.

"Oh, come on," Patrick laughed. "Did you really think that I didn't know that Dylan still stays over sometimes? Or Dylan's parents? She has been sleeping here off and on for over a year, and I hate to tell you, son, but nothing you do makes this room smell like lavender. I may not be able to text two hundred words a minute, but I'm not an idiot."

Charlie let out a huge sigh of relief.

"Dad, I don't know what to say."

"I do," he said as he took a step toward his son. "You have been keeping a really big secret and breaking a really big rule by having her here without asking my permission first. You lied, and you've been sneaking around behind my back. And if you had been doing all this with any other girl, I'd be furious."

Then, Patrick turned to Dylan and continued, "But I'm not furious. Dylan, you were there for my son at the hardest time in his life. You did what I couldn't do. You saved him, and I am eternally grateful to you. You will always be welcome in my home."

Patrick smiled and embraced Dylan in a warm and welcoming hug.

"Thank you, Mr. Everett," Dylan stammered.

"Please, call me Pat. You're family to us."

Dylan smiled and nodded.

"Dad, you're the coolest," Charlie said enthusiastically.

"Yeah, I'm great," Patrick replied. "But please don't test how cool me and Dylan's parents have been so far. You guys are getting older, and I'm not sure the sleepovers are as appropriate as they used to be."

Charlie nodded as his face turned red.

"Dad, can we talk about this a little later?"

"Of course. I'll meet you guys downstairs."

Charlie and Dylan got ready for school in comfortable silence. Every once in a while, one would catch the other staring, and they would both start to laugh. Without any words, everything that needed to be known for the time being was known, and both Charlie and Dylan were happy. There would be plenty of time to figure out what came next in their relationship.

When they arrived at school, Sydney met them at the front door.

"Charlie, I've got a very special Ultra-Man ready to go out today. I think you're going to like it."

Sydney extended a copy of the latest issue to his best friend.

Charlie looked down at the cover and read, "Ultra-Man versus the Pretend Preacher."

The front cover artwork showed Ultra-Man, looking a little more muscular and heroic than usual, holding a dirty, ragged-looking pastor by the shirt collar. The preacher strongly resembled Christian in every way, except the character had holes in his shoes, yellow teeth, bags under the eyes, and a receding hairline.

Sydney smiled and asked, "Look like anyone we know?"

"Syd, you're the best," Dylan said approvingly. Sydney blushed and ran ahead to grab the door for his friends.

As Charlie passed by, he put his arm on Sydney's shoulder and said, "Thanks, man. You really are the best."

Sydney felt pride swell within him, and he walked inside with his two favorite people.

The trio didn't make it more than five steps inside the building before an obnoxious southern boom of joyous rapture met them.

"Ladies and gentlemen, the great Charlie Everett!"

A crowd had already gathered, and several students were holding large posters of the photo Christian had taken and blown up just for this moment of public humiliation. Some people laughed, but most of the kids were just watching in stunned silence.

Before the laughter died down, Christian continued, "I'm surprised you were able to walk in here today after our little encounter."

Charlie was about to speak up and defend himself, but Dylan crossed the room and slapped Christian across the face before he got the chance. Christian recoiled momentarily. Charlie wasn't sure if anyone else noticed, but a wild, uncontrollable fire flashed briefly across Christian's face, but in less than a second, the bully regained his composure and yelled out, "Oh, this one is fiery. I can see why you like her, Charlie. Although I have no idea why she likes you."

"Everyone knows that picture is a fake, Christian," Dylan asserted. "It isn't even Charlie."

The students holding the posters looked closer at the photo to see if what Dylan said was true.

"Oh, Darlin', I think we all see what you're trying to do, but no one here believes your lies."

"You're the one who's lying," Sydney yelled out. "The three of us were working on the new Ultra-Man comic all day yesterday. Ultra-Man versus the PRETEND PREACHER!"

Sydney and his printing partner, Amy, started handing out copies of the new issue, and all the kids immediately picked up on the resemblance between the preacher in the comic book and Christian.

Charlie saw the fire return to Christian's face, and this time, he wasn't able to recover so quickly.

"TELL THEM THE TRUTH, CHARLIE!" Christian yelled out. "TELL THEM WHAT HAPPENED!"

Charlie casually walked over to Sydney and grabbed one of the issues of Ultra-Man.

"To be honest, Christian, I haven't read the ending yet, so I'm not sure what happens, but I'm sure the Pretend Preacher gets what he deserves."

Everyone in the crowd laughed, and Charlie turned to start walking away before a fight began. Seeing his moment of triumph slipping away, Christian sprinted toward his nemesis and lifted his shirt while screaming, "You see the bruises! You see! I made him bleed! I made him…."

Christian looked down at Charlie's chest and was horrified to see that there wasn't a single mark on the boy's body. Charlie twisted out of Christian's grip and stepped back.

"How did you heal so quickly? It's not possible."

By this time, the crowd had mostly dispersed. Charlie shrugged and started walking away again but paused and looked over his shoulder at his despondent classmate.

"Hey, Christian," Charlie called out. "Don't forget, the Lord works in mysterious ways."

Sydney laughed, and the two boys continued down the hallway and into their first-period class.

Christian fell to his knees, completely confused and mortified by the drastic turn of events that had just occurred. Before he had a chance to rise, he felt a tap on his shoulder. He turned and felt an unbelievable force strike him on his left eye. The boy screamed out in agony and fell to the floor. He looked up to find Dylan standing over him.

She leaned in and quietly said, "If you ever touch Charlie again, I'll make sure the whole school sees the next time I lay you out like this."

Then she flipped her hair over her shoulder and walked into her first-period class, leaving Christian in a puddle of tears and regret.

21

For three days in a row, the weatherman called for sun, but the rain continued to fall. After the first day, the news reporters treated the unexpected storm as a joke. One anchor said he was grateful because he didn't have to water his lawn. Another welcomed the rain as a relief from the heatwave that had been going on for almost a week. The weatherman just shrugged his shoulders, laughed, and promised that the sun would return the next day.

On the second day, the news anchors maintained a somewhat diminished sense of humor despite reports of localized flooding and poor road conditions. The weatherman did his best to explain the cause of the storm even though all of his training and expertise told him there was no good reason for it.

On the third day, no one was smiling or laughing as the rain continued to fall harder than ever. More accidents were being reported, and property damage was piling up. Many people were starting to lose power. The worst part was that there was no explanation about where the rain was coming from or when it would stop.

Day after day, the storm intensified and spread throughout the entire state. A few religious fanatics began speaking in front of the local churches that the end of the world had come, and God had sent a second flood to wipe everyone and everything off the planet. Those who hadn't lost power and were still able to watch the news were encouraged by local authorities to remain in their homes as the Governor declared a state of emergency and closed all major roads and highways. No one attended work or school because travel conditions were so dangerous that there was no way to guarantee anyone's safety. Everyone was trapped.

Charlie was no fool, and even though he was still a beginner, he knew magic when he saw it. Someone or something was creating the rain for a reason. Charlie knew that he and his grandfather had to figure out a way to stop it, or people could get hurt and maybe even die.

Charlie pulled out his phone and dialed his grandfather's number, but the call went straight to voicemail, so he decided to leave a message.

Grandpa, you've probably seen the news. I don't know. Maybe you haven't, but I'm sure you've noticed it won't stop raining. You knew from the first day of this storm that something was going on. I could see it on your face when you were teaching me about dragons. We have to do something. Call me back when you get this.

When Charlie ended the phone call, he looked down and noticed that he had a text message from Dylan.

"Can you believe this rain?! I hope you've got a boat."

Charlie thought about ignoring the text, but he was beginning to get nervous and needed his friend to calm him down.

"Yeah, we were going to build an arc in tech class this week too. Guess I'll have to inflate my air mattress."

"LOL. Swing by and pick me up when you float past my house."

"No problem. Should be enough room for both of us and Zag."

"You and that dog. I swear you love it more than me."

"..."

"JERK!"

Charlie was about to type an apology when he heard his father call him, so he put his phone in his pocket and went to see what his dad needed. Patrick was sitting at his desk in the office attached to his bedroom. The lights were off, but some natural light came in through a small window.

"What's up, Dad?"

"Charlie, I'm sure by now you've guessed what's going on outside."

Charlie wasn't sure exactly what to say, so he nodded and quietly replied, "I think it's magic."

"It is magic," Patrick agreed. "Something magical and dangerous is happening, and I think it's going to be up to you to stop it."

Charlie felt a wave of fear pass through his body.

"What am I supposed to do? I don't know anything yet."

Patrick could see panic starting to take hold of his son, so he stood up and walked over to him.

"I think I told you once that your mother and I met in college. Besides the fact that she was beautiful, she had this magnetic personality that people have always been drawn to. Whenever I was in the same room with her, I couldn't look anywhere else. One day, we were in class together, and she caught me staring. I tried to look away, but it was too late. She came over to where I was sitting, and I thought she was going to yell at me or embarrass me, but she didn't. She just extended her hand and said, 'Hi. I'm Jillian Weston. I like pizza.' I was so surprised that she was even talking to me that I just took her hand and stupidly said back, 'Hi. I'm Patrick. I like pizza too.'"

Patrick cringed with remembered embarrassment and continued, "Your mom giggled, and I just kept shaking her hand, completely mesmerized by her. After a few seconds, she looked down, and I realized I hadn't let go of her. I blushed, but before I could apologize, she asked if I wanted to have pizza with her. I just nodded like an idiot. She laughed again, left her phone number on a piece of paper, and walked away."

"Wow, Dad. You've never told me that story before. Sounds like it was a miracle I was even born."

"Yeah, your mom was… well, she was way out of my league, but for some reason, she decided to give me a shot, and I promised myself I wouldn't waste it. I have a lot of great stories about your mom, and I'm going to start telling you all of them because you deserve to know who she is. I told you that particular story because it shows one of the many ways you are just like her. You both approach everything you do with confidence. If your mother was nervous about coming up and talking to me, she didn't show it. As I got to know her and the secrets of her life, she would tell me about her work with your grandfather, and it was clear how much that belief in herself was worth. You are your mother's son. I know you've only had one lesson so far, but there's nothing your grandfather can teach you that will prepare you for the first time you face a truly dangerous situation. You just have to believe in yourself, Charlie. Magic or no magic, I believe that you can handle this."

Charlie wanted to thank his dad for the words of encouragement, but before he could say anything, the disembodied voice returned and whispered, "It's time. The boy is ready."

Charlie looked up at his father, but it was clear that the voice had not come from him. Without excusing himself, Charlie walked out of the office and began chasing after whatever was calling out to him. Patrick didn't bother following his son. He had given all the help he could, and Charlie would have to find his own way from there.

When Charlie arrived back in his bedroom, he asked the empty air, "Who are you?" He waited for a moment, but there was no response, so he asked louder, "Who are you?!" Again, Charlie waited for an answer, but the only noises he could hear were the sounds made by the rain. Charlie sat on the edge of his bed and looked around for any sign that he wasn't alone, but when nothing happened, he yelled out in frustration, "Who are you?!"

All at once, several voices shouted back. Charlie struggled to understand everything they were saying, but he listened carefully and was able to pick out two distinct words: Weston and book.

The noise in Charlie's mind quickly rose to deafening levels, and the room started to spin. Charlie tried moving toward the door but found that his legs wouldn't cooperate. A deep sense of imbalance was followed by intense nausea as the gravity in the room shifted from side to side.

Helpless to fight or flee, Charlie tried apologizing to the voices for shouting at them, but it was no use. He was trapped inside a weightless sense of falling in every direction. With great effort, Charlie managed to focus himself long enough to grab a nearby pillow. He covered his ears, hoping to block out some of the noise, but the pillow didn't help. The voices were inside Charlie's mind, and there was no way to keep them out.

Charlie swayed back and forth unsteadily as darkness started to creep into the corners of his vision. Unconsciousness was coming quickly, and Charlie knew that he was probably going to pass out. With a final desperate effort, he tried collapsing onto his bed but only managed to hit the side and roll off onto the floor next to his closet.

"FOCUS, CHARLES!"

"I'M TRYING, BUT YOU'RE KILLING ME!" Charlie shouted back.

"NOT WITH YOUR BODY! FOCUS YOUR MIND!"

"I DON'T KNOW HOW! I DON'T KNOW HOW TO TALK TO YOU!" Charlie yelled out again.

An intense heat settled between Charlie's eyes like a laser beam burning a hole in his brain.

"SPEAK TO US FROM HERE!"

Despite the pain, Charlie started to recover his senses, and he had a vague idea of what he needed to do. He pushed everything out of his mind except for the voice he was trying to communicate with. Instinctively, he imagined having a conversation with his mother, and that made everything easier. He pictured her as best as he could from memory. The harder he focused, the more she came to life. When he had conjured her enough that he could see the sparkle in her blue eyes, all the noise in his mind went quiet, and the pain in his head vanished.

"That's better," the voice said calmly. "The living and the deceased cannot generally communicate because they speak using different frequencies. The process you just endured, while painful, was necessary to grant you access to the frequency used by the dead. Now that you have found your focus, we can communicate freely."

Charlie tried opening his eyes, but he had shut them so tight that all he could see was blurry darkness. When his eyes finally focused, they settled squarely on one thing: the unopened birthday present from his grandfather that he had flung off his bed in frustration. Charlie sat on his knees and reached into the closet to grab the gift.

Without hesitation, Charlie ripped a chunk of wrapping paper off of his grandfather's present, and to his horror, a giant eye stared back at him. Charlie immediately recognized the gift as the book from his dreams, and he dropped it in disgust.

"Nope! I'm out. Hard pass!"

Charlie vigorously wiped his hands on his bedspread, trying to remove the unclean feeling from his whole body. Every few seconds, he looked down to see if the eye was still watching him, and it was. Never blinking, never sleeping.

"We are the living memories of your ancestors," the voice explained. "We are the Cryptozoologists of the Weston family who came before you for many generations. The Weston Family Book is the vessel we will use to guide you through your trials."

Charlie shuddered as he reached out his hand toward the book, but he quickly recoiled when he saw the eye following his movements.

"I'm sorry. I can't do it. It's too disgusting. Is there a Weston Family eye patch I can use or something?"

The sharp pain between Charlie's eyes returned, and the voice shouted back, "You are already one year behind in your training, and the world is in danger. There is no time for your weakness!"

Charlie rubbed his forehead, and the pain gradually diminished. He was embarrassed and frustrated by what his ancestors had said. It wasn't his fault that he was a year behind on his training or that the world was in danger, but Charlie also knew that sitting in his room and feeling sorry for himself wasn't going to help anyone.

"This is ridiculous. It's just a stupid book," Charlie said reassuringly as he slowly began to reach for the gift. Then, just before making contact, Charlie gasped and yelled, "What the hell is that?!" To his surprise, the eye looked off in the direction he pointed, and Charlie scooped up the book in triumph.

Somehow, holding the bizarre text made Charlie less afraid of it. The eye was still looking at him, but it didn't seem so sinister or accusing anymore.

The book itself was light and surprisingly thin. The cover was a dark red leather and had a clasp with the same dragon head featured in several places at Weston Manor. The paper was old and worn around the edges, but the texture was surprisingly smooth for the book's age. Each page was a light cream color and noticeably heavier than ordinary writing paper.

Charlie was so impressed by the beauty of the notebook that it took him a few moments to realize that the first page was blank. The next page was empty too. After flipping through the entire book, Charlie realized there wasn't a single word, picture, or marking anywhere.

Not sure what to do next, Charlie took out a pen from his desk drawer and was about to write his name on the first page when the book closed forcefully.

"You will add your story to this book someday, Charles, but it won't be with a pen."

"I'm sorry. I didn't mean to offend you guys," Charlie replied as he carefully set down the writing utensil. "It's just that… the book is empty. There aren't any instructions, and I don't know how to find what I'm looking for."

"Simply ask, Charles, and we will share with you all the knowledge we have collected from the beginning of the Weston family through your mother's work."

"You know my mother?" Charlie asked excitedly. "Is she alive? Where is she?"

"You have many questions, Charles, and if we knew the answers, we would tell you, but we are not omniscient. All we can say for certain is that your mother is not with us, which means she still lives."

"She's alive."

Charlie repeated the words to himself several times.

"How do I find her?"

The voices did not answer.

"Please! Tell me! How can I find her?!" Charlie begged.

"Charles, we cannot say what we do not know. But, at present, there is a larger issue."

"There is no larger issue," Charlie yelled. "I need to find my mom."

The book opened suddenly to one of the blank pages, and a picture began to take shape. Charlie watched as the invisible hand of the Weston family began drawing a large creature unlike anything he had ever seen. The animal was clearly some kind of bird based on the feathers, sharp black talons, wings, and beak, but when the drawing was complete, the legendary creature rose from the page and took flight around the room. Energy coursed through the bird's body, and streaks of lightning shot off in every direction, turning the tip of the feathers an electric blue that matched the creature's powerful eyes. Thunderclaps and strong gales of wind roared with each flap of its greyish, blue wings.

"This is a Thunderbird," the voices explained. "It is a creature of Native American myth, although I'm sure you can see that this bird is far from imaginary."

Charlie couldn't take his eyes off of the beautiful and graceful being soaring around his room and shooting raw power from its eyes.

"What does the Thunderbird have to do with me?" Charlie asked without looking away.

"You already know the answer to that, Charles. The Thunderbird has woken from its long sleep, and the rain has come. This storm will not stop until the Thunderbird is put back to rest."

Charlie's eyes widened. "I'm supposed to make that thing go to sleep?! How the hell am I going to do that?!"

The magical Thunderbird flew back into the pages of the book, and a new picture began taking shape. When the drawing was finished, Charlie saw some kind of old musical instrument that looked like several wooden pipes lashed together by a thin rope.

"This is a powerful artifact that has the ability to put many mythical creatures to sleep if you know the correct song. You must find this instrument and use it to help the Thunderbird rest. If you fail, the storm will continue to get stronger and spread. It will not be long before the whole world is consumed by it."

"Oh, that's it?" Charlie replied sarcastically. "Let's see. I just have to find the magical flute thing, wherever that might be, learn to play the special song, track down a legendary Thunderbird, and put it to sleep before it lights me up with a massive thunderbolt. What an interesting way to die."

Suddenly, the book closed, and for the first time Charlie had ever witnessed, the eye on the front of the book also closed. He tried yelling out to his ancestors for more information, but they were gone, and the dragon clasp on the book wouldn't open.

"I guess I've gotten all the information from them that I'm going to get. There's only one person who can help me now."

22

Charlie was surprised to find his father putting on his rain jacket and boots by the front door.

"Dad, what are you doing?"

"I'm getting ready to take you to your grandfather's house. There's no way I can let you ride your bike in this weather."

"So, I guess you heard everything going on in my room?"

Patrick grabbed his blue umbrella off the coat rack and replied, "Nope. Didn't need to. One look outside tells me you've got work to do, and you can't do it here."

Charlie ran down the remaining steps and hugged his dad.

As the two men headed for the front door, Zag came barreling into the room, ready for adventure. Charlie knelt next to his constant companion and said, "Not this time, girl. I don't know what's going to happen next, and I'd feel better if I knew you were here with Dad."

Zag pushed her nose into Charlie's chest and knocked him over. Then, she put her giant paw on his stomach and held him down.

"I don't think she's going to let you leave without her," Patrick said with a laugh.

"Fine. You can come," Charlie gasped under the weight of the huge dog.

Zag took her paw off Charlie's chest and licked him vigorously on the face.

"Gross. Like we aren't about to get wet enough."

Charlie put on his rain gear and took a few deep breaths to brace himself against the harsh weather he was about to face. He could hear the storm pounding against the roof of the house and could see the limbs of the trees bending in the powerful wind.

"Now or never, Charlie," he murmured to himself.

Then, in one quick motion, he flung the door open and took two quick steps outside before barreling into someone standing on his front porch. Charlie and the mystery guest crashed hard into the bushes lining the walkway, completely soaking themselves in an instant.

"My apologies, Charlie. I did not expect you to emerge so vigorously."

Charlie wiped the water from his eyes and looked at the figure sitting next to him. He couldn't see the face of the person he had knocked over because whoever it was had completely covered themselves in protective rain gear from head to toe, but Charlie was pretty sure he recognized the voice.

"Sydney, is that you?" Charlie asked as he got to his feet.

Sydney nodded, and Charlie extended a hand to help his friend up from the ground.

"What are you doing here?"

Sydney attempted to look down at himself, but the excessive clothing severely limited his range of motion.

"It's the end of the world, Charlie. Where else would I be?"

Charlie couldn't help but smile. His friends kept coming through for him without being asked, but unlike Dylan's impromptu visit to his house, Sydney was putting himself in danger that he couldn't possibly understand.

"Sydney, I appreciate you coming here. I really do, but this is a lot bigger than I could have ever guessed. The whole world is in trouble, and I think it might be up to me to do something about it."

After a moment of quiet contemplation, Sydney replied, "I have considered your warning and have decided that I will continue with you into the imminent danger."

Without giving Charlie a chance to protest, Sydney made his way to Patrick's car and climbed into the back seat. Charlie turned to his father watching from the front porch and shrugged his shoulders.

The weather was like nothing any of them had ever seen. The water wasn't just falling to the ground; it was hurtling towards it with a speed and force that made the raindrops sting a little if they made contact with any exposed skin. What had been small puddles three days earlier had become giant lakes of collected water. The roads were barely passable, not that anyone else was crazy enough to try and drive on them.

Charlie and his dad sat in the front seats of the car. Zag took up almost the entire back seat with her head resting comfortably in Sydney's lap. Zag was the only one who didn't seem to mind that she was completely drenched. She stretched out her paws and laid down sleepily as though they were all going for a nice leisurely drive on a perfect spring day.

Nearly all the roads were flooded, and the quickest route to Weston Manor was not safely passable, so Patrick had to improvise by using side streets, sidewalks, one-way roads, and even one person's front lawn. It didn't matter how they got there as long as they got there quickly and in one piece. Charlie wanted to say something to lighten the mood, but he didn't want to break his dad's concentration. Besides, there was no point in trying to pretend like the world wasn't ending.

When the group finally made it to the Weston Manor entryway, Charlie's dad parked the car and turned toward his son.

"This is as far as I can take you. There's no way the car can get up that driveway. You three will have to walk the rest of the way. Can you make it?"

Charlie looked out the window at the terrible storm. The water was striking the car so quickly and violently that he could barely hear his dad speak over the sound of the drops crashing against the metal roof.

Patrick grabbed his son's hand and said, "You can do this, Charlie. Whatever has to be done, I know that you can do it. I'm proud of you, and so is your mother, wherever she is."

"I'm scared, Dad. I don't know when I'll see you again."

"Just as soon as you're done saving the world," Patrick calmly replied.

Charlie nodded and turned to the back seat.

"You ready, guys?"

Zag sat up and prepared to exit the car. Sydney attempted to clean his glasses on his rain jacket, but it was no use, so he removed the frames from his face, tightened the drawstring on his hood, and nodded his agreement. Charlie put his hand on the door handle and hesitated. Then, without turning back toward his father, he said, "I love you, Dad," and jumped out of the car.

Patrick sat silently and watched until his son was out of view. When he could no longer see Charlie in the distance, he said quietly, "I love you too, Son. Good luck."

As the three companions made their way toward the drawbridge, Charlie could feel the water seeping deeper into his clothes, making him cold at his core. There was no escape from the rain and the wind. There was nowhere for him to stop and catch his breath. He just had to keep going. No matter what happened, he had to find the strength to keep moving forward.

After about ten minutes of hard running, the group was within sight of the house, but Charlie stopped dead in his tracks when he saw that the drawbridge was up.

"Oh, come on," Charlie yelled in frustration.

"What about the intercom?" Sydney suggested. "Someone might be listening on the other end."

Charlie ran over to the intercom and pressed the talk button. "Grandpa, let me in!"

There was no response.

"Grandpa! Please!" Charlie pleaded. "I need your help! Lower the bridge."

When there was no reply a second time, Charlie stepped away from the intercom and yelled at the raised bridge, "ENTER AS FRIENDS, LEAVE AS FAMILY! NOW, HELP ME!"

Again, nothing happened, and after a few moments of depressing silence, it became painfully clear that no one was going to lower the bridge.

"You said you were going to help me!" Charlie shouted. "You said that we could save her, but you lied! Keep your dragon egg and your unicorn and your crazy elevator because I don't want any of it! I just want my mom! I just want my...."

Charlie's voice trailed off as he suddenly remembered something important. One of the manor's elevator stops was the horse stables, which were located outside the moat. If the group could make their way there, they could call the elevator and use it to get inside the house.

"Come on, guys! I have an idea!"

The small group took off around the outskirts of the moat. After ten more minutes of running, they rounded the furthest corner of the main house and could see the stables in the distance.

"We're almost there," Charlie said breathlessly. He could feel his lungs starting to burn, and his feet ached from sprinting through the soft, rain-covered ground. He thought about stopping half a dozen times, but every time he slowed down, Zag put her nose into his back and urged him forward.

When the group finally made it to the stables, Charlie was devastated to find it locked. He kicked at the large wooden door angrily and was about to start screaming for someone to let him in when he heard yelling from the other side of the building.

The trio walked cautiously toward the shouting, but as Charlie got closer, he realized that what he heard wasn't yelling; it was singing. Terrible singing, but for some reason, the loud, melody-less song put him at ease, and he moved toward the music. When Charlie finally came into view of the mystery vocalist, he was shocked to see that it was his grandfather, but the old man did not look like himself.

Normally, Morris Weston was dressed in a full suit and tie, jacket buttoned, black shoes polished, white hair combed back, with a different cane for each day of the week. He walked with excellent posture, his head held high, and he had a smooth vocal tone that never fluctuated no matter what situation he faced.

However, the Morris Weston that stood before Charlie now had no jacket, a white shirt half unbuttoned, long gray hair in his eyes, and noticeable facial stubble. Charlie stared in disbelief as he watched his grandfather wildly flail his arms through the air and sing at the top of his lungs.

Charlie wanted to approach but didn't know how. The person in the field wasn't someone he recognized. Luckily, Zag was there to make the first move, and she barked loudly through the storm.

Morris whipped around, and his heart sank in his chest.

"Charles! No! You can't be here! Why are you here?!"

Charlie took a step toward his grandfather, but Morris held out his left hand to keep his grandson at bay. With his right hand, he grabbed a fancy bottle off the ground and upended it, but there was nothing left inside.

"Grandpa… what are you doing?"

Morris threw the empty bottle into the field and replied, "I killed her, Charles. It's my fault. It's my fault that she died. It should have been me, not her."

Then, the old man put his face in his hands and began weeping uncontrollably.

"What are you talking about?" Charlie asked as he ran to his grandfather's side.

Morris ignored his grandson's question and pushed past his unexpected visitors toward the locked door. He used his master key to let himself into the stables, and Charlie, Sydney, and Zag followed him inside.

The disheveled man went straight for a bottle sitting on a nearby desk. Charlie's eyes read his grandfather's intentions, and he intercepted the bottle before Morris could get there.

"What is this stuff?" Charlie demanded.

"It's a potion, Charles. A special potion that helps me forget, but it's not working."

Charlie looked down at the bottle and then back at the shell of the man who looked a little like Morris Weston.

"What are you trying to forget?"

"Everything, Charles," Morris whispered to the floor. "I want to forget everything."

Charlie tossed the bottle to Sydney, who read the label and announced, "I don't believe this is magical, Charlie. It's just alcohol."

He tossed the bottle back to his friend, who turned it over in his hands.

"A lot of people have used this potion to forget about their lives," Charlie said.

He pulled the cork out of the top of the bottle and continued, "But they don't forget anything. They just become lesser versions of themselves."

Then, Charlie turned the bottle upside down and poured the dark liquid onto the ground.

"Be careful, Charlie," Sydney cautioned. "Your grandfather might not be himself right now."

Charlie didn't respond. He simply continued to pour until there was nothing left.

"I want to know what's going on. I'm sure you've probably noticed that the world is ending right now, and you won't even return my phone calls."

Morris was shivering from the rain and the cold. He had never felt so small and frail in his life.

"I'm sorry I haven't been returning your phone calls, Charles. Things were going so well. You're such a bright boy, a fast learner, just like your mom. I see so much greatness in you, so much strength. I was hopeful that we would find your mother together. But then the rain came. I knew almost immediately that this weather did not have a natural cause but a magical one. I knew that, even though we had just begun your training, your time had come to save us."

Charlie watched his grandfather pace back and forth, regaining more of the man that Charlie knew with each step. His posture improved, his voice steadied, and he took a small comb out of his shirt pocket to remove the hair from his eyes.

"I never hesitated to send your mother out into the field. I knew she could be seriously hurt or killed, but I never stopped to think about the consequences. It was her destiny, our family's legacy. Now that she's gone, I can see now what I should have seen then. Destiny be damned."

Charlie found his grandfather's cane on the floor next to the desk. He picked it up and handed it to the man who had become Morris Weston once more.

"Mom didn't have to choose this life. She could have said no. From what I remember about her and from things Dad has told me, you couldn't have made her go anywhere that she didn't want to go."

Morris chuckled.

"That's true, Charles. Your mom could do anything, but no one could make her."

"I don't think Mom did this work for the glory or the power," Charlie added. "She did it because keeping magical animals safe is important."

Morris steadied himself with his cane and knelt next to his grandson.

"It's not just about the animals, my boy. These myths and legends are part of history. They are part of the culture that makes up the core of the world. The stories we protect are powerful enough to change everything. Time marches on, and we find new stories to tell, new Gods to worship, but they are all built from what we know. They exist because of what came first. Those myths, those legends, all the Gods, they are still out there. They are still alive in the hearts and minds of the few who know and the fewer who still believe."

Morris dropped his cane and pulled his grandson in for a hug.

"Thank you, Charles," he whispered in Charlie's ear. "Thank you for saving me from myself."

When the two men broke the embrace, they stood and looked out of the open stable door. The rain was still falling and would continue unless they found a way to stop it.

"Excuse me," Sydney interjected. "It seems like this might be a good time to mention that we have a tremendous amount of work to do and very little time to accomplish it."

"Right you are…Sammy," Morris said with a rejuvenated laugh.

Sydney recoiled at the failed guess of his name and frustratingly began cleaning his glasses as he replied, "I think I preferred, Sadney."

Charlie grinned, feeling hopeful and confident that his mission to save his mom and the world was finally getting on track.

"Hey, Grandpa. Tell me what you know about Thunderbirds."

23

When everyone was safely inside Weston Manor, Charlie, Zag, and Morris went straight to the fireplace to get warm. Sydney was too entranced by the artifacts and displays scattered across the room to care about how cold he was, and he immediately began investigating all the treasures around him. Every few seconds, Charlie heard Sydney mutter something like "Unbelievable" or "Amazing."

Charlie decided not to let Sydney learn about the dragon knights the hard way and shouted, "Just be careful around the red egg sitting on the pillow, Syd. Those knights might look fake, but I promise they will cut you to pieces if you get too close."

Sydney gulped hard and nodded in agreement.

After a few minutes of getting comfortable, Charlie decided he was ready to start talking about everything that happened with the voices in his room.

"The book came to life, Grandpa. It spoke to me."

"My boy, the book didn't come to life. It has always been alive. It is the living mind of our family. All of the Weston's who have ever studied or ever will study Cryptozoology add their knowledge, memories, and stories to the book before they die, and the book is passed down from generation to generation as a teaching tool."

"Mom didn't talk to me through the book," Charlie said excitedly. "I never heard her voice!"

"Exactly!" Morris shouted. "That is how we know that she is still alive. She is still out there somewhere, and we are going to find her."

"Do you think this storm has anything to do with her disappearance?" Charlie asked tentatively.

Morris reflected on the question for a moment as he stared into the fire.

"It's hard to say, Charles," Morris said pensively. "Thunderbirds are powerful creatures. The Native Americans who believed in them and worshiped them knew their power. They feared it and respected it. Some tribes even believed that the flap of the first Thunderbird's wings was what created the world and when that bird flaps its wings again, that is when the world will end."

Charlie thought about the picture he had seen in the Weston family book. It was hard to tell exactly how large the Thunderbird in the illustration might be in real life, but he knew for sure that it was massive.

"Your mother has as much knowledge about the Thunderbirds as I do," Morris continued. "Which means that she knows that they cannot be captured or tamed. I can't imagine anyone holding her hostage wouldn't know that themselves, so it is unlikely that this storm has anything to do with her disappearance."

Charlie felt a sting of disappointment. He had been holding out hope that knowing his mother was alive would be enough to bring her home, and any strange occurrences would inevitably put him on the path to finding her. Charlie walked over to the window and watched the rain continue to fall harder and harder with each passing minute, knowing that the storm was spreading and that it would continue to spread unless the Thunderbird was put back to sleep. He decided that even though stopping the storm might not bring him any closer to finding his mom, it was still what he had to do.

"So, what should we do, Charlie?" Sydney asked.

"With all due respect, Sydney," Morris interjected, "I don't believe there is any role in this adventure for you. I am thrilled that Charles has such supportive friends, but the things we do and the creatures we protect are supposed to be a family secret."

Charlie noticed that his grandfather was looking directly at him when he stressed the part about the family secret.

Sydney looked down nervously at his shoes.

"I'm sorry. I never meant to…."

"Grandpa, Sydney is connected to all of this somehow. He has some kind of magic."

"Charles, we have been over this a hundred times. There are no magical people, only magical things."

"I know that's what you taught me, but Sydney can see my dreams," Charlie said emphatically.

Morris's eyes narrowed as his stern expression turned to one of skepticism, signaling that he needed more convincing.

"Every night, I have the same dream," Charlie continued. "It doesn't have anything to do with the Thunderbird, but Jade is there, and so is the Weston Family Book. There is a blinding light and a person in a red hood too. I don't know what any of it means, but Sydney can see all of it."

Morris looked over at Sydney for confirmation.

"It's true, Mr. Weston. It's like I'm standing behind Charlie while he's dreaming. He can't see me, but I can see him and everything around him."

"When did all of this start?" Morris asked.

Sydney shrugged his shoulders.

"I'm not sure. I don't see anything else he dreams about. Just the one with the unicorn and the person in the red hood."

Morris went back into his million-mile stare, trying to solve the mystery put before him. After a few moments of silent contemplation, he said, "I think you are right, Charles. There is something special about your friend. I don't know exactly where his power comes from, but dream sight is very rare, and I've never heard of anyone being able to do it without a dream sphere. I'm assuming Sydney does not possess one, as there are only five in this world, and none of them are on this continent."

Sydney shook his head to indicate that he did not possess a dream sphere.

"Grandpa… what do you mean 'this world'?" Charlie asked.

"Another topic for another day, Charles. We need to do something about this first," Morris said as he pointed to the storm outside the large windows in his parlor.

The boys both nodded their agreement.

"And I'm afraid we don't have much time," Morris continued. "Unless the Thunderbird is put back to sleep, this storm will flood the Earth, washing away all human and animal life on the planet."

"I'm sure Charlie is up to the task," Sydney responded confidently.

Charlie smiled, but he also felt like he might throw up.

"Before the book…fell asleep or whatever, it showed me another picture," Charlie said. "It was of some kind of musical instrument. It looked like a bunch of different-sized blow darts held together by leather straps. I'd never really seen anything like it."

Morris burst out with an uncharacteristically loud laugh and shouted, "PAN!" Then, he walked quickly over to the fireplace and summoned the elevator. Charlie and Sydney hurried after him.

"What do you mean, 'Pan'? What the hell is Pan?" Charlie asked.

As he waited for the elevator, Morris began talking to himself excitedly.

"Of course! I can't believe I didn't see it. Pan will do the trick perfectly. I must be getting old because…."

"GRANDPA," Charlie interrupted. "What are you talking about?!"

The shout was enough to break the old man's concentration, and he turned to his grandson, who was looking confused and a little afraid.

"Are you referring to the Greek God?" Sydney asked.

"Yes! Precisely! Pan is a Greek God. He had a flute that possessed many special abilities, not the least of which was the ability to put magical creatures to sleep!"

"Grandpa, that's awesome news! So now all we have to do is find Pan's flute and use it to put the Thunderbird to sleep! Day saved!"

"It gets better, Charles," Morris added with shared enthusiasm. "I own Pan's flute. He gave it to me himself many years ago. It is locked up safely in my vault as we speak!"

Charlie couldn't believe his luck as he felt a wave of relief wash over him. All he had to do was play the flute, the Thunderbird would fall back to sleep, and the rain would stop.

Morris climbed into the elevator, and just before the doors closed, he added, "As long as you survive the lightning strike, we should be in good shape!"

"Wait! What did you just say?!" Charlie asked with real panic in his voice. "Survive the lightning strike?! Grandpa, wait!"

As the elevator ascended into the ceiling, Charlie turned to Sydney.

"Did he say 'survive the lightning strike'? What the hell does that mean?"

Sydney shrugged and did his best not to look worried.

As the boys waited for Morris to return, Charlie began pacing around the room while thinking about how much he didn't want to be struck by lightning. He gave serious thought to waking his dog, grabbing his friend, and running right out the door, but before he could go, something his father said popped into his mind.

"You are my son. You are your mother's son. Magic or no magic, I believe that you can do this."

The words gave Charlie courage. The world needed a hero, and even though he wasn't sure he was the right man for the job, Charlie knew that if he didn't find a way, no one would.

"Going somewhere, Charles?" a voice asked from the other side of the room.

Charlie had barely noticed that his hand was on the door, ready to make a hasty exit. He let go of the handle, took a deep breath, and said, "No. I'm not going anywhere. What do I have to do?"

Charlie made his way back toward the center of the room. The elevator had retreated up into the ceiling, and the fire was burning once again. Morris held an old flute carefully in both hands. The instrument looked delicate, and Charlie was afraid that he might break it.

Sensing the boy's hesitation, Morris said, "Don't worry, Charles. This flute is stronger than it looks. It has survived thousands of years and countless battles between men and Gods."

Charlie reached out and grabbed the flute with both hands. Despite the instrument's age, the wood was smooth and fresh. The leather straps that held the pipes together were strong and thick. By all appearances, the magical instrument was brand new and in perfect condition. Instinctively, Charlie put one of the pipes up to his lips and turned his eyes towards his grandfather for permission. Morris nodded, and Charlie blew into the flute. Nothing happened, so he tried a different pipe, and still, no sound came out.

"You need to learn the Song of Storms," Morris explained.

Charlie pulled the flute away from his lips.

"How can I learn to play a song if I can't even get any sound to come out?"

Morris gently took the flute from his grandson's hand and placed it on a nearby table.

"The Song of Storms is not really a song. It is a magic spell. The spell is powerful enough to put almost any legendary creature to sleep. It doesn't work on every known magical animal, but I believe it will do the job perfectly for a Thunderbird. To acquire the ability to perform the Song of Storms, you need to absorb the life force of the creature creating the storm."

Charlie looked back at his grandfather nervously. He was pretty sure he knew what that meant, but he couldn't bring himself to say it.

"Charles, to play the Song of Storms and save the world from being washed away, you need to be struck by lightning while playing Pan's flute."

"Woah! Hold on a second," Sydney shouted. "How does Charlie being killed by a lightning bolt help us save the world?"

"The odds of surviving a direct lightning strike are surprisingly good. About one in ten," Morris replied.

"Sure, but the odds of him being incredibly injured are about ten in ten. Even if he survives the lightning strike, he could be in a coma or have serious internal and external injuries. We can't exactly get him to a hospital right now."

Charlie swallowed hard and contemplated his predicament while his grandfather and his friend argued about the merits of the plan. He couldn't help but think about the pain he would experience. Sydney was right. Being struck by lightning could be a death sentence.

Charlie interrupted the argument by stammering out the only question he could think to ask.

"Will it… kill me?"

"I hope not," Morris replied quietly.

That was not the answer Charlie wanted to hear. He could feel panic beginning to settle into his mind when his grandfather surprised him by adding, "It didn't kill your mother."

"Mom knows the Song of Storms?"

Morris grabbed the flute again and handed it back to his grandson. This time when Charlie held it, he felt something different. He couldn't say for sure, but somehow, he felt connected to it.

"To my knowledge, your mother does not know the Song of Storms, but she was about your age when she faced her first life-or-death situation. A rival of mine had somehow located a very powerful source of magic called an element stone. To this day, I'm not sure how he acquired it, but he used the power of the stone to amplify his water magic and create a summer snowstorm. By the time I made it to his home to confront him, the storm was already quite dangerous and getting stronger by the hour. As I feared, he was ready for me and had me subdued before I could try and stop him. He summoned an army called the White Knights of Winter and sent them after your mother. I don't know if he planned to kill or kidnap her, but I never got the chance to find out. Before his soldiers could return, a ball of fire ripped into the room where I was being held captive and set me free. Before my captor had a chance to recover from the unexpected attack, I destroyed his element stone and ended his plan. When I got back to the house, I found out that your mother had somehow learned a very advanced spell called "Prometheus' Fire." She used the spell to destroy the White Knights and sent the fireball that set me free. She never fully told me about how she managed to acquire the spell that saved us, but I know from my own research that the person using the magic must willingly walk into the living flame and allow themselves to be burned away."

"Mom burned herself alive? Like, to death?" Charlie asked with a somewhat anguished look on his face.

"Well, not exactly. Those deemed worthy are born again from the ashes and flame with newfound power. Those who are unworthy… feed the fire and keep it burning for eternity."

"So, if I had an element stone, would I become as powerful as the guy you were fighting?"

Morris vigorously shook his head and replied, "Remember when I told you that there were no magical people, only magical things?"

Charlie nodded, and Morris continued, "Well, magic is an art that must be studied. Technically, anyone can acquire a spell, but you need to know where to look and what to use and what to do at exact moments, or trying to learn any spell can be potentially fatal. This particular Elemental had spent most of his life studying water magic. He was formidable in his own right, but the element stone enhanced his powers to the point of being capable of destroying the world. Without the proper study, trying to use that level of magic would most likely just freeze you to death."

Sydney raised his hand. "Mr. Weston, sir, what is an Elemental?"

"My apologies, gentlemen. An Elemental is a person who specializes in the magic of various elements. Typically, a mage focuses on only one element and grows their magic in that area. In this case, the Elemental who had summoned the summer snow had become very powerful using ice, which is, of course, a branch of the element of water. Charlie's mother, despite having almost no training in any of the elemental magics, managed to acquire a spell reserved for the highest level of fire mages."

Charlie reflected on what his grandfather had just told him and tentatively asked, "So, Mom was already fighting ice wizards when she was my age?"

"Your mother wasn't supposed to be fighting anyone. She was still very new to magic and didn't have any defensive or offensive skills that would be useful, so I left her at home with several armed guards to keep her safe. Unfortunately, most of the men and women here to protect her died trying to do so. She was very broken up about one man, in particular. She grieved for a long time and blamed herself for not being able to save him. After that night, she never attempted any fire-related spells again. I think the trauma was just too much for her to bear."

"It wasn't her fault, though," Charlie argued. "The knights were probably going to kill her, and she didn't even know any spells to protect herself until she figured out how to do the fireball thing."

"Believe me, Charles. I tried arguing that point with her many times. She was young and at the beginning of her training, just like you. None of what happened was her fault, but she still felt the weight of it just the same. Your mother was thrust into an impossible situation with unrealistic expectations. Somehow, she managed to pull through, but not entirely unscathed. You don't get to choose when the world needs you. Ready or not, the world needed her then, and it needs you now."

When the elevator arrived, the door opened, and the three men prepared to step inside, but before Charlie could climb in, Sydney grabbed the back of his shirt.

"Wait, Charlie. Are you sure about this? I mean, being struck by lightning could kill you. Even if it doesn't, you might never be the same again."

Charlie smiled and repeated Sydney's words from earlier that day.

"I have considered your warning and have decided that I will continue with you into the imminent danger."

The boys both laughed nervously and joined Morris in the elevator. Once inside, he pressed the button that took the group to the top of the Weston Manor observatory.

Lightning lit up the entire sky, and thunder shook the earth. The rain was falling so fast that Charlie couldn't even see the individual droplets. It was as though every step he took was through a wall of water. Seeing no point in wearing his rain gear anymore, Charlie took off his jacket and walked up one flight of steps to the summit of the outlook point. There was a single chair on a stone platform, which made Charlie think that his grandfather probably sat there from time to time and looked out at the world, maybe searching in vain for his lost daughter.

Charlie held the magic flute in his shaking right hand. He started to put the flute up to his lips but stopped suddenly. He looked back at his grandfather and yelled, "I'm afraid. I don't think I can do this."

Morris walked out into the storm and hugged his grandson.

"The lightning won't kill you, Charles," he replied. "You were meant to do this, just like your mother."

Sydney joined Charlie and Morris on the platform and added, "Don't worry, Charlie. I'm not going anywhere. I'm with you until the end."

Charlie turned back towards the sky and looked directly into the lightning bolts. He focused all of his thought on the Thunderbird's flapping wings, the sharpness of its beak, the strength in its talons, and the power in its bright, blue eyes.

Then, Charlie put the flute up to his lips and began to blow. To his surprise, music came out. Charlie lost himself in the beautiful melody of the song. He could barely stand the sadness of it but didn't want to stop playing. Charlie felt the storm begin to settle over him. The

Gods who could still hear the flute's song had heard it, and they were ready to meet Charlie face to face.

As the magical song reached its climax, a bolt of lightning came down from the sky and struck the flute. If the human eye could perceive such things, they would have seen the electricity pass through the instrument and into every cell of Charlie's body. The power filled him in an instant, and for a brief moment, he was nothing but pure, white-hot light.

When the lightning retreated, Morris looked out at the place where Charlie lay motionless, his body still smoking from the direct hit. The old man immediately dropped his cane and ran over to tend to his grandson. When he put his hand on Charlie's shoulder, he could feel the heat radiating from the boy's skin. Morris listened carefully for a moan or a cough or even labored breathing. He prayed for his grandson to speak or to open his eyes or make any movement at all, but, the undeniable truth was, Charlie was dead.

PART 3
THE THUNDERBIRD

24

The Song of Storms rang in Charlie's ears and forced his consciousness to return to him. He tried looking around for his grandfather, but a bright light in the distance made it impossible to see anything, so he balled up his hands and rubbed his eyes vigorously to remove some of the haze from his vision. When Charlie opened his eyes again, he found that he had managed to clear the blurriness, but the strange light hadn't faded at all, so he took a few deep breaths and gave himself a moment to adjust. When he could finally see properly, Charlie immediately recognized the landscape around him. It was his grandfather's field, but all of the buildings were gone. There was no Weston Manor or horse stables or moat. Everyone and everything had disappeared. The only other creature in the bright, open field was Jade, Charlie's unicorn. Even in a world bathed in light, Jade stood out as a beacon of pure beauty.

"What happened to us, girl? Did you get struck by lightning too?" Charlie asked nervously.

Of course, Jade didn't answer, but Charlie felt somewhat comforted by her presence. He spent a couple of minutes running his hands through her silver mane while thinking about where he was and what he was supposed to do next. Charlie considered the possibility that he might be asleep or unconscious. The open field and the mysterious light seemed a lot like his reoccurring dream, but the person in the red hood was nowhere to be found. Charlie also noticed that the rain had stopped, which made him wonder if he had somehow succeeded in putting the Thunderbird back to sleep. But then Charlie remembered that he might not be in the real world, so even though it wasn't raining wherever his spirit was, it was probably still pouring where he left his body.

"Umm… Charlie, I think you might be dreaming," a voice called out.

Charlie turned to find Sydney standing several yards behind him. "Syd? What are you doing here?"

"Don't you recognize this place?" Sydney asked as he jogged over. "It's exactly like the dream you've been having."

Charlie nodded in agreement. "If I'm dreaming, how can I suddenly see and talk to you? We've never been able to do that before." Sydney shrugged his shoulders as he cleaned his glasses on his shirt. "Wait a minute," Charlie exclaimed. "If you're here and I'm dreaming, maybe that means the lightning didn't kill me!"

"Yeah, or it killed both of us," Sydney deadpanned.

Before he had a chance to dwell on the idea of being killed by a lightning bolt, Charlie noticed something strange about his shadow. It was no longer directly beside him. Instead, the shadow had been cast several feet back. The light that had been shining directly overhead mere moments ago had moved to a spot at the top of a hill several hundred yards away. Now, the two boys were standing in a place of relative darkness compared to how bright the same spot had been only seconds earlier.

Charlie wasn't sure what was happening. He didn't know if he was dreaming or if his current surroundings were somehow part of the magic of the spell. For all Charlie knew, he had died while playing a magic flute in the middle of a storm. While he didn't like the idea of being gone from the world or failing to save it, Charlie had done everything he could and knew that his father and grandfather would be proud of him even if it had all been for nothing.

"Well, if I'm dead, nothing on the top of that hill is going to hurt me, so we might as well check it out."

As if Jade understood, she lowered herself to the ground so that Charlie and Sydney could climb on, and then, without warning, the three of them took off like a bullet shot from a gun. Charlie had seen Jade run before, but seeing something with true, godlike speed was much different from riding on its back. At first, Charlie was afraid of falling off. But then, he remembered he might already be dead, or at the very least, his body was somewhere else, so he allowed himself to relax and feel the brisk air whip across his face as Jade ran faster and faster towards the light on the hill.

As the unicorn continued to pick up speed, Sydney's grip on Charlie got tighter and tighter. He successfully fought back the urge to scream but could not make himself relax enough to enjoy the ride.

Charlie, on the other hand, felt completely free. He closed his eyes and spread his arms out at his side. He found himself thinking about the Thunderbird again, and he wondered if this is what it felt like to fly. The sensation was exhilarating. With his eyes closed, he could almost imagine the weightlessness of flight and the wonder of soaring through the clouds.

Unfortunately, the revelry of the moment did not last long. Even with their eyes closed, the light from the top of the hill was becoming blinding for the boys. At first, the brightness was merely annoying, but the closer they got to the source of the light, the more painful it became. Jade continued to run, seemingly unfazed, but Charlie and Sydney struggled.

"Charlie," Sydney shouted. "I don't know if I can take much more of this!"

Even with their eyes closed as tightly as possible, the light still got inside somehow. It was all Charlie could do to keep himself from crying out in agony. He wanted to yell for Jade to stop and turn around, but he couldn't. He knew there was nothing for him back in the empty field, and if his life, and possible death, were going to mean anything, he had to keep going, so he put his hands over his face and screamed into Jade's mane.

Just when Charlie had suffered as much as he ever thought possible, Jade stopped. Charlie opened his eyes, expecting to be immediately blinded, but instead, he found that his vision had adjusted, and he could easily tolerate the light that had been torturing him only moments earlier.

Charlie looked out over the empty field and saw everything for miles in every direction. He saw forests, mountains, hills, lakes, and rivers. He saw every blade of grass on the ground and every brilliant star in the sky. From the top of this hill, Charlie could see all life and light, death and darkness. It was overwhelming and spectacular and perfect.

When Charlie turned to focus on the source of the blinding light, he saw a figure standing in the center. At first, he thought it might be Sydney, but it wasn't. That was when Charlie realized that his friend was nowhere to be found. He looked all around the hill, but there was no sign of Sydney anywhere.

Then, with a soft, sweet voice, the person in the light spoke.

"I've been expecting you, Charlie."

Charlie recognized the voice immediately and, as if to confirm his heart's greatest hope, his mother stepped into view.

"Mom? Is it really you?!"

Charlie could barely form the words, but he managed to repeat his question several times before he stopped long enough to allow her to answer.

"Yes, my boy. It's really me," she replied as she wiped the tears from her son's eyes. "I know you must have a lot of questions, and I want to tell you everything, but we don't have much time."

"But mom, I need to know what happened to you. I need to know where you've been. We've all missed you so much."

Jillian kissed her son on the forehead and whispered, "I know, my love. I missed you too."

Suddenly, Charlie heard a strange noise in his ears, like a fly buzzing around his brain, but he shook off the distraction and returned his attention to his mother.

Jillian grabbed her son's hands, took a deep breath, and said, "Your grandfather was right. A group of Elementals took me. They wanted something, a staff to increase their group's power tenfold. It was dark, dangerous magic, and I refused to help them. I held them off for months, and they treated me…unkind."

Charlie's mother closed her eyes, and a tear fell down her right cheek.

"I didn't care what they did to me as long as you were safe," Jillian continued. "I trusted your grandfather to keep you hidden, but eventually, they found you too. Once they were able to prove to me that they knew where you were, I couldn't hold back any longer. I went on several assignments for them. I chased down leads. I stole things. I even hurt a few people. I didn't care as long as I could protect you. Finally, I found the staff, and I gave it to the Elementals with the understanding that you would be left alone."

Jillian released her son's hands and turned away.

Again, Charlie heard the loud buzzing in his mind. This time the sensation knocked him off balance, but he quickly regained his composure and moved toward his mom.

"I'm sorry, Mom. I'm sorry you had to go through that, especially for me. I feel terrible."

"Don't feel terrible, even for a second. Everything I did was for you, and I would do it all again if it meant protecting you from danger."

Charlie smiled. It was a real smile. Perhaps the first one he could remember since the day his mother had disappeared.

"It's over now, Mom. Whatever you did wasn't your fault. We'll get the staff back from the Elementals, and we will make them pay for what they did."

Jillian looked down at her son with sad, knowing eyes.

"Sweetheart, don't you understand where we are?"

Charlie looked around again at the whole universe laid before him. He understood the importance of the place but didn't know what it was. Before he could venture a guess, the loud buzz struck again with force. It was more than just distracting this time. Charlie's vision blurred, and he lost his balance. He grabbed onto his mother for support, and she lovingly grabbed his chin and turned his eyes up toward hers.

"After I turned the staff over to the Elementals, they killed me. With my dying breath, I used my last bit of magic to keep my soul here so I could wait for you. We are standing in the world between life and death. From here, you can see all of time if you know how to look into the stars and read the signs."

Jillian's revelation opened a floodgate of emotions, and Charlie could feel the panic welling up inside him.

"I'm…dead?" Charlie asked, trying to gain comprehension of the situation.

"Not yet, but very soon, you will be. Any moment your soul could be whisked away into those stars as a permanent fixture of the past. You will become part of the tapestry of the universe, one of an infinite number of creation's memories."

Through his red, tear-filled eyes, Charlie saw a gentle look on his mother's face. For the first time in his life, he noticed how beautiful she was. Her features didn't merely show signs of kindness, understanding, and love; they were the definition of those things. It was as though her human body could not contain all that was inside her. Her personality was stronger than the vessel holding it, and that personality came through every line on her face, every glance from her eyes, and every tiny gesture and movement of her body.

"This doesn't have to be the end for us," Jillian continued lovingly. "The reason I have been waiting here for you is to give you a choice.

The lightning bolt that struck you sent your soul to this place. You aren't quite dead, but you aren't quite alive either, so you get to choose your fate in a way that most people never do."

Jillian turned her son around to face two doors standing about six feet away.

"Where did those come from?" Charlie asked.

"The magic of this place can produce whatever is needed. However, the choice you make now must be with action, not words."

Charlie walked over and inspected the doors. Neither was supported by any kind of frame, but they both managed to stand upright in the middle of the grass. The door on the right was painted bright blue. It had a round, golden doorknob and a flower basket hanging under an ornate semi-circular window. The door on the left was made of damp, rotting wood. There was no window, but there were holes in the door that looked like some small animal had burrowed its way through. Instead of a doorknob, Charlie found a large, golden handle in the shape of a dragon's head. It was the same as the door handles at Weston Manor, but the gold was severely tarnished, and the dragon looked disfigured from thousands of years of damage from age and the elements.

Charlie turned back toward his mother. "What do I have to do?"

Jillian moved past her son and approached the blue door first.

"If you pass through this door, you will be taken to a world much like this one. It is a magical paradise where the Weston family resides. You will be united with our entire line, and I will follow immediately behind you. We can stay there and be together forever. There will be no more loss, no more pain, and no more magic."

Then, Jillian gestured vaguely towards the second option.

"This door reflects the condition of a dying world. Walking through here will bring you back to your body at Weston Manor. You will live until you die, but you will not come back to this place the next time you perish. You will not be given a choice. Having forsaken our family's paradise, your soul will join the other stars in the heavens, and you will be a forgotten story, lost in the hourglass of eternity."

"Are you saying that if I go back to the world, I'll never see you again?"

Jillian nodded gravely.

"But what about all those people? What about Grandpa and Dad?"

"I understand how you feel, Charlie. I really do. The responsibility of our family is tremendous. It's too much for a child. But the truth is, if you go back, you aren't going to save the world. You will only die trying."

Charlie was stunned to hear his mother's blunt words. He knew that there was still a lot to learn and that he may not be the hero the world needed, but he couldn't believe that she would be so willing to condemn every soul on earth to death.

"Mom, I have to try and do something. If I don't go back, the Thunderbird will destroy the whole world. Everyone will die!"

"Everyone is already dead," Jillian responded in a dark, low voice. "There is no hope, Charles."

Charlie looked at his mother with surprise.

"Charles? You never call me...."

Before Charlie could finish his thought, the buzzing in his mind returned and echoed loudly in his ears. The sudden sensation dropped him to his knees, and he screamed in agony. When he managed to regain himself, he stared at the woman standing before him. Somehow his mother didn't strike him with the same beauty he had seen moments earlier. Instead, she looked tired and worn. Her skin appeared loose, and Charlie could almost see down to the bone.

Her hair no longer appeared golden and radiant. Instead, it was more of a thin, silvery gray.

"I'm sorry, Mom," Charlie said as he slowly backed away. "I love you. I will always love you, but I have to try and do something."

Charlie put his hand on the disfigured dragon handle of the rotted door that would lead him back to his body, but before he could pull it open, he heard someone from the other side of the gateway shout, "CHARLIE! LOOK OUT!"

Charlie felt a strong hand grab his shoulder, and out of the corner of his eye, he saw skeletal fingers gripping him tightly. He screamed with terror and spun around, expecting to find some creature holding his mother hostage, but instead, he saw her rotting corpse.

"Fool! If you will not make the wise choice on your own, then I will make it for you!"

The imposter's human features were quickly disintegrating, and Charlie was able to see the monster who had been posing as his mother all along.

At that moment, Sydney emerged from the door that led back to the real world.

"Don't listen to it, Charlie!" Sydney proclaimed triumphantly. "It wants to stop you from coming back!"

"Sydney! Where the hell have you been?!"

"As soon as we got to the top of the hill, this thing's magic started blocking me out. I was sent back to my body. Your grandpa and I tried calling you, but you weren't hearing us. He used a potion to put me back to sleep, and I could see you, but I still couldn't get to you. Every time I yelled, you looked like you heard something but not my voice."

"You were the buzzing in my head! You were trying to warn me!"

Before Sydney could respond, the deathly being lunged forward and knocked both boys to the ground.

"What are you?" Charlie yelled defiantly.

The smooth, porcelain skull turned its gaze towards Charlie, and even though its mouth did not move, both boys could hear the creature speak.

"I am a guardian of fate and gatekeeper for the dead."

The nightmarish demon had shed all of its former disguise and towered over Charlie and Sydney as a ten-foot-tall creature of hardened bone. It wore a bright, white cloak with black trim around its shoulders, and its eyes glowed with many bright colors that changed often. Charlie noticed the monster was holding something in its right hand between its thumb and index finger. He only saw the object for a second, but it looked like some kind of marble.

"What do you want from me?" Charlie demanded.

The voice from inside the demon bellowed with a rumble that shook the ground.

"I want nothing. My service is to those who came before and those who will come again. They are the ones who want you gone."

Charlie tried to lunge for the rotting door, but the undead gatekeeper drew a white staff from under its cloak and struck him in the chest. The blow knocked Charlie backward and stole the air from his lungs. Sydney ran to Charlie's side and helped pull him away from danger.

"If your masters want me dead, why not just kill me?" Charlie choked out as he gasped for air.

The creature repositioned itself in front of the gateway concealed by the rotting door and prepared to stand guard.

"No one can kill what is already dead. You are not yet deceased, but neither are you alive. If your soul stays here long enough, your body will die on its own. You were supposed to choose the blue door. I could have held you there for eternity in a cage that looked and felt like paradise, but you chose to be a hero, so you and your friend will die here and live out eternity in oblivion."

The boys rose to their feet and brushed themselves off.

"We will beat you," Charlie said with steady determination.

Sydney tugged on his friend's sleeve and whispered, "Charlie, not to state the obvious, but if you have any magic spells you have been saving for a rainy day, I will remind you that we are in the midst of a never-ending storm, both physically and metaphorically."

"Sorry, Syd. I left my anti-skeleton gun with my body on earth. We'll just have to try and do this the old-fashioned way."

With that, Charlie let out a yell and ran toward the skeletal guard holding him captive. The powerful demon easily swatted Charlie away with its staff, completely unfazed by the boy's sudden, enthusiastic rush.

"Pathetic," mused the undead gatekeeper. "I thought that a Godmaker would be a more formidable opponent."

The monster loomed over Charlie and raised its staff to strike the final blow when Sydney jumped onto its back and yelled, "Go, Charlie! You have to get back to the world!"

The undead gatekeeper laughed and shook the small boy from its shoulders.

"You're not going to hurt my friend," Sydney proclaimed as he stood to face his foe.

"And how exactly do you plan to stop me?" the demon asked. "A child with no magic or strength cannot hope to stand against a Guardian of Fate. You have wasted enough of my time."

The undead gatekeeper swung its staff directly at Sydney's head, but to its surprise, the weapon passed right through him. At first, Sydney thought maybe the attack had missed, but the creature quickly rebounded with another mighty swing. Again, the staff passed through the boy's body, leaving him completely unharmed. The skeletal Guardian of Fate approached Sydney with rage, reaching out its bony hand to grab the boy by the throat but was unable to make contact of any kind.

The demon shuddered and dropped its staff as it took a tentative step backwards. The skull's once glowing eyes had diminished to nothing more than small dots of light, and the huge guardian submissively hunched down to far less than its full height.

"It's you…" the undead gatekeeper said meekly. "You have returned."

Several questions formed in Sydney's mind at once, but before he got a chance to ask any of them, Charlie called out, "Try and stop this move!"

Sydney had managed to distract the skeletal guardian long enough for Charlie to get into an attacking position. By the time the demon turned its head to see what was happening, Charlie was already running at full speed. His rage and determination gave him strength and power that he had never known, and he could feel every muscle in his body tense as he braced for impact. As Charlie barreled into his captor, he could feel the skeleton's body break apart and fly away in pieces.

Charlie's momentum carried him right into the door, hitting it with tremendous force. He waited for the pain to begin rushing through his body, but it never came. He looked around and saw pieces of the former guardian of fate scattered all over the ground. Whatever life force had been holding the creature together had been destroyed. Charlie laughed out loud and screamed in triumph.

"Did you see that?! I made that guy explode! I broke him into a million pieces!"

"I don't think we are out of the woods quite yet, Charlie," Sydney said as he spun his friend around to face a newcomer.

Charlie's excitement quickly turned to fear as he saw the red-hooded man of so many of his dreams. The red cloak concealed every distinguishable feature of its wearer and almost willfully contorted itself to hide the person underneath. The only thing Charlie could make out clearly was a ball of fire hovering over the palm of the mage's outstretched hand. Charlie looked at the dancing fireball and then down at the remains of the skeleton. He sighed with disappointment.

"You did that, didn't you?"

The red hood nodded in affirmation.

"Well, that's embarrassing."

From somewhere inside the red cloak, Charlie heard a voice say, "What you did took great courage. The easy choice is often not the right one. You could have allowed yourself to be deceived by the vision of your mother. You could have left your friend here to die. Both times, you chose to do the right thing no matter what it cost you. That is a rare trait, indeed."

"You're an Elemental, aren't you?" Sydney asked.

The red hood nodded again and bent down to pick up the marble that Charlie had seen the skeleton holding.

"What is that?" Charlie asked, but the Elemental did not answer.

Then, the red mage dropped the fireball from his hand and was instantly enveloped in bright flame. Charlie and Sydney shielded their eyes, and when they opened them again, they were alone.

"Okay then. Nice meeting you," Charlie said with heavy sarcasm to no one in particular. He turned back toward the doors but was surprised to find that the blue one was gone and in its place was a pile of ash.

"I guess the Red Wizard doesn't want us changing our minds."

"Charlie, did you see me fighting the skeleton?" Sydney asked sheepishly.

"I sure did," Charlie exclaimed. "It was awesome. The perfect distraction."

"But did you see the skeleton hit me in the head with his staff?"

Charlie grimaced.

"No. I must have been getting in position for my useless charge. Are you okay? That staff really packed a punch."

Sydney nodded that he was fine, but it was only because the demon's staff had passed through him somehow. Even more alarming was that the undead gatekeeper seemed to know who he was and was scared of him for some reason, but that was a problem for another day, so Sydney removed his glasses to clean them and said, "Yes, he barely made contact. I guess I got lucky."

Charlie walked over and slapped his friend heartily on the back.

"Thanks, Syd. I wouldn't be walking out of here if it weren't for you."

"What are friends for?" Sydney replied.

Both boys laughed and pushed on the old, rotted door that led back to the real world. It swung open with ease, and they walked through together.

25

Charlie felt a wet, sloppy tongue move across his face. He opened his eyes to see Zag doing her best to revive her fallen master. He slowly raised his hands to push the giant beast off him, but the slight movement overjoyed the loyal dog, and the kissing continued with renewed vigor. After a minute or two, Charlie had regained enough of his strength to sit up and look around. He was lying on one of the black couches inside his grandfather's parlor. Zag was doing her best to contain her excitement and sit calmly next to her master, but her efforts were in vain, and she ended up mainly in Charlie's lap.

At either end of the couch, Charlie saw that the two knights, usually posted as guards for the incubating dragon egg, had been repositioned to guard him. He was touched by the gesture, and it dawned on him how worried his grandfather must have been.

Charlie looked across the room and saw Grandpa Morris and Sydney peacefully sleeping on the couch opposite from him. Charlie stood to stretch but fell back down on the couch when the knights closed in on him in a tight, defensive formation.

"Woah! Easy boys. I've been dead all day. I need to walk around a bit."

Charlie moved towards the large glass windows that overlooked the fields behind Weston Manor. His procession of bodyguards followed close behind. He sat on a large, cushioned window seat and put his head against the glass. Charlie sat and watched the rain fall for a while. He told himself that he wanted to let his grandfather get some much-needed rest, but the truth was that he was nervous about finding out what would happen next.

At first, Charlie barely noticed that he had been itching his arm the entire time he sat on the window seat. It was only a minor annoyance, and he scratched at himself automatically. After about ten minutes, the irritation had only gotten worse, and Charlie was no longer able to concentrate on the relaxing sounds of the rain. He clawed at his sleeve, but no relief came. Finally, the itch became so unbearable that it had stolen his full attention. He pulled up his sleeve and, to his horror, looked down to see a tattoo covering the spot he had been scratching.

"Oh, no… No. NO. NO!" Charlie stood up abruptly and walked right into one of his armored protectors.

The noise shook Morris out of his sleep, and he turned to see his grandson scrubbing at his arm with a piece of cloth and what appeared to be the contents of a thousand-dollar bottle of limited-edition scotch.

Morris leaped to his feet and shouted, "Charles, my boy! You're alive! I'm so relieved. I'm also a little sad that you're wasting my good scotch but mostly relieved."

Charlie barely noticed that his grandfather had addressed him, and he continued to scrub at the mark on his arm. It was no use. If anything, the tattoo was only getting darker and more permanent. Finally, Charlie flung the cloth down in frustration and held his arm out for his grandfather to see.

"Look at it! LOOK AT IT! I might as well have gone through the blue door because dad is going to kill me. Saving the world is one thing but my dad does not like tattoos. Like, at all."

Morris began laughing hysterically.

"Oh, this is funny? Fine. You can call my dad and tell him you did it because I'm not doing it."

Morris took the expensive bottle of alcohol out of Charlie's hand, replaced the cork, and said jokingly, "Rule number one, Charles, is never to use Grandpa Weston's good scotch for anything. When you're old enough, I will teach you how to use this important tool properly."

Charlie rolled his eyes.

"But seriously, Charles. You did it! You acquired the Song of Storms! I'm so proud of you."

"How do you know that I learned the song?" Charlie asked as he continued to scratch his arm.

"Because you bear the mark of the spell," Morris replied while pointing to the tattoo.

Charlie looked down at the magical ink and listened as his grandfather explained, "Every spell in the world has its mark. When you have acquired new magic, it becomes part of you. It can never be taken away or forgotten. The mark is proof of what you have accomplished. It shows prominently on the skin for the first few hours and any time you are actively using the spell. At all other times, the mark is invisible."

Charlie looked up hopefully. "You mean, it's going to go away?"

Morris laughed again. "Yes, Charles. The mark should fade soon. Unfortunately, new spells can have a bit of an irritating effect on the skin. Don't worry, though. I have an ointment that should make the inflammation and itchiness subside."

Charlie let out a deep sigh of relief as he wandered back towards the couches and threw himself down on the closest one. He buried his face in the soft leather and was content to stay there for a while, but his grandfather had other ideas.

"What did you mean when you said you should have gone through the blue door?" Morris asked.

Charlie didn't want to move, so he shouted into the cushion, "The test. The blue door and the rotted door."

"Charles, I have no idea what you are talking about," Morris replied as he sat down on the arm of the couch.

Charlie raised his head and looked up at the confusion on his grandfather's face. It had never occurred to him that he might have had an experience that his grandfather had never had.

"Oh, right… You don't know the Song of Storms spell," Charlie said.

"It wouldn't matter even if I did know it. Every journey to acquire new power is unique to the person trying to attain it. As I have told you before, anyone can learn magic, but it takes strength, courage, conviction, and luck to succeed. Many have lost their lives in the pursuit of acquiring new magic. Even the most powerful among us only know five or six spells because learning them is often dangerous and can come at a great cost."

Charlie looked down again at the mark on his arm. He noticed that the tattoo was in the shape of the same flute he had used to play the Song of Storms. There was also a lightning bolt going through the magical instrument. When Charlie touched the bolt, he could almost feel its power running through his body. He traced the outline of the mark with his finger while he asked, "So I really could have died in there?"

Morris simply bowed his head in reply.

Charlie looked over at Sydney, who was still sleeping on the couch.

"Is he going to be okay?"

Morris glanced over at the small boy.

"You wouldn't know to look at him, Charles, but that is one brave young man. His determination to follow you into danger was like nothing I have seen in all my years."

Charlie walked over to where Sydney lay and looked down at him. He was soaking wet, his Batman t-shirt was ripped in places, his glasses were smudged, and he was caked with dirt and mud.

"After you were struck by lightning, you collapsed, and I ran over to check on you. You barely had a pulse, so I scooped you up in my arms to carry you back into the house. I yelled to Sydney to come to help me, but when I turned back to where he was standing, I saw that he had also collapsed. I thought maybe he had fainted, but I quickly realized that he was in a deep sleep. I remembered what you had told me about him being active in your dreams, so instead of waking him up, I carried him back into the house as well and settled you both on the couches here in the parlor."

"That's right," Charlie said. "Sydney was there with me. But it wasn't like the dreams from before. This time he was able to talk to me and do stuff. We rode Jade up a huge hill towards a bright light. I could feel Sydney holding on to me, but when we got to the top of the hill, he was gone."

"Quite right, Charles," Morris said, picking up where his grandson left off. "I was watching over both of you when Sydney suddenly shot up off his couch and told me that you were in great danger. We tried shouting at you, shaking you, and I even used a few magical communication amulets, but nothing worked. Finally, Sydney decided that the only way to reach you would be for him to go back to sleep, so I offered him my strongest sleeping tonic, and he swallowed the entire potion without hesitation. A few moments later, he was dreaming again."

Charlie recounted the rest of the adventure in the land between life and death and filled in the blanks that Sydney wasn't able to communicate when he had woken so abruptly. Charlie hesitated when he got to the part about seeing his mom because he wasn't sure how his grandfather would react.

Morris sensed his grandson's hesitation and felt confident that he knew what the boy was holding back.

"It was your mother, wasn't it?"

"Yes…Well, not really," Charlie replied with his eyes lowered. "It was just some creature that made itself look like mom."

"What kind of creature?"

Charlie explained how his fake mother's beautiful appearance had worked to disarm him and how being in her presence made him feel calm and under control. Then, he explained how her form eroded as he began to challenge her until all of her features melted off, and there was nothing left but a skeleton wearing a white cape.

Morris had a look of fear on his face. He stood up from the couch and walked over to a wall of shelves filled with old books, faded newspapers, and dusty scrolls. He climbed a ladder attached to the wall and searched the top shelf frantically for something in particular. When he finally found what he was looking for, Morris returned to the couch with the biggest book Charlie had ever seen.

Charlie watched as his grandfather quickly flipped through the pages of the old book. After a few moments of searching, Morris stopped on a page and pointed at an illustration.

"Is this the creature you saw?"

Charlie looked down at the drawing and was shocked to see the same demon he had fought in the land between life and death.

"It's a Moirai," Sydney said as he rose from his couch. "They are powerful mystics of the old Greek religion and the guardians of the past, present, and future."

Morris and Charlie both turned towards Sydney with surprise.

"Very good, young man!" Morris said enthusiastically. "According to myth, the Moirai worked exclusively for Hades. If you look at the picture here, the object the Moirai is holding is one of the three eyes of fate. As the legend goes, one orb shows the past with perfect clarity, the second orb shows the present from a single perspective, and the third orb shows the most likely outcome for the future. How do you know about these creatures, Sydney?"

Sydney stood shakily and walked over to the other two men in the room.

"I'm not sure. I just woke up and knew."

Charlie got up from the couch and hugged his friend.

"Thanks for coming back for me, Syd. You're a real friend."

"You two meeting a Moirai is impossible," Morris said as he continued to pour over the book.

"Why is it impossible?" Charlie asked.

"Because they have been dead for thousands of years. Some of the mystical animals from that period survived for a time. Now and then, we will discover a griffin or minotaur, but they are incredibly rare. The Gods, demigods, and their acolytes are another story, though. They are supposed to be gone. Long gone. Even if the Moirai did survive, they are only supposed to take orders from Hades. Did the Moirai say anything to you while you were with it?"

"It said something about serving those who came before and those who would come again." Charlie paused and looked up at his grandfather. "Then it said that they are the ones who want me gone."

Morris closed the book and took both boys by their hands. "Clearly, there is more going on here than we originally suspected. I'm beginning to believe that it is no accident the Thunderbird has woken." Morris turned his attention to Charlie and added, "We will find the answers together."

"First, we have to put the Thunderbird back to sleep," Charlie said confidently.

"Right you are, my boy," Morris replied.

Charlie started collecting his things and making his way toward the parlor exit.

"Where do you think you are going in this storm?" Morris asked.

"I almost died today," Charlie explained as he put on his jacket. "I intentionally got myself struck by lightning. Some kind of monster of fate that shouldn't exist impersonated my mom and tried to trap my soul in a cage. Someone or something is still out there trying to kill me. I know what I have to do, but now, I also know what's at stake. I need to go home and say a couple of goodbyes before we go off and fight this thing. I might not get another chance."

Morris was visibly nervous, but he could see that there was no changing his grandson's mind, so he relented and said, "I will have the car pulled around. Sydney and I will stay here and begin working on a plan."

As Charlie prepared to venture out into the storm, Morris asked, "Is there anything else of note that took place on your journey between worlds?"

"Yeah. Sydney and I didn't make it back on our own," Charlie added tentatively. "A Fire Elemental saved us. I have been having dreams about him ever since you told me the truth about everything. The mage was able to hold a fireball in his hand and used one to destroy the Moirai that was trying to kill us."

The old man straightened his tie and ran his hands through his silver hair.

"He didn't try to hurt me," Charlie continued, "but he did take the orb that the Moirai had been holding. Then, he disappeared."

"I don't know the identity of this Elemental, but I am thankful he saved your life, even if that was not his purpose," Morris replied gratefully. "The Moirai are indistinguishable, so it is impossible to know which was killed or which of the orbs the fire mage now possesses, but anyone who obtains all three will be a powerful, all-knowing entity. It is too soon to know if this person is a friend or foe, but we need to be on our guard from this point on."

26

Charlie sat with Zag in the back of his grandfather's car as the chauffeur did his best to navigate the mostly flooded roads. He shifted nervously in his seat as his mind wandered between facing the Thunderbird and telling his father that the moment of greatest danger had finally come. Even though Charlie had barely spent any time working with his grandfather, he tried to focus on all the things his mother had taught him over the years because, whether he liked it or not, there was no more time for training or planning.

When the car finally pulled into the driveway, Charlie still had no idea what he would say, but he decided he would speak from the heart and try his best to keep his dad from worrying too much.

Without turning around, the driver said in a thick Irish accent, "Don't take too long, Mr. Weston. These roads aren't getting any better."

Charlie put his hand on the door handle and hesitated.

The Irishman chimed in again, "Look, your old man knows what's what. He isn't gonna be happy about what you've got to do, but he already knows it's gotta be done, so go in there, say what needs sayin' and let's get gone."

Somehow the straightforward, no-nonsense attitude of the driver gave Charlie a small boost of confidence. He took two deep breaths, flung the door open, and ran into the house where he found his dad waiting for him. Before Charlie had a chance to say anything, Patrick threw his arms around his son and welcomed him home.

"I was worried about you. I had a horrible dream earlier that you were in danger."

Charlie shrugged and gestured with his hands from head to toe. "Nope. All in one piece."

The moment of truth had come. It was time for Charlie to tell his dad what he was about to do and find some way to get through a difficult and emotional goodbye. He was about to speak when his father grabbed his arm.

"What the hell is this?!" Patrick shouted

Charlie looked down with dread, having completely forgotten about the magical tattoo.

"It's not what you think, Dad. It's a... mark."

Patrick licked his index finger and began rubbing his son's arm vigorously.

"It's a mark that won't come off, Charlie! See! I'm rubbing it, but it's still there!"

"Dad, stop. You're going to rub the skin off."

"Good! I can't believe you got a tattoo! If your mother were here, she would kill you. Then, she would kill me for letting this happen!"

Patrick brought Charlie's arm up to his face to take a closer look, but before he got the chance, the mark faded right before his eyes.

"It's gone," they said in unison.

Charlie and Patrick looked up and caught each other's mutual look of anger and panic. Then, both men burst out laughing hysterically.

"You should see the look on your face!" Charlie said as tears streamed from his eyes.

"ME?! You should see your face!" Patrick added between booming laughs. "You looked like you just took a flying leap off the world's tallest building!" Then, Patrick did his best imitation of his son's horrified expression, and they laughed together even harder.

Over the next several minutes, Patrick made several attempts to compose himself but eventually surrendered to the ridiculous moment and reached out for the wall to steady himself. Charlie laughed so hard that his stomach hurt. He doubled over with a combination of amusement and pain before he collapsed to the ground.

When the laughter finally died away and both men had regained themselves, Patrick asked, "What just happened?"

"The mark isn't a tattoo, Dad," Charlie answered. "It is part of a magic spell that I had to learn to stop the rain. It's called 'The Song of Storms'."

"That's right!" Patrick said as he smacked his forehead. "I completely forgot about the spell marks."

Patrick grabbed his son's arm again. He turned it over, and sure enough, there was no sign that the mark had been there only minutes earlier.

"In all the years your mother and I were together, I only ever saw her magic tattoos a few times, but she did tell me about them. I guess seeing one on my teenage son made me forget."

Now that the ice had been broken, Charlie felt much more relaxed. He remembered that his father had been through this before and had some vague idea of what needed to be done and how dangerous it could be.

"Dad, I have to put a Thunderbird back to sleep."

Patrick gave a weak but knowing smile.

"I know you do. I found the Weston family book in your room."

Patrick could see a worried look forming on his son's face, so he quickly added, "It's okay, Charlie. I saw that book a lot when your mother and I were dating. I know what it is. She trusted me with everything. I hope you can do the same."

Charlie let out a deep breath and relaxed again.

"Were you able to read it?"

"No, I'm not a Weston. I can't read the book, but I saw it on your desk, so I knew it must have spoken to you and told you what you were up against. A Thunderbird, huh? Is it dangerous?"

Charlie nodded his head.

"Of course, it is," Patrick sighed. "You know, Charlie, when I first started seeing your mother, I fell in love with her immediately. It had nothing to do with magic. I had no idea that she helped protect the rarest, most powerful creatures or that she had assisted your grandfather in saving the world once or twice. What I fell in love with was her strength of character and her conviction. She had a clear view of right and wrong, and she made it her mission to protect what was right and fight against wrong. I had never met anyone who saw the world with such clarity. You have that strength of character. You aren't willing to settle for living in the world as it is. You fight to make the world into what it should be. No matter what you learn or how many magic tattoos you get, you already have what it takes to save the day."

Charlie didn't know what to say. He wondered how many times his dad had given his mom a similar pep talk and if she had ever felt the way that he was feeling now, that his dad had found the exact, perfect words to say.

"You may not be a Weston, Dad, but there is no way I could do this without you."

Patrick held a hand out to his son and helped him to his feet.

"Before you go, I have something for you."

Charlie's dad disappeared around the corner and returned a moment later with an oversized red rain jacket.

"Yours is in pretty rough shape and barely even fits you. I have been meaning to get you a new one, but for now, just take mine. It might be a little big, but it will keep you dry."

Charlie tried on the red jacket and pulled the hood over his head. It fit surprisingly well.

"I'll come home as soon as I can."

"I know you will. Try to stay safe. The world needs you, but not as much as I do."

The two men embraced one more time, and Charlie ran back out the door, leaving Zag looking on anxiously from the window in the front room of the house. From the back seat of the car, Charlie could see his father comforting the sad dog, probably telling her the exact right words she needed to hear because, apparently, that was his father's magic power.

As the driver carefully made his way through the flooded roads, Charlie called from the backseat, "Can we please make one more stop?"

The driver shook his head.

"That's not a good idea, Mr. Weston."

"Please, you can call me Charlie."

"Okay, Charlie. Your grandfather instructed me to take you home to see your father and then right back to the manor. There is a lot of work to do."

"Do you know where we are going and what we have to do?"

"No, but I know it is very dangerous."

Charlie unbuckled his seatbelt and leaned closer.

"What's your name?"

"My name? Well, you can call me Cain."

"Cain, you're right. When we get back to my grandfather's house, we have to do something very dangerous. I'm nervous about what might happen, and that's saying something because I've already died once today."

Cain's eyes widened, but he kept staring straight ahead.

Charlie continued, "I need to say one more goodbye, just in case I die again and can't find my way back this time."

Cain stopped the car in the middle of an intersection. There was no need to worry about traffic because there were no other cars on the road.

"Where would you like to go, Charlie boy?"

Charlie smiled and gave his driver directions to Dylan's house.

When they arrived, Cain parked the car in the driveway, and the two men sat in silence.

"Well, are you going in, or did you just want to look at the house?"

"I'm going! I just need a minute," Charlie replied defensively.

"You seem awfully scared for someone who died once already today."

Charlie frowned.

"Not cool, Cain."

Emboldened and slightly embarrassed by his driver's taunts, Charlie got out of the car, giving Cain an "I'm doing it" look as he passed by the driver's window. He quickly made it to the covered front porch but immediately thought about turning back and pretending like no one was home when the door opened, and Dylan walked outside.

"Hey, Dylan," Charlie said with an embarrassingly lame wave. He used his other hand to pull down the awkward gesture.

Dylan gave him a mocking wave in return.

"Did you swim here or something?"

Charlie noticed that Dylan was wearing a dress. He had seen her dressed up before but only on rare occasions, and it never really struck him as strange to see her this way until right then. She was beautiful. Distractingly beautiful.

"What's with the dress?" Charlie asked.

Dylan blushed.

"My grandfather is here, and he doesn't come over that often, and it's a whole big thing and...."

"Woah! I'm sorry," Charlie interjected with his hands held up in surrender. "I didn't mean to make you freak out. I just don't see you dressed up that often. You look... really nice."

"Do you want to come inside? It's pouring out here."

Charlie took a step back.

"I can't. I have this thing I have to go do."

Dylan stepped out onto the front porch and closed the door behind her.

"A thing? What kind of thing?" she asked curiously.

Charlie took another step back and found that he had retreated as far as possible without going back into the storm.

"I can't really talk about it. All I can tell you is that it's kind of dangerous."

Dylan took another step forward, and Charlie had nowhere to go.

"Charlie, you're scaring me. What's going on?"

"I'm sorry. I can't tell you everything, but it's for your own protection."

An angry look appeared on Dylan's face, and before Charlie got a chance to say anything in his defense, she punched him hard in the shoulder. Dylan could see that she had knocked Charlie off-balance, so she gave her best friend one giant push, and he fell backward onto the ground in the pouring rain. Without a moment of hesitation, she followed him into the storm. Charlie stood up quickly and was about to yell, but Dylan beat him to it.

"Do I look like some damsel in distress? Do you think I need your protection? I can protect myself, and you need to treat me better."

Charlie was ashamed. She was right. They had been best friends for as long as he could remember, and he wasn't treating her as an equal. The two stood together in the storm, waiting for the other to say or do something to break the tension.

After a few seconds of awkward silence, Charlie managed to find his nerve.

"I'm sorry. You're right. It's been a strange few weeks, and I don't know how to talk about it, even with you. The truth is, I think my mom might be alive. She's in trouble, though, and I'm working with my grandfather to save her."

Dylan's angry expression changed to one of genuine concern.

"Oh my God, Charlie! Are you serious?"

Charlie shook his head and continued, "There's more, and I promise I will tell you, but there isn't time right now. I have to go. I just wanted to come by and see you before I… went and did that thing. I'm sorry I underestimated you. You're the most special person in the world to me, and I wouldn't want to hurt you for anything."

Charlie started to walk back toward the car, but he felt a hand rest on his shoulder. He turned around and looked at his best friend again. She was soaked. Her hair was wet, her dress was clinging to her body, and the little makeup that she wore was smeared on her face. She was still beautiful. She was always beautiful. Before he had a chance to say anything, Dylan leaned forward and kissed him. A couple of years earlier, the two had shared their first kiss. It was a light peck on the lips. It was nice and comfortable because they were best friends, and they wanted to share that experience. This kiss was not like that kiss. It was deep and tender with feelings that had been lying dormant for both of them, feelings that were awake now and might never rest again. Charlie wasn't exactly sure what a kiss like this would mean, but he did know that it changed everything.

"What was that for?" Charlie asked when Dylan pulled away.

"Because you're my best friend and because I love you." she replied sweetly.

Charlie smiled his biggest smile, at least twice the size of his actual mouth.

"I love you too. I will come see you when I get back."

The two friends hugged, and Charlie stumbled back to the car completely drenched. Despite the upgrade in rain jackets, he had been standing out in the storm long enough to be soaked all the way through, but he didn't care one bit. As the car backed out of the driveway, he looked out the window and saw Dylan watching him leave from her front porch. He wondered why he had never noticed how amazing she was or how he could have been so blind to his feelings for her.

"Are you always that smooth, lover boy?" Cain teased. "Your arm is gonna have a nice bruise on it. Maybe your back too."

"Probably, but you know what, Cain? I can die a happy man…again."

27

Charlie practically floated back into the parlor at Weston Manor. His mind lingered on the kiss he had just shared with his best friend and the encouraging words he had received from his father. The danger he faced had transitioned from a general sense of dread to a more specific threat against the people he loved. It wasn't just that the world needed saving. Charlie had to stop the storm for his family's sake.

Charlie's thoughts were interrupted by his grandfather's voice calling out from somewhere in the room.

"We will be with you shortly, Charles. I am experiencing a few technical difficulties."

Charlie looked around but saw no signs of his grandfather or Sydney anywhere.

"Where are you guys? Are you using some kind of magic spell to talk to me?"

"It's an intercom system, Charles," Morris said with amusement. "Not everything here is accomplished through magic. There are small speakers and microphones placed throughout the house so that we can communicate with each other from any two points in the manor."

Charlie scanned the room for the speakers, but they were well hidden, and he couldn't find any.

"How was your farewell tour?" Morris asked. "I trust your father didn't give you too much trouble."

"Actually, dad was great," Charlie said as he plopped down on one of the leather couches. "Ever since he gave me his blessing to hang out with you, things between us have been awesome."

"Yes…Well, your father was always supportive of Jillian, despite his personal feelings for me."

"Dad likes you, Grandpa," Charlie said while looking around for a speaker to talk to. "He is just dealing with losing mom in his own way. You can't blame him for trying to protect me."

After a long pause, Morris replied, "Actually, Charles, I think that is the very thing your father dislikes the most about me. He never believed I took the risks of what we do seriously enough. Maybe he was right, but nothing like this has ever happened in our family's history. Every generation, a member of the Weston family entered the magical world in one field or another. We have been Cryptozoologists since your great-grandmother, but before that, we were unicorn breeders, dragon trainers, and even a few explorers in our line who all did very dangerous work with little to no negative consequences aside from some bumps, bruises, and burns."

"What kind of places did our family explore?" Charlie asked.

"Oh, Charles, my boy. Just as there are mythical creatures in this world, hiding in plain sight, there are worlds in this universe that remain accessible but are still a vast mystery, even to experienced practitioners such as myself."

This wasn't the first time Morris had casually mentioned the existence of other worlds. Charlie was eager to ask for more details as he imagined himself traveling through the galaxy and visiting places no one had ever been, but before he could, Sydney asked, "How did things go with Dylan?"

The question immediately brought Charlie plummeting back to Earth with a mixture of embarrassment and emotional butterflies.

"What makes you think I went to see her?" Charlie responded defensively.

"You had a near-death experience, and it might not be the only one you have today. There was never a question of whether or not you would see Dylan. What did she say?"

Sydney was right, and Charlie knew it, so he decided to embrace the truth and excitedly yelled out, "She kissed me, man! It was awesome!"

Sydney gave no audible reaction to the news of the kiss. Instead, he asked, "Did you tell her about the Thunderbird?"

"No, we didn't really get into all that," Charlie said, slightly deflated. "I just told her that I was going to do something dangerous and that I couldn't tell her the details."

"And then, I'm guessing she punched you," Sydney remarked with a laugh.

Charlie's jaw dropped.

"Geez, Syd. Can't you just let me have my moment?" Charlie asked frustratedly.

"I'm sorry, Charlie. I just know both of you very well, and I think you might be oblivious to how obvious your feelings for each other are to the rest of us."

Charlie blushed.

"Fine. She punched me. Then, she pushed me off her porch, and I fell in the mud. BUT AFTER ALL THAT, SHE KISSED ME!"

Charlie could hear Sydney and his grandfather laughing through the intercom.

"It was a nice moment, guys. You had to be there."

Charlie was about to continue his self-defense when he heard loud squeaking noises coming through the room's hidden speakers. It also sounded like his grandfather was exerting himself tremendously.

"What the hell are you two doing?" Charlie asked tentatively.

"Almost there," Morris mumbled to himself. "I just need to suck in a little bit. A little bit more. And…… done!"

A moment later, the elevator descended into the room. Charlie walked over to meet Sydney and his grandfather so they could tell him about the plan they came up with while he was gone. Before anyone had a chance to say anything, though, Morris stepped out of the elevator in the ugliest magenta suit that existed anywhere in the universe. Charlie immediately burst into uncontrollable laughter that left him barely able to breathe.

"Oh my God! Grandpa, what in the world is that?!"

"This, Charles, is my best latex rubber suit. I have had this outfit since the late '80s, and it still fits perfectly."

"You say that like it explains why you are wearing it," Charlie teased.

Morris attempted to maintain his usual posture and sophisticated swagger, but the suit's tightness and restrictive material made normal movements impossible, and the more the old man tried to conduct himself with dignity, the more Charlie burst out laughing, to the point where he collapsed on the floor.

Morris hovered over his grandson.

"Oh, fine. Die of laughter and forget about saving the world."

Charlie composed himself a little bit after the rebuke.

"Okay. You're right," Charlie said with a grin. "It's not that bad, but why are you wearing a rubber suit at all?"

Morris Weston, always the gentleman, ignored his grandson's childish demeanor and retorted with confidence, "We don't all possess the Song of Storms, Charles. Your new ability will provide you some protection from the lightning produced by the Thunderbird, but I will be completely exposed."

"The suit will help to deflect any direct hits," added Sydney. "I had no say in the color choice. I didn't even know they made rubber in magenta."

Now, Charlie felt bad about laughing. He hadn't considered that the suit could save his grandfather's life or that the Song of Storms would help protect him from any major damage.

"Sorry, Grandpa. I didn't mean to laugh."

"Function over fashion, Charles," Morris replied. "Not everything is always as it seems."

Charlie looked down at his shoes, and Morris immediately softened at the sight of his sorrowful grandson.

"Truth be told," Morris said casually, "I hate the color."

With that, all three men laughed, and their spirits immediately improved.

"So, how are we going to find the Thunderbird?" Charlie asked.

After a generous swallow of his freshly poured drink, Morris replied, "Why don't you ask Sydney? He's the one who figured out where we need to go."

"Finding the Thunderbird is the easy part," Sydney said happily. "The storm has grown large enough to have an epicenter, and according to the weather maps, that epicenter is located in the Appalachian Mountains. I have precise coordinates. I would be willing to bet that when we get close enough, the Thunderbird will reveal itself to us."

Charlie rolled his eyes.

"Yeah, like the Thunderbird is just going to roll out the welcome mat and say, 'Here I am. Come defeat me.'"

"Defeat him?" Morris asked with surprise. "Charles, you are looking at this all wrong. I will be the first to admit that there is something strange happening. Thunderbirds don't randomly wake up from a sleep that has lasted centuries. Something or someone has been the engineer of everything that has happened, but the Thunderbird is not our enemy. It is a powerful, beautiful creature that is being used for a malicious purpose. Our job is to put the great bird back to sleep, not to "defeat" it."

Charlie hadn't thought of it that way. He had been so caught up in the idea of being some kind of hero and needing to save the world that he had begun seeing the Thunderbird as a villain.

"You're right, Grandpa. I was being stupid. I'm sorry."

Morris smiled compassionately and labored over to his grandson.

"There's no need to apologize, my boy. I understand. Believe me. There are powers at work here that even I don't fully comprehend. You just started your education in this new world, and already you're being asked to save it. It's a lot to take on. You will make mistakes. I will make mistakes. We will learn from them together and try harder the next time. Just never lose sight of one thing. This world will continue to go on with or without us. Morris Weston, Jillian Everett, Charlie Everett; we, and many others fight to make sure that when our time has passed, the world will be a little better from what we did and what we tried to do."

Charlie absorbed his grandfather's important message and nodded with new understanding just as a loud thunderclap interrupted the somewhat serious moment and brought the group back to the task at hand.

"So, how are we going to get to the mountains?" Charlie asked. "Cain was barely able to get me back here from my house."

To Charlie's surprise, his grandfather wordlessly handed him a broom.

"Oh my God! Are you serious?!" Charlie exclaimed as he straddled the broomstick. "I knew it!"

Now, it was Morris and Sydney's turn to laugh hysterically.

Between gasps, the old man shouted, "You should see the look on your face, Charles. You look ready to clean the kitchen, not save the world."

"I told you he would believe it, Morris!" Sydney added. "I told you!"

Charlie was not amused.

"Apparently, I still have a few things to learn," Charlie responded between clenched teeth.

"Apparently, you have learned nothing," Morris retorted. The old man laughed again, but he apologetically added, "I'm sorry, my boy. We simply couldn't resist."

Charlie laughed along with them, but he knew he would never be able to look at a broom again without feeling embarrassed.

"Okay, so if we aren't flying there, then how are we going to make it to the mountains?" Charlie asked again.

"Oh, we're still flying, Charles. I think you will find that Cain has more talents than you give him credit for."

28

Charlie stared out at the helicopter from inside the plane hangar, and he wondered exactly how rich his grandfather was. The main parts of Weston Manor were impressive in their own right, but there seemed to be some new vehicle or structure or wing of the property that Charlie had never seen before every time he went there.

"It's an old army helicopter."

Charlie turned to see Cain approaching him. He hadn't gotten a good look at Cain when they were together in the car, but now he could see that the man was much more formidable than he had initially thought. While Cain wasn't particularly tall, probably a little over six feet, he was very filled out and muscular, making him look larger than he really was. He had dark black hair with a few streaks of gray and stubble on his face that he kept well-groomed to look neat but also like he wasn't trying. Charlie could see, though, that nothing about Cain's look or presentation was by accident. He had a distinct walk, smile, and manner of speaking. He was a man who didn't need to brag about what he could do because his mannerisms and his personality did all the talking.

"It's really cool," Charlie replied when Cain was standing next to him.

"Your grandfather has a good eye for resources that can help him. He is always on auction sites looking for deals. Of course, he makes a lot of trades too. Still, he has always been fond of saying that talent can make you rich, but intelligence will keep you rich."

Charlie nodded. That was definitely something his grandfather would say.

"So, everything here is second-hand or traded?"

"Don't get me wrong, Charlie. Your grandfather has a fortune, and he has spent his fair share on more than a few toys, but he makes it a point to indulge himself as little as possible. Most of what he acquires has a purpose, something that helps him get the job done. You know what I mean?"

Charlie knew exactly what he meant but wasn't sure what to say because he had no idea how much Cain knew about what was really going on in the world. Charlie barely understood it himself and certainly didn't want to be the one to let it slip that a Thunderbird was the reason why the world was ending.

Cain sensed Charlie's hesitation and added, "I know, Charlie. About everything."

"Okay?" Charlie asked hesitantly. "But how can I know you know? Maybe you think you know, but you really have no idea."

Cain gestured outward with his arms. "Look at all of this, Charlie. This place is huge. Have you ever met anyone here besides me?"

Charlie shook his head.

"So, how do you think this place is maintained? There are no servants or butlers or maids or stable keepers or anything like that. I certainly don't spend my time shoveling unicorn shit. The whole place is run through magic."

Charlie thought for a minute and realized that Cain was right. He had never seen or even heard of anyone else setting foot on the grounds.

"But Grandpa said there are no magical people, just magical things."

"That's true, and there is a nifty little treasure locked up in his vault called the Orb of Order. The owner of the orb speaks a task into the magic eight-ball, and the orb takes care of the rest. Your grandfather is smart enough to know that he can't have dozens of people walking around this place. So, he set the orb to running and maintaining the manor so he could focus all of his energy on protecting the world's mythical creatures and training you to do the same."

Before Charlie had a chance to respond, Morris approached his companions slowly and steadily in his magenta rubber suit.

"Looking good, Morris," Cain said sarcastically.

Charlie was about to interject on his grandfather's behalf, but Morris chuckled and replied, "I'm glad you like it. Yours will be ready for our next adventure."

"No thanks, Morris. I think I'd rather die from a direct hit by a lightning bolt than from the embarrassment of wearing that thing."

Charlie watched the two men continue to banter back and forth. There was no formality or hierarchy between them. Cain wasn't just his grandfather's employee; he was also a close friend who could get away with teasing the old man because there was an unspoken trust between them that had developed over many years. They had probably fought together, maybe even saved each other's lives once or twice. It was becoming clear to Charlie that Cain was not just the driver or the pilot. He was the man his grandfather turned to when there was no magical solution.

"Well, gentlemen. Shall we take off?" Morris asked enthusiastically. "The world certainly isn't going to save itself."

"Ready to go, sir," Cain replied with a mock salute. "Can you make it to the chopper, or should I just roll you out there like an old tire?"

"You'll be wishing you had one when you get struck by lightning."

"Wait a second," Charlie interrupted. "What about Sydney?"

"Ah, yes. Sydney will not be joining us in the helicopter, Charles. He is going to stay here and operate the radio and navigation systems. We will be able to hear him through our headsets once we are inside the chopper. If anything happens, he can send help."

Charlie nodded with slight disappointment. He was hoping that Sydney would come for moral support, but he also understood the need for having a backup team member at the manor in case of an emergency.

Cain ran out into the storm first to start the helicopter. Charlie helped his grandfather out into the driving rain and then into the aircraft. After a few minutes of safety checks, the three men were off to find the lair of the Thunderbird.

Charlie immediately put on his headphones and tried out the communication system.

"Hey, Syd. Are you there?"

"Affirmative," Sydney answered. "I can hear you perfectly. I am uploading the coordinates to the epicenter of the storm in the helicopter's navigation system. The flight should be fairly smooth until you get within a couple of miles of the center of the storm."

"What happens a couple of miles from the center of the storm?" Cain asked hesitantly.

"Well, the intensity of the electromagnetic activity in that area could mess with the navigation system and with the radios. There is a chance we will lose contact at that point, but I don't think it will be a problem. From that distance, you should be able to see the source of the storm, maybe even the Thunderbird itself."

"Great," Charlie said sarcastically. "So, if the Thunderbird comes out and attacks us, I'll just take a picture and text it to you before we die."

"Please do," Sydney replied excitedly. "I mean, take a picture. Try not to die, though."

Cain laughed and yelled into his microphone, "No promises!"

The ride was smooth at first. Charlie could see the landscape outside his window, and there was barely any turbulence. He spent most of the trip talking with Sydney about things they wanted to do when he got back. They pretended like nothing out of the ordinary was going on, and they never even entertained the possibility that Charlie might fail. After about an hour, though, the winds picked up, and the storm intensified significantly. The radio began cutting in and out sporadically, although the worse the storm got, the less anyone had anything to say. Charlie looked down, and all he could see was the damage being caused by the water. Roads were flooded, fields were drowned, and power lines were either down or ineffective as Charlie noticed that not a single light was shining anywhere. There were a few cars on the road, but they weren't moving, and Charlie hoped that they had been abandoned, but he had no way of knowing.

Another thirty minutes later, and all visibility was gone. Cain struggled to keep the helicopter from falling out of the sky, and Charlie was terrified that they would die before he even had a chance to do anything.

Charlie was in the middle of thinking about what he might say in a final text to his dad when Cain pointed abruptly and shouted, "That's gotta be the place."

Charlie looked out the front of the helicopter and saw lightning being shot continuously out of the mouth of a cave. A loud thunderclap accompanied each bolt. There was no doubt that it was the home of the Thunderbird.

"Oh my God!" Charlie yelled into his microphone. "Sydney, we found the spot! It's unbelievable!"

There was no response. Charlie tried yelling a few more times, but it was no use. They had lost communication with Weston Manor.

"Don't worry, Charles," Morris said. "If things get really bad, we have a beacon that can break through the storm. If there's any serious danger, we will send out the emergency signal, and Sydney will be able to find us."

"There's a ledge at the mouth of the cave large enough for the chopper," Cain said as he pointed to his intended landing spot. "I'm going to try and set you…."

BEEP! BEEP! BEEP!

"Warning," a robotic voice said calmly. "Malfunction detected."

A bolt of lightning had grazed the helicopter, threatening to knock the team out of the sky. The aircraft pitched violently, and Cain did his best to steady the controls.

BEEP! BEEP! BEEP!

"Warning. Malfunction detected."

"Strap in, boys!" Cain yelled.

Charlie did his best to tighten his seatbelt but still found himself being bounced around with each attempt to level the flight path.

BEEP! BEEP! BEEP!

"Warning. Malfunction detected."

"Shut the hell up!" Cain shouted at the control panel. "We understand the situation!"

"What if we…" Morris started.

"Not now, Morris! I'm busy trying to save our lives."

BEEP! BEEP! BEEP!

"Warning. Malfunction detected."

"I SAID NOT NOW!" Cain yelled out as he punched the screen of the emergency warning system. "Just one more little adjustment and…"

The helicopter leveled off and hung steadily in the air.

Cain let out a huge sigh of relief and then shouted, "Woo! It's gonna take more than that to knock this bird out of the sky!"

But before the group had a chance to celebrate, a beam of blue-streaking light shot out from the cave. Waves of lightning rippled through the air, and thunder crashed down all around them. A creature of unnatural size moved to the ledge of the cliff at the mouth of the cave and spread its wings to their full, majestic length, far enough to touch both sides of the canyon inside the mountain ridge at once. The Thunderbird let out an ear-piercing screech as it pushed off the ledge and took flight. Charlie's eyes lit up and reflected the blue glow of true, unlimited power.

The Thunderbird wasted no time approaching the intruders, circling them inside a tornado of wind, rain, and electricity. Every few seconds, the bird let out another screech, and the circle it was making around the helicopter grew smaller and smaller as the hunter closed in on its prey.

"Anyone have any bright ideas?" Cain shouted as the Thunderbird continued its measured approach.

 "Does this thing have any weapons?" Charlie asked hopefully.

Cain shook his head. "The only weapon we've got is you!"

"Of course! That's it!" Charlie exclaimed.

Charlie took out the pan flute and began playing the Song of Storms. At first, he couldn't hear the soft melody coming from the instrument, and the legendary bird continued circling the helicopter, snapping its razor-sharp beak at the machine that was just out of reach, but as Charlie continued to play, the music cut through the sounds of the thunder and the wind of the storm. After a few minutes, the great bird ceased its pursuit and hovered in the air in front of the helicopter, giving the trio their first good look at the creature. It was even larger than Charlie had imagined, and he knew without any doubt that it didn't even need to use its magical power to disable or kill them. All it would take was one well-aimed flap of its wings or one quick swipe from its beak, and that would be the end of the adventure for all of them. But the great bird did not attack or make any effort to disable the aircraft. It just hovered in space, glowing with heat and raw energy. Charlie watched the lightning dance around the tips of the Thunderbird's wings, and he saw blue sparks ignite inside its large, watchful eyes. After a few moments of hovering, the Thunderbird shot up into the sky, leaving streaks of lightning in its wake. The whole mountain range boomed with thunder. Finally, it descended into its cave, and the light slowly dimmed as it moved deeper and deeper into the mountain.

The three men sat in stunned silence as the final streaks of lightning came shooting out of the cave from the tips of the Thunderbird's tail feathers. Charlie looked over and saw that his grandfather was crying.

"Grandpa, are you okay?"

"In all my years, I have never seen anything so beautiful," Morris responded as he dabbed at his eyes with his kerchief.

"Yeah, simply gorgeous," Cain replied sarcastically. "But hey, no one gets you closer to the action than this guy! Am I right?! Or am I right?!"

Before anyone had a chance to answer, the helicopter shook violently again, and a bright light filled the cabin of the vehicle as a stray lightning bolt nailed the chopper with a direct hit.

BEEP! BEEP! BEEP!

"Warning. Malfunction detected," the robotic voice intoned again, this time sounding more demonic due to Cain's assault during their first life-threatening emergency.

"Oh, what now?!" Cain groaned, but before he got a chance to do anything, all the electronics inside the machine shut down, and the helicopter started falling out of the sky.

As the men plummeted to their inevitable death, Cain continued to play with the controls, and Morris sat perfectly still with his eyes closed and his lips moving rapidly, possibly reciting a final prayer. Then, from inside his latex suit, the old man pulled out a large feather, and a tattoo of a pair of wings suddenly appeared on his neck.

Charlie leaned forward in his seat to get a closer look at the magic mark when he realized that the helicopter should have already crashed, but it hadn't. Looking out his window, Charlie saw that, while they were still losing altitude, the aircraft was navigating itself slowly towards a clearing that was just big enough for the helicopter to fit comfortably. After a few minutes of careful descent, the giant machine came to rest softly on the grass.

"That was amazing! Grandpa, you saved our lives."

Charlie leaned forward and grabbed his grandfather by the shoulder, but Morris was completely limp and lifeless.

Hot tears immediately began streaming down Charlie's face as grief threatened to consume all reason, but before Charlie completely broke down from imagining the worst, Morris managed to turn his head slightly and whisper, "Don't worry, Charles. I will be fine. That was just a particularly difficult spell."

Charlie let out several heavy breaths and did his best to swallow the lump in his throat.

"You have to teach me how you did that," Charlie said as he wiped the tears from his cheeks.

Morris nodded and put his hand on his grandson's arm to reassure him.

"I think I can get this baby working again," Cain said, breaking the silence. "But your grandfather is in no condition to get up to that cave. So you're going to have to go alone, Charlie. Think you can handle it?"

"What do you mean?" Charlie asked with dread. "I already played the flute before we got hit. The Thunderbird went back into its cave. Aren't we done here?"

"Sorry, kid, but I'm sure you've noticed that it's still Armageddon weather conditions out here," Cain said as he gestured to the dark storm clouds overhead. "If I had to guess, I'd say proximity matters, which means you're probably going to have to be standing right in front of that thing when you use the spell to give it the full whammy."

"He's right, Charles," Morris added breathlessly. "Only playing the Song of Storms directly in front of the Thunderbird will end this."

Charlie froze up thinking about how he had almost died again. It was his first time in the field, and he had been inches from death twice already that day.

Cain unbuckled his safety harness and turned to face Charlie directly.

"Hey, if you get scared, just think about that girl who knocked you on your backside. Save the world, get the girl."

Even though Charlie knew what Cain was doing, it still worked.

"You're right. No guts, no glory."

Charlie cast a worried glance toward his grandfather, who looked to be trying to regain his strength.

"Don't worry, Charlie. I won't let anything happen to him. You just worry about yourself. We'll be ready to take off when you get back. If I can't get this bird back in the sky, we'll use the beacon, and your boy will send us some help."

Charlie hugged his grandfather and prepared to exit the helicopter, but just as he put his hand on the door, Cain pulled him back.

"Hold up a second. Take this," Cain said as he put a long, black cylinder into Charlie's hand.

"Is this some kind of magical weapon?" Charlie asked hopefully as he studied the object.

Cain sighed.

"It's a flashlight, Charlie." He reached out and pushed the button on the side that made the light turn on.

Charlie felt his face turn red.

"Not exactly a smooth start."

"Don't worry. I'll chalk that one up to nerves."

Charlie graciously nodded and ventured out into the storm. Each drop of rain that made contact with his skin felt like someone pinching him because of how hard and fast it was falling. He wondered if he might end up with bruises from the impact.

Luckily, Morris' spell had managed to get the helicopter relatively close to the mouth of the Thunderbird's cave, so Charlie wouldn't have to do any serious rock climbing. Still, the ground was wet enough, and the slope was steep enough that he couldn't afford to stop paying attention to each step he took. After a few minutes of walking through the woods in the general direction of the cave, Charlie noticed a small trail breaking off to one side. As far as he could tell, the new path went straight up and might not provide him with access to the Thunderbird's lair. The trail Charlie had been following was relatively flat and steady, but he guessed that continuing in that direction would put him several hundred feet below the cave entrance. He decided to gamble and turned up the inclined path. As he walked, he half expected the trail to disappear and leave him stranded somewhere in the woods, but luckily that never happened as the trail widened and became easier to follow. As Charlie continued to climb upward, the forest became less dense, and he could see that he had made a good decision because the road was winding back in the direction he needed to go.

By the time Charlie reached the peak where the cave was located, he was out of breath. He paused for a few moments and looked around. He could see everything for miles. Despite the storm, the view was breathtaking. Charlie couldn't believe he had climbed so high, but somehow, he had done it.

As he worked his way around the mountain to the mouth of the cave, the trail narrowed significantly. There was enough room for Charlie to walk straight but not much width beyond that. One wrong step would mean falling over the side, and the wind was strong enough to push him right off the cliff. Charlie was not interested in taking any chances, so he turned his body and clung to the side of the mountain as he sidestepped toward the cave entrance.

When Charlie reached the ledge just outside the mouth of the cave, everything was dark and quiet. He tried to peer inside, not sure what to expect. Unfortunately, he couldn't see anything, so he pulled out the flashlight Cain had given him and clicked it on. Slowly, Charlie made his way into the darkness. He couldn't believe how quiet it was, hearing only the sounds of the rain outside as he moved deeper and deeper into the cave. Eventually, Charlie had gone deep enough that he couldn't see the light from outside anymore. His heart raced, and he wrestled with the idea of turning back.

"I'm just a kid," Charlie thought. "If anyone should be doing this, it should be a guy like Cain. I've had almost no training, and I only know one spell that might not even protect me! Even if it does protect me from magic, nothing will stop this bird from just killing and eating me the old-fashioned way. What the hell am I doing here?!"

Before Charlie even had a chance to wrestle with his fears, the Thunderbird let out an ear-splitting scream and began to glow with intensity. Suddenly, the whole cave was illuminated with the same white light that had overwhelmed Charlie in the world between life and death, but because his eyes had already adjusted to that painful sensation, he found that he had no difficulty seeing straight through to the legendary creature. And just as Charlie saw the Thunderbird, the mythical animal opened its glowing blue eyes and saw Charlie.

29

For a moment, all Charlie could do was stare in terrified wonder. Cowering in the bright and powerful glow of the great bird, he had been reduced to exactly what he was, a scared child. Charlie wondered if he had ever felt anything besides fear because he certainly couldn't remember a time when his heart was filled with any other feeling. The legendary creature completely and utterly dominated his mind and all of his senses. Charlie vaguely recalled that he was there to do something, but he couldn't remember what it was. The only thought he could form clearly was to run away but running meant moving, and he couldn't even blink, let alone get his legs to work.

"Ow! What the hell was that?" Charlie yelled out.

A sharp needle had pinched his skin, and Charlie reflexively grabbed at his arm. A moment later, another needle jabbed him, and then another and another. Charlie recoiled from the stings. Every few seconds, he felt sharp pain somewhere on his body, but he couldn't figure out where the sensation was coming from. At first, he thought maybe a swarm of insects from the cave was attacking him, but that was impossible. His skin was completely covered. No bug would be able to penetrate his rain jacket and his clothes, but the pain was undeniable.

Charlie decided to roll up his sleeve and inspect one of the areas where he thought he would find a wound, but there wasn't one. Instead, he discovered his magical tattoo, and it was glowing. Each time he experienced a painful sensation, the tattoo on his arm pulsed in reaction. Then, he realized a bug in the cave wasn't stinging him; tiny sparks of electricity coming off the Thunderbird were striking him. Charlie also noticed that each time he was hit, the pain intensified. The Song of Storms was not going to protect him forever.

Charlie quickly reached for the pan flute in his messenger bag. The moment the flute touched his fingers, he felt something like a sledgehammer strike him square in the chest. It was a direct hit from a lightning bolt, and it didn't come off the Thunderbird by accident. The bird had fired that electric missile intentionally to either disable or kill him. Luckily, the Song of Storms protected him enough so that the strike was not fatal, but the force of the blow brought Charlie to his knees and knocked the wind out of him.

Charlie coughed and struggled to his feet.

"That's nice. Thanks for that!" Charlie yelled. "I'm trying to help you!"

Charlie reached for the flute again, and this time he was able to get it out of his bag despite a few more shocks to his torso. Unfortunately, it had become apparent that the Thunderbird was not interested in making this any easier. Still, the repeated shocks were helping Charlie replace his fear with anger, and his anger allowed him to act instead of standing helpless.

"I guess maybe you are helping me," he mused. "Just don't help me so much that I die. Okay?"

Charlie held the pan flute in both hands and stared down at it, wondering if it was glowing with its own magic or just reflecting the power of the Thunderbird. He worried for a moment that his nervousness would keep him from remembering how to play the Song of Storms before he realized he had never played an instrument of any kind before doing it perfectly on his grandfather's roof while being struck by lightning. Besides, the flute wasn't really a musical instrument, and the Song of Storms wasn't really a song. They were magical tools, but like any tool, they were useless without someone to wield them.

Charlie raised the flute to his lips, but as he did, another spark hit him directly on the hand.

"OUCH! COME ON! That really hurt! I can't even feel my hand now!"

Charlie nursed his hand for a few seconds before realizing that the flute was not resting at his feet. He scanned the floor of the cave frantically, and when he saw where the pan flute had landed, his heart sank. The salvation of the world, the one thing that could end the storm, was resting just below the beak of the Thunderbird.

Until then, Charlie had wisely kept a safe distance from the Thunderbird, but with the flute well out of reach, safe distance was no longer an option.

"I can't beat you, okay?" Charlie yelled out in frustration. "I'm not a Cryptozoologist or a great mage. I only have one spell, and you won't let me use it! I'm not a hero! I'm just Charlie."

The final words hung in the air and echoed throughout the cave. "I'm just Charlie," repeated over and over again until they triggered a memory in his mind.

"No matter what you learn or how many magic tattoos you get, you already have what it takes to save the day."

Those were the words of encouragement Charlie's dad had given him. They were his shield against self-doubt and fear. Patrick knew that his son hadn't had much training and how difficult and dangerous his task would be, but still, he believed that Charlie was capable of getting the job done.

Charlie stood and faced the Thunderbird again. Either he stepped up right then and there, or no one would.

"Hey! I'm not dead yet! Let's finish this!"

The words came out strong and confident. The Thunderbird threw its head back and let out a piercing scream in response. Charlie saw his opportunity and ran directly into the lightning storm towards the great bird. With each step, bolts of power shot out from the creature's massive wings. The electric missiles flew past Charlie, glancing off his body, narrowly missing a direct hit that would stop him in his tracks. The bird continued to cry out, and Charlie could feel sparks bouncing painfully off his skin, but he didn't care. There was no stopping now. As he moved within striking distance, the Thunderbird lifted its enormous leg and swiped with one of its razor-sharp talons. Charlie saw the bird shift its weight, so he anticipated the move and was able to sidestep most of the blow, but he didn't move quickly enough, and the tip of the talon scraped him down his left shoulder. Charlie screamed in agony, but he didn't dare stop and inspect the gash even though he could already feel the blood running down his back.

Charlie's eyes remained focused on the goal, and nothing was going to stop him. As he bent down and reached for the flute, the Thunderbird lowered its head and opened its massive beak. Charlie had counted on the bird snapping at him when he got close enough, and he knew exactly what he needed to do to avoid the attack, but he really didn't want to do it. Unfortunately, there was no time to half-measures, so he lunged forward, sliding his stomach across the rocky cave floor just underneath the strike of the bird's beak. Charlie could feel the loose rocks scraping his skin and opening cuts all over his torso. As he slid within reach of his target, Charlie grabbed the magical flute with one hand, and with the other, he pushed himself up off the ground and slammed into the wall on the other side of the cave.

Without hesitation, Charlie put the flute to his lips and began to play. Luckily, he had been right about the song being a magical tool that he was capable of wielding at any time. The spell flowed through him and the flute effortlessly, and the bittersweet melody was as perfect as though Charlie had played it a thousand times before. The great bird turned its head towards the magical lullaby and reared back to strike the final, decisive blow. Charlie closed his eyes in anticipation of the attack, but he stood firm and continued to play the melody in the face of certain death.

The Thunderbird lunged forward with all its power, but to Charlie's great surprise and relief, the creature froze just inches from his face. Too afraid to stop playing, Charlie continued the spell and watched as the blinding glow in the cave gradually began to dim. The bird remained in its attack position, and Charlie could feel the hot breath of the mythical beast on his face, but the sparks coming from the Thunderbird's body were getting smaller and shooting off less frequently.

The cave was too small and narrow for the massive bird to stretch out completely, but that didn't stop it from spreading its wings out as far out as they could go, pressing them firmly against the cave walls. Then, the Thunderbird settled on the floor and put its head down in a peaceful, submissive position. The glow from the creature's body was almost completely gone, and the only light left was from the blue sparks still flashing in the bird's eyes. Charlie met its gaze for the last time as he played the final few notes of the Song of Storms. Finally, the Thunderbird closed its eyes and fell asleep.

Beams of light immediately began to shoot into the cave from small holes in the walls. The storm had stopped, and the sun was shining bright in the afternoon sky. Water continued to drip from the ceiling, but Charlie knew that the rain was finished. The sun would do its work, and the world would dry out. There was no telling how much damage had been caused by the Thunderbird, but at least now, there would be an opportunity to fix whatever had been broken.

"I did it," Charlie said softly to himself. He tried to jump for joy but found that every part of his body hurt. His clothes were spattered with blood, and his shoulder was significantly gashed. He raised his shirt to find bits of rock embedded in his torso. Charlie also found several bruises on his arms and legs. He had no idea how he would be able to make his way back down to his grandfather in this condition, but he knew that his wounds were a small price to pay, considering that death was the alternative.

Charlie turned and faced the sleeping Thunderbird. For the first time, he looked at the legendary creature entirely without fear or anger. It was magnificent. Charlie tried to remember what the great bird looked like as it flew through the air. He imagined himself riding it but quickly shook off the notion. This beast would never be tamed. No one could ever ride it. No one ever should.

"Grandpa was right. You're not the bad guy," Charlie said tenderly to the sleeping legend.

He gently placed his hand on the bird's large head and felt the most incredible sensation of his life. Even while sleeping, the Thunderbird radiated energy, and it surged through Charlie's body. Unlike the hit he had taken from the lightning bolt, this power lifted him up instead of knocking him down. Instead of stealing his air, it breathed life into him.

Then, Charlie felt a strange, warm feeling in his chest under the skin. He lifted his shirt and found that his wounds were healing right before his eyes. The blood evaporated from his body. The cuts mended themselves, and the skin that had been scraped away was replaced. Even the bruises on Charlie's arms and legs disappeared. Somehow, the Thunderbird's energy was passing through him like an electric current and healing him. Charlie didn't know how it was happening, but he really didn't care.

The one injury that would not heal was the gash on his shoulder. Charlie touched the remaining wound and winced in pain, but then he began to laugh. One bad shoulder was nothing compared to the pain he had felt a few moments earlier. He would have no trouble making it back to the helicopter now.

After a few moments of rest next to the Thunderbird, Charlie decided it was time to leave and find Cain and his grandfather. He couldn't wait to tell them what had happened, and he started thinking about everything he was going to say when he heard something move behind him. Charlie turned around quickly but saw nothing except the sleeping bird.

"Hello? Grandpa?" Charlie called out.

There was no answer.

Charlie tried not to panic as he backed away from the Thunderbird and towards the mouth of the cave, but he kept hearing noises all around him, and the echoes from the cave made it impossible to know where the sounds were coming from.

Charlie meekly called out again, "Cain? I did it. I'll meet you back down at the helicopter."

Still, no one answered, and Charlie's heart raced with fear. Something or someone was definitely getting closer. Charlie grabbed the flashlight from his bag and pointed the beam down into the cavern. He could see shadows dancing on the walls from something moving toward him. Without thinking, he dropped the flashlight and turned to run out of the cave, but before he could make his move, a sharp blow landed on his head, knocking him to the ground.

Charlie lay on the cave floor as he struggled to steady his vision, fighting against the darkness trying to overtake him. With a final effort, Charlie looked up just in time to see the Red Wizard pick something up off the ground and run out of the cave.

"Wait. Come back," Charlie said weakly, but he was unable to remain conscious.

The whole world went black, and Charlie passed out under the enormous wings of the Thunderbird.

30

Pain was the first thing Charlie felt as he began to regain consciousness. His head and shoulder both throbbed, and he wondered if he might be bleeding but couldn't bring himself to touch his head and find out. Luckily, the assault had not woken the Thunderbird, as Charlie could hear it breathing heavily beside him.

"This doesn't make any sense," Charlie thought. "Why would the red mage save me from the Moirai and then attack me after I put the Thunderbird to sleep?"

After a few minutes of motionless reflection, Charlie finally dared to open his eyes. The light shining into the cave seemed incredibly bright, but he was glad to be seeing anything at all. He turned his head toward the mythical creature lying beside him.

"Apparently, it takes more than a little tussle to wake you up, big guy," Charlie said to the sleeping bird. "How did you wake up in the first place? Better question. Who woke you up? Wait. Best question. Why did someone wake you up?"

Charlie stood and dusted himself off with his uninjured arm. The left one was completely useless after the gash the Thunderbird's talon had given him. As Charlie picked up his bag, he quickly glanced inside and saw that Pan's flute was missing. Figuring that it had fallen out when he was attacked, Charlie grabbed Cain's flashlight and began to look around.

"Please tell me the flute isn't under this bird!"

Charlie looked over at the sleeping animal, took a deep breath, and began lifting up massive feathers in search of the magical instrument. The energy that flowed from the creature was exhilarating, and it made Charlie's head feel a little bit better. Unfortunately, there was no sign of the flute anywhere.

"He stole it," Charlie said to himself. "That jerk stole the flute!"

Charlie closed his eyes and felt the anger well up inside him. He no longer cared about being cautious, and he screamed out in frustration. The magic flute, literally the priceless and irreplaceable prized possession of a Greek God, was gone. Charlie didn't know how he could go back to his grandfather without it. He spent the next few minutes looking for a clue about the Elemental, anything that might reveal the mage's identity or location, but it was no use. The Red Wizard could hold fire in his hand, he could travel to the world between life and death, and he was strong enough to defeat the Moirai. A wizard that powerful knew what he was doing and wasn't about to leave clues behind that would unravel whatever plan he was carrying out. Charlie had to accept that he had been beaten, and the first point of whatever game he was playing had gone to his enemy.

Charlie gave the Thunderbird one final stroke on the head. The powerful sensation of pure energy made him smile and forget his sadness for a moment.

"Don't worry. No one is going to bother you anymore. I promise."

Then, Charlie turned toward the mouth of the cave and began to make his way out. As he descended back down the mountain in the direction of the helicopter, he tried to think about what he would say to his grandfather. Charlie thought about apologizing profusely or possibly making excuses and blaming everything on the traitorous Elemental in the hope that his grandfather's anger could be redirected toward their common enemy.

"I just have to tell him the truth," he decided. "Maybe it won't be so bad. I mean, he probably won't trust me with his stuff for a while, but who could blame him?"

The journey back to the clearing seemed to take twice as long as the journey to the cave of the Thunderbird. Both trips filled Charlie with fear and a sense of dread but for very different reasons. Charlie wasn't sure which was worse. Physical danger was one thing but disappointing his grandfather was emotional pain. It hurt his heart and made him afraid that all of his training was going to come to an abrupt end. Even worse, Charlie worried that his mistake would be the end of spending time with one of the most important people in his life. It might even mean the end of the search for his mother.

When Charlie finally spotted the clearing, he paused. He still wasn't sure what he was going to say, but just like in the cave, he knew that something had to be done, and he was the only one who could do it, so he took a deep breath and approached.

"Charles, you did it!" Morris shouted when he saw his grandson. "I knew you could!"

Morris looked like he had completely recovered from his exhaustion. In fact, he looked younger than ever as he twirled around the clearing in celebration.

"Piece of cake, huh?" Cain said as he emerged from the pilot's side of the helicopter. "You took your sweet time getting back here though. Probably had more trouble finding us than putting that thing back to sleep. Am I right?"

Cain made his way over to Charlie and slapped him on the back, making the young man fall to his knees in pain. Morris moved quickly to his grandson's side and helped the boy steady himself.

"What happened up there, Charles?" Morris asked.

Charlie still wasn't sure what to say, so instead, he removed his rain jacket and showed the men his shoulder wound. Cain jogged to the helicopter and was back moments later with a first aid kit.

"Sorry about that slap on the back, pal. I had no idea you were injured."

"It's fine," Charlie responded unconvincingly. "It looks worse than it is."

Cain recognized the tough guy act and paid Charlie the courtesy of going along with it.

"Well, I'm going to stitch you up so the arm doesn't fall off, and when we get home, I'm sure your grandfather has some kind of magic first aid kit to speed things along. Another bit of good news, we got your friend Sydney back. He's been talking us through some repairs from the headset. He said to tell you congratulations and that he has a surprise for us when we get back to the house."

Charlie nodded his head and looked down at the ground.

Morris knelt in front of his grandson and attempted to meet his gaze.

"I'm sorry for what happened to you, Charles," Morris said softly. "It's not fair to ask a young man to do this job. Nothing that's happened to you is fair, but you've done it, my boy! You've saved us all!"

Charlie couldn't accept his grandfather's praise. It was all too much. He was exhausted and had given everything he could, including his life, and still, he had managed to fail. He didn't deserve adulation because he had been tricked into doing exactly what the Red Wizard wanted. He was a fraud. With that final thought, Charlie couldn't hold back the truth any longer.

"I lost the flute, Grandpa," Charlie yelled out more aggressively than he intended. "I'm so sorry. I was in the cave, and the Thunderbird knocked it out of my hand, so I had to charge at it, and it scratched me in the shoulder because I couldn't move out the way quickly enough, and then I slid under its mouth and scratched my stomach to get to where the flute was. I got it back and played until the Thunderbird fell asleep, but the stupid fire mage knocked me out, and when I woke up, he was gone, and so was the flute. And… I'm sorry."

Now sobbing, Charlie raised his head to face his grandfather. To his surprise, he did not see anger in Morris's face. Instead, he saw pain and sadness and tears streaming down his grandfather's cheeks.

"You did all that?" Morris asked in stunned disbelief. "I can't believe you… I don't know how you… You are my hero."

"But what about the flute?" Charlie asked despondently.

Morris threw his arms around his grandson and held him tight.

"I don't give a damn about the flute. I only care that you're safe."

With those words, an indescribable wave of relief washed over Charlie. He buried his head into his grandfather's shoulder and wept. Everything Charlie had been holding inside, his fears, his doubts, they were all coming out.

Charlie wasn't sure how long he cried, but he felt like a different person when he finished.

"Are you gonna sew me up or not?" Charlie called to Cain as he wiped the remaining tears from his eyes. "I'm ready to get out of here."

"Right away, boss," Cain answered with mock seriousness as he pulled out his first aid kit and began working on Charlie's shoulder. He also handed Charlie an ice pack for the bump on his head, which Charlie accepted gratefully. Once Charlie was well enough, the three men climbed back into the repaired helicopter and prepared for the flight home.

"How did you get it working again?" Charlie asked.

"I've got my own magic, kid," Cain answered with a mischievous grin.

Charlie pulled on his headset and was immediately greeted by a friendly voice.

"You saved the world, Charlie. You're a real-life Ultra-Man," Sydney exclaimed.

"Not Ultra-Man. Just me. Charlie Weston."

"Either way, I never doubted you for a minute. When you get back, I have some pretty cool stuff to show you guys."

"That's great, Syd. Can't wait, but for now, I'm just going to relax for a bit. We'll see you soon."

Charlie found himself looking down at the world once again, but this time the landscape looked completely different. There was still a lot of water on the ground, but the sun was shining. Charlie could see animals outside, and even a few people were venturing out of their homes. It would take a long time to fix everything that had been damaged, but the world wasn't going to end anymore.

"The Red Wizard woke up the Thunderbird," Charlie said to his grandfather. "He's the one that made all this happen."

"You might be right, Charles," Morris answered thoughtfully. "What is clear is that there is more going on here than we thought. If this 'Red Wizard' was so intent on getting the flute, why risk the Song of Storms killing you or the Moirai trapping you? Why involve you at all? You have been dreaming about this person for quite some time, and I don't believe that is a coincidence. All I know for certain is that we must be cautious, especially where this Elemental is concerned, until we know more about who he is and what he wants."

Charlie nodded in agreement and turned back to the window.

After a few hours of flight, Weston Manor appeared in the distance. As the helicopter touched down, Charlie saw his father and Zag waiting for them. When the blades stopped spinning, Charlie climbed over Cain's lap, not even waiting for him to exit the aircraft, and ran to his dad. Before he could make it, though, Zag intercepted him and tackled her master to the ground. The tongue bath was brutally wet, but Charlie didn't mind.

"Zag! I was stupid to leave you at home, girl! Next time, you're coming!"

Charlie's father pulled the giant dog off his son and helped him to his feet. He noticed Charlie wince with pain and honed in on the injured shoulder.

"Oh my God! Charlie! We have to get you to the hospital."

"I'm okay, Dad. Besides, there is better medicine for me here than any hospital."

"I guess that's true," Patrick replied as he inspected the wound. "It looks pretty bad, though."

"It's not as bad as it looks, right, kid?" Cain said with a wink as he walked past.

"Nope. Just a scratch," Charlie agreed as they all made their way inside.

Once inside the parlor, Patrick and Morris began talking about everything that had happened. Charlie happily sat back and listened to his grandfather tell the tale of their flight to the Thunderbird's cave, Cain's amazing flying, and the use of the spell that had saved their lives after taking a direct hit from a stray lightning bolt.

When his grandfather got to the part where Charlie went out on his own to face the Thunderbird, Patrick turned to his son and asked, "What happened next, Charlie?"

Charlie's face grew serious, completely changing the tone of the story and the room's mood.

"Dad, the Thunderbird won. It beat me. It had taken my only weapon, and I was lost with nothing to do and nowhere to go."

"But Charlie," Patrick started to say, but Charlie continued.

"I was running out of the magic that was keeping me alive. There was no way for me to succeed, but I also knew I couldn't leave. So, I closed my eyes, and I thought about everyone who loved me. I thought about what I would be losing if I gave up. Then, I remembered what you told me about being brave and believing in myself. In the end, it was what you said that gave me the courage to do what needed to be done. Thank you for believing in me. Thank you for helping me believe in myself."

No one spoke or moved. Having said what he needed to say, Charlie relaxed back on the couch. He was tired. His shoulder hurt, his head ached, and his heart felt heavy. He didn't want to be Charlie Weston anymore. Not for a while, anyway. For now, he just wanted to be Charlie Everett again, a regular kid with a normal family and no obligation to save the world. It was a beautiful dream, a vacation for his mind, but he knew it wouldn't last. He had a destiny, and the world might need Charlie Weston again someday. At the very least, his mother needed him, and it would take everyone in the room to find her and bring her home safely. None of them would truly be done until they got her back.

"Charlie," a voice said softly from somewhere in the room.

The sound of his name snapped Charlie out of his trance. He looked up and saw that his dad had been calling to him.

"I never doubted you," Patrick said. "I knew you would find a way to save us, and you did, but I also know that you're just a kid, and you have limits. The reason why you felt like I was with you in that cave is that I was. I'm always with you. We all are. I'm excited for you and what you've learned. I'm proud of you for what you've done, but I've always been proud of you, and I always will be, whether you continue to pursue this or not. I guess what I'm saying is, it is not solely your job to save the world, and it's certainly not your responsibility to bring Mom home on your own."

Everyone in the room nodded in agreement. For Charlie, just knowing that he could admit to them when he was overwhelmed and needed a break was enough to give him the strength and conviction to keep going.

"I just need the world to not be in danger for a few weeks so my shoulder can heal."

Everyone laughed. It was a real laugh, a comforting laugh that let everyone know that Charlie would be okay.

At that moment, Sydney entered the parlor triumphantly with a big smile on his face.

"As much as I'm sure Patrick enjoyed everyone's description of today's events, I think he might like to see what happened with his own eyes," Sydney boasted.

Cain sat up in his chair. "What's that now? We lost contact with you before the real fun even started."

Sydney began connecting a laptop to a large television monitor and continued, "While it is true that you lost contact with me, I did not lose contact with you. I was still able to hear, and more importantly, see, everything that you were seeing."

"That's impossible," Morris claimed. "My helicopter isn't equipped with that kind of technology."

"It wasn't when the day started," Sydney responded playfully. "But I took the liberty of making some upgrades before you took off."

Then, Sydney pressed a button on the computer, and the recorded stream began to play on the monitor. The entire group watched as the Thunderbird shot out from the cave and began circling the helicopter.

As they watched the replay of the day's events, Sydney stated, "This video will help us study many different aspects of the Thunderbird. I have several programs running that are analyzing the weather patterns that were created, the bird's flight patterns, and the physiology of the creature. All of this data will help us understand how we can protect the Thunderbird better going forward. I was even able to place a GPS tag on the cave, so we will know if there is any new activity happening before we get to another world-ending scenario."

Morris could barely contain his excitement. "Sydney, my boy, this is the most impressive work I have seen in my field in many years. I can't thank you enough for doing all of this."

Sydney smiled as he looked over at Charlie. "I'm just glad to be part of the team."

Charlie shook his head and replied, "No, Sydney, you're not part of the team. You're part of the family."

Everyone cheered in agreement, and Sydney felt a rush of happiness flow through him like he had never felt in his entire life.

Charlie shifted his position on the couch and felt something move inside the right pocket of his jacket. At first, he thought it was the flashlight that Cain had given him, but then he remembered that he had left the light in his bag. Charlie pulled the mystery item out of his pocket and was surprised to find a small bottle wrapped with old, brown paper in the palm of his hand. He removed the wrapping and marveled at the contents inside the bottle.

"Guys! Come take a look at this!"

The other men quickly made their way over to Charlie and stared in wonder.

"What is it?" Patrick asked.

Charlie didn't have to wait for his grandfather to answer this time.

"It's a bolt of lightning," Charlie replied.

Morris nodded in agreement. "Quite right, Charles. Remarkable."

Charlie put his hand on the cork, but his grandfather quickly stopped him.

"No, Charles! We dare not open it. This is no ordinary magic. Lightning is a rare gift and something not easily lost. Whoever this belongs to is very powerful and is most likely searching for it vigorously."

"The Red Wizard!" Charlie shouted. "He must have slipped this into my pocket before he ran out of the cave! Why would he give me this, though?"

Morris shrugged his shoulders and answered, "I don't know, Charles, but perhaps the answer you seek is on that scroll in your other hand."

Charlie grabbed the ends of the paper with his fingers and carefully unrolled the secret message. When it was spread out, Charlie took a deep breath and read, "The old Gods have returned."

Epilogue

The Red Wizard walked toward the edge of the river that stretched forever in both directions. Dark clouds gathered over the water, and thunder began to growl in the sky. Small tines of energy streaked across the horizon with growing intensity. The Red Wizard could feel the electricity in the air, covering every surface with charged anticipation. Without warning, a lightning bolt shot down from the darkest storm cloud and struck the flowing water, making it pulse with glowing blue light. The mage immediately fell to one knee and bowed with submissive deference.

"What have you done?!" a voice boomed from overhead.

The Fire Elemental did not look up and replied reverently, "I am deeply sorry for interfering with your plans, Lord Zeus. I meant no disrespect."

A whirlpool began churning violently in the river, shooting off streaks of energy from Zeus' mighty blast as the water turned faster and faster. From the center of the vortex, another voice spoke, "You interfered with our plan when you destroyed the Moirai, one of our brother's favored minions. You ruined it when you allowed the boy to put the Thunderbird back to sleep before capturing the creature's essence to create a new bolt for Lord Zeus."

"The Thunderbird's power is derived from the Earth." the Red Wizard replied calmly. "Its energy cannot be stolen. I explained this, but you woke the creature all the same."

"You will fulfill your oath to us, or you will suffer a fate worse than death!" the godly voice from the sky declared.

Then, the black clouds parted, and the thunder and lightning retreated with their master. Zeus' departure also stopped the whirlpool in the river, and the water returned to its calm, soothing flow.

"Do you not understand the full weight of the situation you are in?" asked a voice from the water's edge. "You made a sacred promise. Helping us is not an option, nor is it negotiable."

The Fire Mage turned to see the man-fish swimming near the shore.

"Your instructions were simple," the man-fish continued. "My brother and I used what was left of our godly powers to wake the Thunderbird, the Moirai was in position to remove the little Godmaker and keep him from interfering with our plan, and you were supposed to capture the essence of the Thunderbird to help restore Lord Zeus to his former glory."

"Lord Poseidon, with all due respect, the Thunderbird's power cannot be taken. It must be given by the creature freely. Even if I could find a way to harness some of the bird's energy, how were you going to put it back to sleep before it destroyed the world?"

"We were prepared to kill the creature once it had served its purpose," the man-fish scoffed as though it had just been presented with a trivial detail. "After all this time, Zeus and I are not interested in having any rivals for power."

"I'm sorry, Lord Poseidon," the Red Wizard replied hesitantly, "But even with your trident and your brother's original bolt, you would not be powerful enough to kill the Thunderbird. Its strength is directly connected to the living Earth. Your power comes from the belief of your followers, of which there are very few in the world right now."

The man-fish frowned as he slapped his tail fin on the surface of the water, creating a wave that crashed down hard on the shore, leaving the Fire Elemental drenched and gasping for air.

"I needed the boy to put the Thunderbird back to sleep," the Red Wizard said between coughs. "And I needed the Moirai's orb of fate as part of my new plan that will see you and your brother's original power restored, not borrowed from a secondary source. Hades is the key."

The mention of his older sibling made the man-fish wince, but a moment later, a sly grin returned to the old God's lips.

"And your sudden reluctance to do as you are told has nothing to do with the fact that the boy is your son?"

The Red Wizard removed her hood, revealing Jillian Everett underneath.

"He is a means to an end, my Lord, but as a Godmaker, I think he will prove more useful to us in play than tucked away in some realm of the Underworld."

"We shall see. Just remember, Jillian, my brother and I may not be the Gods we once were, but if you betray us, we are still more than capable of killing you and your son, Godmaker or not."

"Don't worry, Lord Poseidon. I will fulfill my oath to you or die trying. Charlie will not stand in my way."

The man-fish said nothing in return as he sank slowly underneath the water until he was no longer visible.

Jillian pulled out the orb of fate from her robe and looked into it. The small marble grew in her hand and showed her the past with perfect clarity. Inside, she saw memories of Charlie from when he was a little boy. Jillian watched wordlessly as her son was born, took his first steps, and said his first words. She felt a brief flare of emotion rise up inside her but quickly pushed her sadness and anger back into the dark place where she kept everything that made her human locked up tight. After a few moments of viewing, Jillian returned the orb to her pocket and pulled the hood back over her head, becoming the Red Wizard again. She held out her right hand, and a fireball immediately materialized and hovered above her palm. When the Elemental dropped the flame at her feet, she was immediately consumed by the inferno as the magic worked to bring her back to the world and one step closer to the end.

ABOUT THE AUTHOR

My name is Trent Gerbers. I am a Hispanic American author who thinks that Paulo Coelho's masterpiece, *The Alchemist*, should be mandatory reading for every person on the planet because of how strongly I believe in the importance of following your dreams. Consider me his disciple.

In my adolescence, I had one special skill that set me apart from my peers: singing. In the small Indiana town where I grew up, being a premiere vocalist did not come with the same social collateral as being an athlete. As such, I was somewhat bullied by a few of my peers. It wasn't until the captain of our basketball team publicly stood up for me and my talent that I began to appreciate my own gift. It's important to note that he and I were not friends, nor did he owe me anything. He simply saw a situation that he considered an injustice and took it upon himself to make it right. His unusual strength of character for a young man of that age and social position is the inspiration for the protagonist of my book.

I spent my late teen years and most of my twenties making music throughout New England, where my family moved when I was fifteen. After a thirteen-year professional career, I had played hundreds of shows, toured around the country, and recorded three albums with some of the finest musicians I had the pleasure of knowing.

Closing in on my thirties, I traded in my late nights and unpredictable schedule for a stable job in the education field and for a chance at having my own family. I now live in southern Connecticut with my beautiful wife and three amazing children. In many ways, I wrote this book for them, so they could see me start and finish something that seemed too big to accomplish. I wanted them to see me struggle, and I wanted them to see me persevere. More than once, my wife nearly saw me quit. But if I'm being honest, I also wrote this book for myself.

When I stopped performing, I feared that my creative life had ended. While I gladly left the stage for my day job and my family, I felt unrest growing inside my mind. A creative channel had been dammed up inside me, and I knew I couldn't be happy if I didn't have some way to get that energy out. What started as a short story became a rough draft that I read to my kids for laughs. The rough draft turned into a better version that I worked on every night after doing baths, making lunches, cleaning up the house, and spending some time with my wife. The final drafts were slow, painstaking labors of love where I poured over every sentence while fighting off the exhaustion of giving one hundred percent to my job, one hundred percent to my family, and whatever I had left to my passion.

This book, The Never-Ending Storm, is the culmination of years of hard work and belief that writing is my true calling. In many ways, it is a love letter to my children because years after I put down my microphone, they still dance around the house while listening to my music, which means that years from now, they will probably still be reading the words I wrote for them.